Death by
Chocolate

Books by G.A. McKevett

JUST DESSERTS

BITTER SWEETS

KILLER CALORIES

COOKED GOOSE

SUGAR AND SPITE

SOUR GRAPES

PEACHES AND SCREAMS

DEATH BY CHOCOLATE

Published by Kensington Publishing Corporation

Death by Chocolate

A SAVANNAH REID MYSTERY

KENSINGTON BOOKS
http://www.kensingtonbooks.com

KENSINGTON BOOKS are published by

Kensington Publishing Corp.
850 Third Avenue
New York, NY 10022

All Kensington titles, imprints and distributed lines are available at special quantity discounts for bulk purchases for sales promotion, premiums, fund-raising, educational or institutional use.

Special book excerpts or customized printings can also be created to fit specific needs. For details, write or phone the office of the Kensington Special Sales Manager: Kensington Publishing Corp., 850 Third Avenue, New York, NY 10022. Attn. Special Sales Department. Phone: 1-800-221-2647.

Kensington and the K logo Reg. U.S. Pat. & TM Off.

Library of Congress Card Catalogue Number: 2002103435
ISBN: 1-57566-712-6

First Printing: January 2003
10 9 8 7 6 5 4 3 2 1

Printed in the United States of America

This book is lovingly dedicated to
Blanche and George Hald,
who have welcomed me so warmly
into their hearts and their family.

Acknowledgments

The author would like to thank
the newest members of the
Moonlight Magnolia Detective Agency
for their kindness and expertise.

Jennifer Hald
Blanche Hald
Leslie Connell
and
Dan McLeod

Chapter 1

"You're really not too bad-looking, you know, for a chubby old broad."

Savannah resisted the urge to growl and bite her companion as the hair on the back of her neck bristled. "I beg your pardon, sir," she said in her sweetest, most demure imitation of a Southern belle—a belle who might feed you your teeth after a back-handed compliment like that. "But I am not old. I'm . . . forty-something . . . and in my prime. And as far as chubby"—she turned in the passenger seat and stared at the driver's more than ample midsection—"in the years since I met you, that belly of yours has gone from washboard-hard to duvet-poofy, so watch it, buddy."

Dirk shot her a wounded, highly offended look as he steered his ancient Buick Skylark through the ever gathering morning rush-hour traffic. Though in the laid-back Southern California coastal town of San Carmelita, traffic didn't exactly rush—at any hour of the day.

"Man, try to say something nice and you get your head handed to you," he said, reaching for a pack of cigarettes on the dash-board. "And as for the chubby part, I just meant that—dressed up like an old lady, even with that stupid gray wig on and the extra padding under that flowery dress—you still look okay."

"I'm not wearing extra padding. This is all me."

"Oh . . . sorry."

She snatched the pack out of his hand. "You said you were quitting."

"I said I was thinking about quitting. I'm still thinking."

"You've been thinking about getting ready to start thinking about quitting for the past fifteen years."

"Well, no point rushing into anything. Gimme those smokes, woman, before I fly into a blind rage."

Sighing, she slapped them into his open palm. "Roll down the window and blow it outside."

"Yeah, yeah, yeah . . . you and your smoke allergies. What's the matter with you, Van? You're moodier than usual."

She opened her mouth to protest, but then snapped it closed. He was right; she was in a foul mood. Had been for several weeks. And her self-medicating regime of nightly bubble baths by candlelight and chocolate truffles had provided only the briefest respites.

Once, for half a moment, she had considered that she might be going through some sort of midlife crisis. But, of course, that would have meant admitting that she was "middle-aged" and maybe just a tad past her prime.

And if, indeed, her prime had come and gone, exactly on what day had she supposedly peaked? She couldn't recall a twenty-four-hour period in the past forty years when she hadn't felt fairly dragged out and grouchy.

Then she had an even more depressing thought: maybe a body only peaked for about five minutes. If so . . . she had missed the big event.

"Come on . . . what's the matter?" Dirk asked, reaching up to scratch under his own ratty gray wig. "Is it because we didn't nab somebody this time out?"

She looked down at the senior-citizen sensible black shoes and baggy hose she was wearing. The giant white patent-leather purse on the seat beside her. The monstrosity of a floral polyester dress that she had purchased at the local thrift store for a buck.

"I do feel a mite rejected," she said. "There was a day when I could dress up in a black leather miniskirt and fishnet hose and hook any bad guy in fifteen seconds. Now I go out of my way to look the part of a sweet, totally vulnerable old lady hanging around the ATM with her big 'Come Snatch Me' white purse, and I can't even get mugged. It's a sad situation, Detective, this downward trend of mine. I used to have to fight the boys off with a stick. Now they don't even get within smacking distance."

"Eh . . . what do you need with more men in your life? You've got me."

Mental pictures of Dirk with his feet propped on her coffee table every Monday night, swigging her beer, eating her pizza, watching Monday Night Football on her TV, shoving her potato chips into his face and spilling crumbs on her sofa, using her toilet and leaving the seat up, often missing the bowl.

He had a point there. Why would she want more men in her life?

When she didn't reply, he nudged her with his elbow. "We'll get 'em tomorrow morning, Van. If you're up for going out with me again, that is."

She gave him a sidewise grin, and he returned it, the smile softening his street-rough face. Being a cop had taken its toll on Dirk . . . as it had on her. Savannah Reid was all too glad to be a private citizen again without the "Detective" in front of her name. No badge, just a P.I.'s license and a lot less headaches—if you didn't figure in the stress of self-employment. Or rather, the even more nerve-racking bouts of self-unemployment.

"Yeah, I'll play decoy for you tomorrow, too," she said. "We've gotta get this guy before he really hurts somebody. And as long as the San Carmelita P.D. is too cheap to assign you a partner . . ."

She was giving him the benefit of the doubt, blaming his single status on departmental frugality. Last she had heard, everybody else in the squad avoided partnering with Dirk with a vengeance. Having worked with him for more than fifteen years, on and off the force, she understood that Detective-Sergeant Dirk Coulter was an acquired taste.

She loved the crotchety geezer. But she couldn't think of any reason why anybody else would.

"Really, we gotta get 'im," Dirk said, the gleam of righteous indignation lighting his bloodshot eyes. "Even if it's a water pistol he's using, sooner or later one of these poor old ladies is going to fall over dead of a heart attack right in the middle of the robbery."

She lifted her chin a notch and nodded, her own eyes glittering with the same icy warmth. "Don't worry. We'll put a stop to his nonsense, jerk a knot in his tail, and hang him up by it . . . somehow or another."

For the first time in several days, she felt a sense of well-being trickle through her . . . along with the mental picture of herself slamming some scumbag over the head with that white purse, which carried not some vulnerable senior lady's social security check, but a brick from her backyard. She'd stand by, grinning like a goat eating briars, while Dirk cuffed him and read him his rights. Yes, that would certainly brighten her day.

Maybe that was all that was wrong with her. It had been too long since her last "Get the Bad Guy" fix. Adrenaline and justice—it was a heady mix.

Dirk guided the Buick off the highway and onto a palm-tree-lined street that led up the hill and away from the ocean and the downtown area where they had been playing decoy.

"Hey, you're not taking me home, are you?" Savannah said, suddenly alert and suspicious.

"Well, yeah." He nodded but stared straight ahead, avoiding eye contact. "You said you were hungry and wanted breakfast. I figured I'd get you home as fast as I could so that you could scramble up some of those Western omelet things you make and maybe some home fries and . . ."

"Don't you even start with me, Coulter. You head this buggy for the nearest restaurant . . . like the pancake house on Luther Avenue. If I haul my tired butt out of bed and dress up in this garb and stroll up and down in front of an ATM for four hours, the least you can do is feed me."

Dirk grumbled something under his breath, and even though she caught only a couple of words, she got his drift.

"No money on you is no excuse. There's a bank right there on Luther, two doors down from the Flap Jack Shack. We'll stop there first. And you'd better get a bundle while you're at it, 'cause I worked up quite an appetite on that stroll."

Rather than risk being charged a fifty-cent ATM fee, Dirk pulled the Skylark into a spot in the bank's parking lot next to a meticulously restored 1963 Oldsmobile Starfire. "Hey, look at that," he said. "What a beauty! Same year as my Buick."

Savannah sniffed. "It ain't the years, darlin'; it's the mileage, and I can hear this poor jalopy of yours groaning with embarrassment just to be sitting next to that lovely machine."

She waited for him to flare, as always, when she insulted his car, his driving, or his table manners. But he sat there, his hand on the door handle, staring at the bank's rear wall.

Or more specifically, at one of the two small windows.

"Look at that," he said.

"I'm looking."

"What do you think?"

She studied the small, crudely scribbled paper sign that had been shoved between the glass and the venetian blinds in the window on the right. "I think somebody's a bad speller," she replied.

In writing that looked as if it had been done by a five-year-old with a large black marker were the words *We're being robed.*

"Robed? Maybe they're having a pajama party. But I doubt it." Dirk reached inside the old flannel jacket that had completed his senior-citizen ensemble, and at the same time Savannah checked inside the waistband of the flowered dress for her Beretta.

"You don't have to have a piece of this," Dirk said. "I can call for backup and wait."

"Maybe you can wait and maybe you can't." She squinted against the late morning sunlight that was shining on the glass

door to the bank. She saw movement inside but couldn't make out details. "Depends on what's going on in there," she said. "If somebody had time enough to write that sign and stick it in the window, it's been going down for a while."

"One thing for sure," Dirk said, opening his door, "we gotta stop Grandma Moses there from joining the party."

Savannah saw who he was talking about—an elderly woman shuffling toward the bank's door with a walker. Considering her lack of agility, she was making pretty good progress and had nearly reached the entrance.

But Dirk was faster. He bounded out of the car and across the lot with Savannah right behind him.

"Hey, lady," he called out to her, keeping his voice low. "Come back here. Don't go in . . . I think the place is being—"

"Holy shit!" the old woman yelled as she stood outside the door and stared inside. "There's a guy in there with a gun!" She turned, wild-eyed, to Dirk and Savannah. "There's two guys in there! And they've both got guns! Really big ones!"

"Get away from that door. Come back here, honey," Savannah called to her. But the lady was already on the move without aid of her walker, which she was holding straight out in front of her like a lion-tamer would hold a chair.

She ran up to Savannah, who grabbed her by the arm to steady her. "Is that your car, ma'am?" Savannah pointed to the Starfire.

"Yes."

"Well, go get in it and drive away as quick as you can, okay?"

"You bet your sweet ass, I will."

For the briefest moment, Savannah thought, Since when do grandmothers say "sweet ass" and "holy shit?" But then she heard a woman scream inside the bank, then another.

"We've gotta get in there," she told Dirk. He nodded. Turning back to the lady, she said, "May I borrow your walker?"

Rodney Flynn had never robbed a bank before. Until this morning, he had stuck to knocking over all-night convenience stores and the occasional gas station. But his cousin, Ferris, had

convinced him that if they hit just one bank a month, they'd make more money in ten minutes than they'd both made in the past ten years. Flipping burgers at Joe's Grill wasn't particularly lucrative for Rodney, and Ferris hadn't actually worked a full day at a real job in his life.

Rodney had told him he was nuts, but then he got to thinking about how much money there was in those bank tellers' drawers, not to mention what they might get ahold of if they could somehow get the safe open.

Besides, it would be on the news. They'd be on the news. Not their names, hopefully, but a story about the robbery. Rodney had been disappointed that his service station knockover hadn't even made the newspaper. Hell, they'd probably run those little commercials on the L.A. stations: daring bank holdup in San Carmelita . . . daring robbers get away with millions . . . film at eleven o'clock.

Maybe we should have worn masks or pantyhose over our heads or something, he thought, as he stood in the middle of the bank pointing his gun at a huddled bunch of terrified employees and customers. In the corner of the room he spotted a little black box with a lens sticking out of it—pointed right at him. Damn it, Ferris should have thought of some kinda disguises. I got the car filled up with gas. I can't do it all.

Ferris always acted like he was the boss, strutting around with his nose in the air, taking charge, telling everybody what to do, when to wipe their nose and not to. But what kind of a boss forgot something as simple as masks, huh?

"Get that ring off her finger, now!" Ferris yelled at him, waving his pistol in Rodney's direction.

"But she won't give it to me," Rodney tried to explain. He'd already whacked the woman on the head with his own gun. She'd screamed bloody murder, but she still wouldn't surrender the diamond on her finger.

"Then shoot her! Goddamn it, we ain't got all day here!"

Rodney looked at Ferris hard, trying to see if he meant it. They'd already said they wouldn't shoot anybody, except a cop.

He could tell Ferris meant it. Ferris had that same look in his eye that he'd had the night he cut Franky Caruso's nose off with a broken beer bottle in a bar fight.

"You shoot that bitch or I will . . . and then I'll shoot you, too, you faggot! See if I ever pull another job with you."

Rodney felt his blood boil, his face flush red. He felt like he was ten years old again and Ferris was his big cousin, shaming him, making him feel weak and small. He hated that. He hated that more than anything.

He'd show Ferris. He's show everybody on the eleven o'clock news.

Shoving his .357 magnum against the woman's cheek, he screamed, "Give me the fuckin' ring, woman, or I'll blow your brains out. Right now!"

In some dark corner of his mind, Rodney heard himself hoping that she'd refuse. He'd shoot her there and then and the whole world would see; they'd all be watching on TV and—

The door opened right behind him and Rodney spun around to see an old lady and old man toddling in. The woman wore a bright flowery dress and was shuffling along with a walker. The guy was stooped over and moved slow and stiff, like he'd just pooped his pants.

Great, that was just what they needed. A couple more knuckleheads to contend with . . . a couple that probably didn't have a dime between them.

"Hey, you two," Rodney shouted at them. "Get over there with the others and put your hands up."

The woman took several halting steps toward him. "Eh? What did you say? Sorry, but I'm a mite deaf in both ears."

"What's the matter?" asked her decrepit companion as he moved closer to Ferris. "Is the bank closed or something? We thought it was open this time of day."

"You picked the wrong time to go banking, you old fart," Ferris said as he swaggered over to the man and waved his gun in his face. Ferris swaggered everywhere, Rodney thought, with a gagging feeling in his throat. Ferris got a lot of girls with his tight

jeans and wife-beater shirts that showed his muscles and that damned swagger of his.

Rodney would have loved to wear shirts like that, but he had too many pimples on his back and not enough biceps to pull off the look.

He glanced up at the camera and wished for a moment that he'd worn something nicer than his tie-dyed T-shirt with a hole in the front where his chest hairs stuck out.

The gal in the flowered dress with the walker came right up next to him and looked him up and down, like his grandma had before he'd left for school each morning when he'd been a kid. And like Grandma Flynn, she had a disapproving scowl on her face.

"What do you think you're doing there, son?" she said. "You shouldn't go waving a gun around like that. It might be loaded. You could put somebody's eye out with that thing."

Ferris gouged the guy in the ribs with his gun. Hard. The old man stood up a little straighter. "You and your wife better get over there with everybody else before we kill you both," Ferris told him.

"Yeah," Rodney said, feeling a surge of power that he'd never felt before in all of his twenty-two years. "Yeah, you'd better do what you're told or I'll shoot you . . . just like I'm gonna shoot this stupid bitch over here who doesn't wanna give me her ring."

He turned away from the grandma and returned his attention to the young woman with the big, sparkly ring on her finger. "I'm tired of waiting around for you," he said. "I think I'll just go ahead and blow you away. That way everybody here will know that we—er . . . that is—I mean business."

He glanced over at Ferris. Ferris had a stupid little grin on his face, a grin that meant he didn't think Rodney had the balls to do it. Yeah, well, he'd soon see. . . .

"You don't want to do that, son," said the old woman behind him. "And I'll give you three good reasons . . ."

Rodney turned and was somewhat surprised to see that she wasn't looking at him; she was talking to him, but she was look-

ing at the guy she'd come in with. The guy was looking back at her kind of funny. Like they had some sort of secret between them.

But Rodney couldn't immediately figure out what it might be, so—like most things Rodney couldn't understand—he ignored it.

"One," the woman was saying, "when they catch you, you'll be charged with murder instead of just plain ol' bank robbing."

"They ain't gonna catch us." But Rodney wasn't as sure as he had been when they'd walked in. There was that camera in the corner, and there they were with their faces hanging out—no masks or pantyhose—plain as day.

"And two . . ." She fixed him with eyes that were startlingly blue. They cut through him like icy knives and made him feel sick and small, just like he had a second before Grandma had whacked him with Grandpa's big leather belt. "It's just wrong," she said, "and if you do something as wrong as killing somebody, you'll pay a really big price for it."

"Shut her up!" Ferris yelled at the guy. "Shut your old lady up before I blow her head off."

The man's face changed; it actually twisted into some sort of an angry grin. And all of a sudden, it occurred to Rodney that—except for the gray hair and the baggy clothes—he didn't look all that old, or weak.

"What was that you were saying, honey?" the guy asked the woman with the walker.

"I was saying . . . I have three good reasons why you shouldn't be doing this. . . ."

Time seemed to slow down for Rodney. It was a moment he would play over and over again in his mind for years to come and remember every detail: the young woman who wouldn't give up her engagement ring, softly sobbing behind him, the bank employees and other customers shaking and pale in a tight circle behind the counter, the gal with the walker, moving still closer to him, talking. . . .

"Three reasons, and all of them good ones. Like I said: One,

they'll give you the needle when they catch up with you. Two, it's just wrong, and three—"

Rodney didn't know what hit him. At least, not at first. Later, much later, the would realize it was the old lady's walker.

But at the time it was just a blur of silver, the gun flying out of his hand, an awful pain across his face, and the taste and feel of warm blood gushing out of his nose and down the back of his throat as he fell backward to the cold marble floor.

He was only dimly aware of a scuffle on the other side of the room. Ferris's cry of pain. The dull thud as Big Cool Swaggering Cousin Ferris hit the floor, too.

Rodney felt the weight of somebody on him, mashing the air out of him. Somebody heavy. Strong hands grabbed his shoulders and flipped him over onto his belly. His bloody nose smacked against the floor, and for a moment he saw red and white stars of pain flashing through his head. The same somebody twisted his hands behind him, yanking his shoulders and elbows half out of their joints.

In the corner of his eye he could see just enough bright yellow and pink flowers to realize . . . it was Grandma!

He could hear Ferris yelling, "What? What the hell? What do you think you're doing, Pops?"

"Arresting you, numskull. And don't call me Pops or I'll put these cuffs around your neck instead of your wrists and cinch 'em down good and tight."

"Got another pair of cuffs?" he heard the woman on top of him say.

"Nope."

"Here's some duct tape," said a male voice from the crowd behind the counter. "Will that do?"

"Sure. Just wind it around here if you don't mind."

Rodney heard the rip of the tape, saw some brightly polished black shoes appear an inch or so from his forehead. And some gray pinstriped trouser legs.

The bank manager had been wearing a pinstriped suit, he recalled, as the gravity of his situation began to press down upon

him . . . along with the grandma's knees in the small of his back. The old gal had thrown him around like she was some sort of sumo wrestler or something.

Shit, Rodney thought. It's all on camera.

By tomorrow the whole country, everybody he knew or would ever know, would have seen his disgrace: Old lady and old man take out desperate bank robbers with nothin' but a fuckin' walker. Film at eleven.

Savannah sat on her sofa, pen and tablet in hand, jotting down notes furiously as she stared at the television screen, determined to miss nothing.

"Gourmet Network again?" Tammy Hart asked as she bounced across Savannah's living room to the desk in the corner that served as "Control Central" for the Moonlight Magnolia Detective Agency. Not that there was any business to speak of that needed controlling at the moment.

"Yeah. Shhhh . . ." Savannah said, scribbling ingredients and instructions for the Queen of Chocolate's latest creation: Deep Dark Chocolate Passion Layer Cake. "I gotta get this down. I'm going to make it for you guys tonight when the boys come over for the weekly briefing."

"They're not coming for the briefing," Tammy said as she pulled her long, straight blond hair back with a scrunchy and sat down at the desk. "It would only take a second to 'brief' them on the phone. 'Nothing's happening. No clients. Not a one.' End of briefing. They're coming over for the chocolate."

"Of course they are. That's why I'm having the briefing . . . an excuse to bake something chocolate. At this point in my life, it's my foremost fleshly delight."

Tammy threw the switch on the computer and, once it had booted up, began to enter the accounts, brief as they were. That was one thing Savannah loved about her: Tammy assisted, even when there was nothing to assist with. And that quality nearly made up for the fact that Tammy was young, energetic, bouncy, and thin as a runway model.

"This time, I swear, I'm going to get it right," Savannah said. "No more disasters like that Triple Chocolate Soufflé that turned out more like pudding. I'm going to do it exactly the way the Queen of Chocolate does, and it'll be a culinary triumph."

"Famous last words," Tammy muttered.

"This sucks." Savannah looked down at the slice of cake on her plate and around the table at her faithful friends, who had gathered to discuss the non-details of the detective agency—which Savannah owned, but they all participated in from time to time—and to sample her latest experiment.

"It isn't that bad, Savannah," Ryan Stone said—always kind, always breathtakingly gorgeous as he graced the end of her table radiating "tall, dark, and handsome."

"It's tasty . . . if a tad . . . chewy," added John Gibson, Ryan's life partner who always sat to his right and sipped Earl Grey tea in that quiet, dignified manner that only British aristocracy could achieve. About fifteen years older than Ryan, John sported a full head of snowy white hair and a luxurious silver mustache. He was the only man Savannah had ever known who actually wore tweed hunting jackets in California. And his genteel English accent gave her shivers. John, too, was kind.

Dirk wasn't.

"No," he said as he shoved yet another forkful into his mouth, "overcooked steak is chewy. This is just plain tough."

"Well, I don't see you turning it down," Savannah said, grabbing the plate out from under his nose. "If you don't like it, don't feel obliged to—"

He snatched it back. "Hey, gimme that. Food's food."

"Especially if it's free," Tammy grumbled, making an adolescent "little sister" face at Dirk. "That's your number one criteria, isn't it, when critiquing a dish?"

"It helps," Dirk said, munching heartily.

Savannah dropped her fork onto her plate. "That does it. My jaws are tired. It's going into the garbage."

"Maybe you oughta stick with pecan pie or peach cobbler,"

Dirk volunteered. "Something more in keeping with your Georgia heritage. Hey, don't throw that out. I'll take it home with me."

Savannah stepped into the kitchen, got the coffeepot, and set about refilling everyone's cups . . . except John's. He had his own Dresden teapot and cozy at hand.

"Speaking of the Lady Eleanor, the Queen of Chocolate" John said, "occasionally our paths cross, as they did last evening at a benefit held at the Stardust Ballroom. She mentioned that she's in need of a personal security expert, and I recommended you, Savannah. I hope you don't mind."

The playful twinkle in his eyes told her that he knew she wouldn't mind. Mind? Mind?

"Really? I mean . . . Lady . . . Eleanor . . . bodyguard . . . me?"

"Yes. I told her you were a highly qualified professional, charming, and, above all, delightfully articulate."

"Not in front of celebrities, she's not," Tammy said as she left the table, wandered into the kitchen, and began searching in the refrigerator crisper. "She loses her cool and starts babbling like an idiot. Say, don't you have anything alive in here, like an apple or a carrot?"

"There're some golden delicious in the basket on the counter, nature girl. I was saving them for dipping in a chocolate fondue, but you go ahead and help yourself." She turned to John. "Do you think she'll call? Did she act like she was interested or . . ."

Ryan chuckled, reached over and squeezed her hand. "Don't worry, Savannah. I was there, and after the sales pitch John gave her, I'd bet that you're in."

"I'm in. I'm in." Savannah closed her eyes, savoring the possibilities. "To meet the great lady herself, to walk, even for a moment, in her sweet, chocolate-dipped world. To taste heaven on earth and not even have to go to the mall to buy Lady Eleanor's Confections. To see the place where the Raspberry Delight Truffle and the Lemon Chiffon Kiss began. . . ."

"To pig out on everything chocolate you can get your mitts on," Dirk added, "and then walk around here griping because you gained ten pounds."

Savannah sighed. "Oh, shut up, Dirk," she said with a kind of quiet resignation born of self-knowledge, "before I smack you upside the head with my walker."

Savannah's candlelit bubble bath in her Victorian clawfoot bathtub did the trick that night. Ah, she thought, as she soaked in the iridescent, lavender-scented splendor of mountainous bubbles, nothing like feeling a scumbag's tendons snap as you twist his arm out of socket to put everything right in your world.

To be the instrument of justice, even for a moment, was a fine, fine thing. Almost as fine as the Hazelnut Cocoa Cream in her right hand. Almost, but not quite.

Savannah, along with the rest of the nation, had acquired yet another vice about two years ago, when the self-titled Queen of Chocolate on the Gourmet Network had opened a chain of mall stores known as Lady Eleanor's Confection Shoppes. Like the lady herself—who wore Victorian garb: long skirts and leg-o'-mutton-sleeved high-necked blouses, button-up boots, and a Gibson girl updo with dainty curled tendrils about the face—the clerks in the turn-of-the-century-decorated shops served up candy morsels that sent the happy taster into fits of gastronomic ecstasy.

Since the opening of those stores, Savannah could swear she had gained fifteen pounds. But what the heck, it was all on her butt, which simply made her life that much more cushy. Besides, she prided herself on wearing only the best on her heinie. And Lady Eleanor's confections produced, undoubtedly, the very best fat that money could buy.

One candy at bathtime . . . and another at bedtime, just to ward off any nasty midnight sugar lows . . . and life was good.

A little later, as she snuggled between rose-spangled flannel sheets, a Double-Dipped Praline poised in front of her mouth, the thought crossed her mind that her dentist certainly wouldn't approve of this nightly ritual. But he was all about teeth and gums and warding off cavities; what did he know about feeding a famished soul? One had to be well-rounded in this world.

At least, that was her story and she was sticking with it.

"Thank you, Lord, for chocolate," she prayed as she slipped into a blissful sleep. "Thank you for good friends like John, who recommend me to wonderful people like Lady Eleanor. And most of all, thank you for helping Dirk and me end that robbery today without getting our hides—or anybody else's—perforated."

Yes, Savannah had a lot to be grateful for. Hers was a peaceful, sated soul.

Ring. Ring.

The shrill pealing of a bell pierced her ears and ripped her out of that dark, safe cocoon of sleep.

Ring. Ring.

"What? What the hell?" She sat up in bed and grabbed for the phone, missed it, and knocked her three-pound box of "assorted nuts and creams" onto the floor.

The square red numbers on her digital alarm clock told her it was 2:12 A.M.

"Damn it, this had better be an emergency, 'cause if you're a wrong number, you're dead," she mumbled as she flipped on the nightstand lamp and picked up the receiver. "Who is this and what do you want?" she demanded, every trace of her sugar high and good mood gone.

"This is Eleanor Maxwell," said a nasal, grating voice. "Is this Savannah Reid?"

Eleanor Maxwell? Eleanor Maxwell?

She didn't know any Eleanor Maxwell. And the only Eleanor she knew . . . or knew of . . . had a delicately modulated British accent that fell lightly on the ears of her television viewers like a soft spring rain. This woman's voice was more like the screeching of a Styrofoam egg carton when you closed it.

And she was calling at 2:12 in the friggin' morning!

"This is Savannah Reid. I was sound asleep. Who are you and why are you calling me at this hour?"

"I need a bodyguard. Right away. I spoke to a friend of yours, John Gibson, and—"

"Oh, yes! Of course!" Instantly Savannah was wide awake, her emotions sunny-side up. "Lady Eleanor! I'm such a fan of yours! You have no idea how many times I've watched your show, how much of your candy I've bought, how . . ." She realized she was babbling like a Rolling Stones groupie and reined in her enthusiasm. "I'd be glad to help you anyway I can," she added in her most professional tone. "If you need me to come over right now, I—"

"Now? Hell no. I'm cooking. Nobody is allowed in here when I'm cooking."

"Oh, I just meant that maybe . . . since you were calling in the middle of the night, there was some sort of urgency or—"

"No. I'm calling now because that's when I'm awake."

And to heck with the rest of the sleeping world? Savannah thought. But she quickly pushed the unworthy idea from her mind. Lady Eleanor rude? Why, she was the epitome of—

"Come over tomorrow and I'll tell you what you're going to do for me."

"O . . . kay." A few more unworthy, downright nasty thoughts floated through Savannah's head. John had forgotten to mention that, just maybe, Lady Eleanor might be a bit of a bitch. "Let's see . . . it's now two-fifteen on Tuesday morning, so you'd like me to come over sometime on Wednesday?"

"No, I told you, tomorrow—after I've slept."

"Oh, I see." The lady was one of those people who divided their "days" into the periods after and before sleep, having nothing to do with the clock or the rest of the world's schedule. "And when I shall I arrive? Say, around nine?"

"Nine? Are you nuts? I won't be awake, let alone ready to talk to anybody, before one."

Savannah reinforced her professional persona before opening her mouth again. "Would that be one in the afternoon, then?"

"Yes. That's what I said." A long, impatient sigh. "And John

Gibson said you were the best he knew. Says a lot about the circles he travels in."

Savannah bit her tongue and slowly counted to five before replying, "One o'clock sharp, at your home?"

"Of course at my home. I do everything from here. You do know where I live, don't you?"

"Certainly, Lady Eleanor. Everyone knows your estate there on the beach. I've passed that gorgeous Victorian home a hundred times and thought—"

Dial tone.

The gracious and genteel Queen of Chocolate had hung up on her. What a miserable, rotten, lousy . . .

Savannah glanced down at the box of chocolates on the floor and for one weird, perverted moment, she was actually glad they had spilled. Who wanted candy that was probably now covered with carpet fuzz? Especially if it came from a silver box with a cameo picture of Eleanor on the cover.

But the moment passed. She reached down and gathered the chocolates back into their box. No sign of carpet residue.

The Lady might be an inconsiderate, bossy old bitch who woke people up at two in the morning . . . but she still made a mean truffle.

Chapter 2

At five minutes to one, Savannah pulled her 1965 Mustang onto the cobblestone driveway and stopped at the wrought-iron gate with the ornate, scrolled "E" in its center. On an equally elaborate pole to her left was the communications security box with its assorted buttons and dials. She maneuvered the car close to it, leaned out the window, and punched the button marked VISITORS.

A few moments later, a soft female voice inquired from the speaker, "Yes? May I help you?"

"Savannah Reid, here to see Lady Eleanor," she replied.

Within seconds, the gate swung open and she drove inside, practically giddy with anticipation. She couldn't have been more excited if she had been holding a golden ticket to Willy Wonka's Chocolate Factory.

Hundreds of times she had driven down Seaside Avenue and glimpsed the peaked tops of the Queen's castle, a Victorian-style mansion, one of the oldest and most prestigious homes in the county—though few of the county's residents had seen more than the gray roof with its grand turrets and a bit of its white gingerbread trim.

As she drove along the tree-lined road, past the gatekeeper's cottage and through acres of beautifully landscaped lawns and

gardens, she felt as though she had stepped back in history, to a more gentle, graceful time. She half expected to see women in long skirts playing croquet while their girlfriends protected their ivory complexions by sitting beneath fluttering white canvas pavilions to sip their afternoon tea.

Halfway down the drive, she had to stop the car and wait for a pair of peacocks to cross, their long iridescent plumage sweeping behind them.

Ah, she thought. I have stepped through the looking glass. This is wonderful!

So far Lady Eleanor's domain was everything she had ever dreamed and more. And if she got the job, she might actually get to spend time here in this fairyland. The very thought of anyone's body needing to be guarded in this gentle world seemed inconceivable. What bad thing could possibly happen amid such splendor?

She rounded a curve in the road, and suddenly the house was before her. A dark, dusky rose beauty, trimmed in white with balconies, stained-glass windows, and a wide porch that wrapped all the way across the front of the house. White wicker furniture with thick floral cushions invited the weary traveler to take a load off and enjoy the ocean view beyond.

The estate canines were less hospitable, Savannah realized the moment she opened her car door and set foot on the cobblestone driveway. Three tiny, silky terriers bounded off the chairs on the porch where they had been napping and raced toward her, fangs bared, growling and yipping like a pack of starving mini-wolves.

"Well, hello there," she said in her best dog-wheedling tone as she knelt to hold out the back of her hand for the first one to sniff. "Are you the welcoming committee? Ow! Damn it, you little booger!"

She sprang to her feet and grabbed her nipped finger, which was leaking drops of blood. The mangy pooch had chomped her!

Looking down at the tiny creatures who circled her feet, lips quivering, gaping jaws frothing, the pink bows in their hair belying their ferocity, she wondered if someone had trained them to go for the Achilles tendon.

She glanced up at the house and thought she saw a movement of bright color, like a giant parrot, at an upper window. Thinking better of retaliation, she decided not to kick the fellow who had just sank his fangs into the toe of her new kidskin loafer.

His buddy jumped on her, leaving muddy streaks from the knee to the hem of her taupe linen slacks.

"Back off, you flea-bitten varmints," she said in a low, but menacing tone, "or I'll bring my two cats out here next time, and they'll eat you mutts for breakfast."

"All right, all right, come back here, boys," said the same soft female voice Savannah had heard on the speaker at the gate. "Hitler, Satan, Killer! That's enough!"

Instantly, the terrible terriers tucked their tails and headed back to the porch and their cushioned chairs as a tall, thin woman in full black-and-white maid's garb stepped out of the front door and onto the porch.

"Please, Ms. Reid, come inside. Their bark is much worse than their bite," she said, beckoning Savannah with a dust cloth she held in one hand.

Savannah looked down at the blood drops on her finger. "Their bite's pretty good, too, for their size." She stepped up onto the porch and looked at the dogs, who were circling on the cushions and settling down for naps. "What did you say their names were?" She couldn't believe she had heard correctly.

The maid's pale cheeks flushed, and she shrugged her thin shoulders. "I didn't name them," she said, then lowered her voice and added, "I never would have named poor, innocent animals such . . . but . . . well . . . Please, come inside."

Savannah stepped through the door, heavy with leaded beveled glass, and into a foyer with a black-and-white marble-tiled floor. A mahogany staircase, ornately carved with cupids, roses, and lilies, curved to her right, while an arched doorway to the left opened into a formal parlor.

"If you'll have a seat," the maid said, waving a hand toward the diamond-tucked, burgundy velvet settee, "I'll get you a cup of cappuccino. Mrs. Maxwell will be with you . . . ah . . . soon."

But Mrs. Maxwell didn't join her soon. Savannah had plenty of time to cool her heels, sip two cups of cappuccino from a delicate English porcelain cup, and memorize every piece of antique furniture in the room, from the glass-front bookshelves filled with leather-bound classics to the jeweled dragonfly Tiffany lamp in the corner. It was nearly two o'clock when the maid appeared again and said with subdued enthusiasm, "Lady Eleanor will see you now on the verandah."

Not particularly eager to encounter the furry-faced fiends again, but anxious to get the bodyguard show on the road, Savannah followed the maid through the parlor and a vast dining room to the back side of the house, which faced the ocean.

The San Carmelita beaches and skies were in fine form, the morning fog having burned away and the golden afternoon light glimmering on the waves. Swimmers in wetsuits rode the surf in the distance, and a flock of pelicans, looking like a gaggle of prehistoric pterodactyl, dipped and dove overhead.

And off to the right, sitting at a table beneath a giant umbrella, was . . . a woman who bore absolutely no resemblance whatsoever to Savannah's Gourmet Network heroine. Where was the auburn hair, piled in luxurious profusion on her regal head? Where was the Victorian costume that bespoke of genteel aristocracy?

The woman at the table wore a gaudy tropical print caftan that was cut much too low and displayed an unladylike amount of sagging, unattractive cleavage. On screen, Lady Eleanor looked pleasingly plump, but without benefit of corset and costume, she appeared seriously overweight. Her salt-and-pepper hair looked as though she had cut it herself with scissors, leaving only a ragged inch-long bristle.

On the table before her was spread an enormous breakfast of everything from pancakes to bagels, cream cheese, and lox.

Lady Eleanor was shoveling in the bounty as though she were expecting to be executed at sundown. She barely looked up from her burdened plate to wave a hand at the empty chair on the other side of the table.

"Sit," she commanded through a mouthful of Danish pastry, which she washed down with a celery-sprigged Bloody Mary.

Savannah did as she was told, feeling a bit like a cocker spaniel. Would she be expected to roll over and play dead, too?

"Want some?" Eleanor pointed to a plateful of chocolate donuts.

But Savannah was long past any sign of an appetite. Eleanor's openmouthed chewing and the syrup and butter on her fingers and chin had worked better than any over-the-counter suppressant.

And Savannah had thought Dirk had bad table manners. Next to Eleanor, Dirk was Cary Grant.

"No, thank you," Savannah said. Reaching into her purse, she pulled out a pen and a spiral notebook. "If you don't mind, I'd like to discuss business with you. Exactly what your needs are and—"

"My needs are simple. You shouldn't have any trouble understanding them." A quick swig of Bloody Mary, then she continued in that same, grating, nasal voice she had used earlier on the telephone, the one that had nothing in common with the cultured British accent heard by millions on television. "I need you to find out who's writing me nasty letters. Because once I find out who's doing it, they're dead."

"Oh, I see."

But Savannah didn't see. Looking into those narrow, squinty eyes with their wicked gleam, she wasn't sure if Lady Eleanor meant "dead" as in figuratively or literally. Maybe she should find out before she took the job. The term "accomplice to murder" floated across the movie screen of her imagination in flashing red neon letters.

"And," Eleanor continued, "you have to keep them from killing me . . . if that's what they've got in mind. I want to get them first."

"Ah, yes, of course. I—"

"And most of all"—more food cramming, more chomping—"you have to stay out of my hair, because I can't stand having anybody too close, breathing down my neck. Makes me nuts."

"Too close, hmmm." Savannah couldn't imagine that anyone would want to be close to this person. Chocolate fantasyland or no, Savannah wasn't too hot on the idea herself at that moment.

"Do you think you can manage that?"

Savannah quirked one eyebrow and gave Eleanor her most pointed, professional, semi-sarcastic look. "Piece o' cake, Lady Eleanor, if you're willing to cooperate with me. If you'll behave yourself in a way that will enable me to guard you properly. Are you willing to meet me halfway?"

The Queen of Chocolate paused in half-chew, her mouth hanging open, her eyes slightly bugged. Apparently she wasn't accustomed to having her subjects talk back to her.

She stared at Savannah for several long seconds, then swallowed hard and reached for a cinnamon roll. "Yeah, I guess." She shoved half the roll into her mouth at once and added, "Get lost and let me finish my breakfast. Then I'll show you those nasty letters."

Gee, Savannah thought. I can hardly wait.

"How nasty were they?" Tammy asked as she and Savannah sat at opposite ends of Savannah's sofa and compared notes on their day.

"Nasty enough," Savannah replied, lifting one of her two black cats, Diamante, onto her lap and stroking her glossy coat. After spending the afternoon with the terrible threesome silkies, it soothed her soul to be in the company of a peaceful, benign animal. That, and the cup of coffee generously laced with Bailey's.

"How many were there?" Tammy curled her bare feet under her and nibbled the celery stick in her hand. Tammy was always munching vegetables. "Live" food, she called it.

Savannah had decided long ago to love her anyway. Nobody was perfect.

"Three," Savannah replied. "All mailed from Los Angeles. How's that for narrowing down the possibilities?" She sighed.

"What did they say?"

"In a nutshell? Basically, 'Shape up and treat people better, or you're going to die, you stinking bitch.' "

"That blunt?"

"Oh, yeah. No frills around the edges, just your generic death threat."

"Handwritten?"

Savannah sniffed. "Yeah, right. No such luck. Typed. A word processor. Arial font 14."

"Fourteen? That's bigger than average. Maybe the typer has a vision problem."

"That occurred to me, too. Or maybe they just wanted to make sure Eleanor didn't miss a word. The words were in bold, too. Exclamation marks everywhere."

"Sounds juvenile."

"Maybe."

Savannah's second miniature black leopard, known as Cleopatra, hopped onto her lap and jostled with Diamante for the best petting position. Both had started off their lives as ordinary housecats, but nobody starved in Savannah's household. No one was even allowed to feel a hunger pang. And after years of a never-ending flow of Kitty Kiddles and assorted goodies from Savannah's hand, the oversized twosome could have easily felled a zebra in Africa.

Savannah offered them a sip from her coffee/Bailey cup. Only Cleopatra accepted. Diamante preferred her coffee black.

"I know," Tammy said, "that you think Lady Eleanor is the greatest, but—"

"*Thought* she was the greatest. She's a pig. And I say that with all due respect to the porcine population. I wish I'd never met her in person. Boy, talk about a letdown."

"When goddesses tumble from their marble pedestals . . ."

"Something like that. I gotta tell you, it's a painful thing, losing one of your idols."

"Anyway, I know you thought a lot of her," Tammy continued, "but this gig sounds like it's more trouble than it's worth. Maybe you should pass on it."

Savannah stroked first one cat, then the other, feeling them arch to enjoy her touch to the fullest. She looked down at the

tiny teeth marks in her finger. Hitler, Satan, Killer—how sick was that?

She thought of the woman with the spiky gray hair, the gaudy muumuu, and the voice that felt like a parmesan cheese grater raking across her nerves. The commands to "sit" and "get lost." The harried, weary look on the gentle maid's face. The death threats that had the tone of someone who was, very simply, fed up with Lady Eleanor.

"Maybe you're right. Maybe I don't need the hassle right now," she said, feeling a cloud lift from her head and shoulders, a cloud that had been floating around her since that rude 2:00 A.M. phone call.

"Good." Tammy crunched on her celery. "I think that's wise. Let Eleanor find another flunky to guard her royal heinie."

Savannah thought a few seconds more, weighing all factors. "Did you pay the bills this morning?" she finally asked.

"Some of them."

A long, heavy silence stretched between them.

"How many of them?"

Tammy sighed. "I paid last month's electricity. The phone from the month before last."

"The mortgage?"

"Nope."

"Insurance?"

"Uh-uh. The electric and phone tapped you out."

"When's the last time you paid yourself?"

"Last March."

"That long, huh?"

Savannah drained the last of her coffee. Tammy finished off the celery stick and started on the carrots before she said, "So, when do you report for Eleanor Guard Duty?"

"Tonight at eight P.M. That's when she starts taping."

"A taping. Hmmm. That should be interesting. You know . . . kinda nice."

"Gr-r-r-r . . ."

Chapter 3

"Gee," Savannah whispered to the maid, who she had recently found out was named Marie, "somehow I thought the show was filmed in her actual kitchen, like she says it is on TV."

"A lot of people think that," Marie said as she walked around the set with a garbage bag in hand, picking up the plastic cups and paper plates left behind by the film crew. "At first we taped in the kitchen in the house, but it was so much trouble setting up and breaking down each time. So a year ago they built this studio here in the barn. Well, it used to be a barn, but they got rid of the animals and . . ."

Marie's voice trailed away, and so did she, leaving Savannah standing on the periphery of a bustle of activity that she knew absolutely nothing about. Half a dozen people, wearing strange headgear, T-shirts, and shorts, scurried around, some of them carrying notebooks or stacks of papers, others handling microphones, lights of all different sizes and colors, and other terribly technical looking meter-type equipment that Savannah didn't recognize.

But even more foreign than the taping set in front of her was the transformation of Eleanor Maxwell. Gone was the disheveled, slovenly woman of the afternoon. Standing behind the

kitchen counter, dressed in a high-necked ivory lace blouse, wearing an auburn wig of perfectly coifed ringlets, twists, and rolls, was the Lady Eleanor of Gourmet Network fame.

Speaking with the distinction of a diction coach at a British school for young ladies, the woman stirring the wonderfully fragrant chocolate mixture on the stove seemed to be from another world, far removed from the gal in the muumuu, shoving bagels and lox into her face, washing them down with Bloody Marys.

For half a second, Savannah allowed herself to fantasize about this gracious lady's evil white-trash twin who kept the real Lady Eleanor imprisoned in some sort of dungeon beneath the house and allowed her to come out for air only during tapings.

"A bit more what you were expecting?" asked a female voice behind her.

Savannah turned to see the woman who had earlier been introduced to her as Kaitlin Dover, the show's producer.

From the moment she'd met her, Savannah liked Kaitlin. Petite, slender to the point of looking underfed, the thirty-something Kaitlin looked as though she had inherited her red hair and golden freckles from some Irish ancestor. And maybe a bit of Irish charm, too.

From the way her large brown eyes met Savannah's openly and honestly, to the perpetual half-grin she wore that seemed to be bravely covering some sort of personal pain, Kaitlin Dover came across a genuine person. And after spending the better—or rather, the worst—part of the afternoon with Eleanor, genuine seemed all the more appealing to Savannah.

"Yes, this is who I was expecting when I arrived for my appointment this afternoon," Savannah said, keeping her voice low as the crew moved in a swirl of activity around them. "I've been a fan of Lady Elean . . . well, this person's for a long time."

Kaitlin's freckled face beamed with something that looked like satisfaction. She took the pencil she had been scribbling with on a clipboard and stuck it in her short, tight red curls above her ear. "That's the idea," she said. "To create a character that the world embraces."

"A character? To create?"

Kaitlin gave her a long, measured look, as though deciding how open to be with this newcomer to the set. "Yes," she finally said, "creating characters. Conjuring the magic inside the viewers' minds and imaginations. That's showbiz."

"Even in a cooking show, huh?" Savannah watched as a young man patted the shine off the Queen of Chocolate's nose between takes.

"Lights, camera, action . . . and it's all make-believe . . . done with smoke and mirrors. Even for a cooking show." Kaitlin sighed. Savannah noticed how dark the circles were under her eyes. She was too young to look so tired.

"I was surprised that you started taping this late," Savannah said, glancing down at her watch. It was almost eleven and they had only gotten down to business about half an hour before. "Don't most TV shows tape in the afternoon or early evening? I mean . . . I heard that the *Tonight Show* is done in the afternoon and . . ."

"We tape when Eleanor is ready to tape," Kaitlin said, her eyes trained on the star of the show, who had dropped her genteel facade the moment the cameras stopped rolling and was dishing out verbal abuse to a long-suffering hairstylist who was trying to set her wig right for the next take.

"She's a bit of a night owl, huh?" Savannah said, noting the look of pure, bitter hatred that fleetingly passed over Kaitlin's pretty Irish face. It was gone when she turned back to Savannah and said in a sweet, even tone, "Oh, yes. Eleanor prefers the darkness to the light."

"And why do you suppose that is?"

Kaitlin shrugged. "So many, many things become clear by day."

"Things she'd prefer not to see?"

Kaitlin's eyes cut back to Eleanor, who was shoving a crew member out of her way as she stomped off the set, shouting, "Damned stupid idiots . . . I oughta fire all of you! I'm gonna go back to the house to take a break. And don't call me until you get your shit together!"

"A break." Kaitlin shook her head wearily. "She'll be drunk as a skunk by the time she gets done with her 'break.'" She left Savannah's side and strolled to the center of the set, where nobody seemed particularly surprised. "That's it for tonight, ladies and gentlemen. We'll try again on Wednesday. Thanks."

In less than ten minutes, Kaitlin and her crew had cleared out of the barn-converted studio, and Savannah was left alone to wander down the cobblestone driveway back to the main house.

Perhaps under different circumstances she might have considered the moonlit walk romantic: the silver light spilling over the lawns, the smell of the sea mingling with that of nearby eucalyptus trees, the house's stained-glass windows glowing in the jewel colors of ruby, sapphire, and topaz, and the hypnotic, rhythmic sounds of the waves washing onto the beach below.

But there was another, unsettling sound. The soft snuffling of someone crying. A child.

Savannah saw her sitting in the gazebo, a young girl of about six, with long, straight dark hair that covered her downturned face like a privacy curtain. She had her knees drawn up under her chin, her arms wrapped around her bare shins. She wore a bright pink T-shirt and matching shorts, and in the moonlight Savannah could see sparkles, like glitter, on her sneakers.

Savannah walked across the lawn to the gazebo and stepped into the white, ivy-draped structure. "Hi," she said softly.

The child looked up her with enormous eyes full of sadness that went straight to Savannah's heart. Being the oldest of nine siblings, Savannah had seen more than her share of pouting and whining, but this youngster's sorrow was obviously genuine and deep.

"What's the matter, sweetpea?" she asked in her best big-sister voice as she sat across from the girl on the circular padded bench that surrounded the interior of the gazebo.

Shrugging her shoulders, the child sniffed and wiped her hand across her nose. Savannah reached into her slacks pocket, pulled out a clean tissue, and offered it to her. The girl took the tissue and blew heartily into it before tucking it into her own pocket.

"What's wrong?" she asked again. "Did something bad or sad happen? Did one of those terrible terriers down there take a bite out of your shorts?"

The child shook her head, but Savannah saw a trace of a smile cross her face. "Naw. Hitler's the only one who ever really bit me, and he doesn't do it anymore, 'cause I smacked him on the butt with a flyswatter."

Savannah chuckled. "Well, I can't say that I think hitting innocent animals is a good idea, but"—she held up her bandaged forefinger—"I do understand. I have to admit that if I'd been holding a flyswatter or a rolled-up newspaper this afternoon when I met Hitler, I would have whalloped him, too. Self-defense and all that."

"I know. They're mean, those little dogs. Mommy says that Grandma spoils them rotten and that's why they're bad. Doggies are supposed to be nice, not going around biting people for no reason at all. I told Mommy I wanted a good dog, like a golden retriever, but she said that Satan and Hitler and Killer would eat another dog alive. So I can't have one until all three of them die. Maybe a coyote will come down out of the hills and eat them some night. I hope so."

The wicked gleam in the little girl's eyes took Savannah aback for a moment. She had seen that particular light in the eyes of criminals she had arrested on the force, and it seemed inappropriate on one so young.

"My name's Savannah," she told the girl. "And you are . . . ?"

"Gilly. Gilly Sarah-Jane Maxwell." The child reached into her pocket, pulled out the tissue, and blew into it again.

"And Lady Eleanor is your grandmother?"

"Yeah, but we don't call her 'lady.' Just people who don't know her call her that, because of television, you know. My mommy calls her a bitch."

Savannah cringed. After her own Granny Reid's strict Southern upbringing, she couldn't get used to a child cursing . . . or being cursed around.

"I'm sorry," was all she could think to reply.

"Yeah, me too. I like my grandma okay . . . except for when she drinks booze and smells bad and talks bad. Then she's no fun to be around."

Glancing across the lawns to the mansion, which was now mostly dark except for the kitchen lights, Savannah said, "Like tonight?"

Gilly sniffed and nodded. "Yeah. I went down to visit her, but she was already, you know, weird. She told me to get lost. She doesn't usually do that. Sometimes she lets me watch her cook. I'm the only one who can."

So much for gleaning any chocolate secrets, Savannah thought. "Do you live in the mansion with your parents?"

"No. I live in the gatekeeper's cottage with my mom. Her name is Louise. I never saw my daddy. Mommy says he was rich and very, very handsome, but she didn't want to marry him, 'cause she didn't really like him that much. She says I'm ill'jit-mutt. And the kids at school say I'm a bastard."

Again, Savannah's heart ached . . . and her fingers itched to wrap themselves around any mother's throat who would say something like that to a child.

"Those are ugly words for such a pretty girl," she said softly as she reached over to brush Gilly's long, stringy hair out of her eyes. The child was in great need of a hairbrushing, a hug, and a gentler, healthier environment. "My daddy wasn't around much when I was a kid, either," Savannah said. "But I had other people who loved me. I'll bet you do, too."

Gilly thought for a moment, then nodded. "Yeap. Marie likes me and Sydney, too."

"Who's Sydney?"

"He works for my grandma. Drives her to Los Angeles and stuff. And he lets me help him wash her big, black car sometimes. And my grandma loves me . . . when she's not . . . you know . . . and my mommy does. Mommy's just got really bad nerves because of Grandma being such a bad mom to her when she was a kid. Mommy has to take a lot of nerve pills, or she gets

all mixed up and sad and mad and stuff, and sometimes she has to go away . . . you know . . . for a rest."

"A rest, hmmm." Savannah was fairly sure Mom wasn't checking into the local Motel 6 for her "rests." Rehab clinics, maybe, for popping all those "nerve" pills? "Where do you live when your mom's away . . . resting?"

"With Grandma or Grandpa. He loves me, too, but he doesn't come around here anymore, 'cause Grandma said if he did, she'd call the cops and get his sorry butt arrested. They're divorced."

Savannah jotted that one down in her mental notebook, along with the other information she had gleaned in this small but child-candid conversation. Ten minutes spent talking to a pure soul with no guilty secrets could be more informative than hours interrogating a hardened street criminal.

Savannah glanced around at the dark, shadowed areas of the lawns and listened to a pack of coyotes yipping in the distant hills. Lady Eleanor's estate struck her as more spooky than romantic at night, despite its Victorian elegance.

"Do you usually hang around outside this late?" she asked the girl, who had taken the tissue out of her pocket and was dabbing at her eyes again.

"It's not that late," she replied with a sniff.

Savannah glanced at her watch. "Actually, it's almost eleven-thirty. That's pretty late on a school night. You do go to school, right?"

"Yeah, I'm in first grade. But if I don't want to go tomorrow morning, I'll just tell Mommy that my stomach hurts and she'll let me stay home. Besides, Mommy's already asleep. She doesn't care if I stay up and run around, as long as I don't wake her up when I come in."

Savannah reached over and tweaked the girl's bangs. "Well, I'll tell you what I think . . . and I had eight little brothers and sisters, so I know a lot about kids and bedtimes. I think you're still growing, and in order to grow big and strong, you have to sleep. Because that's when it happens—the growing, that is."

Standing, Savannah took Gilly's hand and pulled her to her feet. The child looked up at her, impressed by her height. "Looks like you got lots of sleep. You're taller than my mommy and Grandma. You're as big as Sydney!"

"That's right. And when I was your age, I was always in bed and snoring by eight-thirty."

Gilly surveyed Savannah's figure. "Is that when you grew big the other way, too?"

Savannah laughed and shook her head. "No, darlin'. I grew tall by sleeping, but I got wide by eating your grandmother's raspberry truffles . . . and a lot of other yummy things."

She took the child's small, warm hand in her own and walked her across the lawn to the road. Pointing her toward the gatekeeper's cottage, she said, "You scoot along home now and get to sleep as soon as you can. You've still got a lot of growing to do."

"Will you be around tomorrow?" Gilly asked as she skipped backward down the road, swinging her arms like a clumsy albatross chick trying to fly.

"I hope so."

"Me too. See you then."

Savannah waved. "Later, gator."

Once the child was safe inside the cottage, door closed behind her, Savannah continued down the road to the mansion and Grandma . . . Grandma who smelled bad like booze, talked weird, and had told her sweet grandchild to "get lost."

"Oh, goodie, all this and Hitler, Satan, and Killer, too," Savannah muttered to the oleander shrubs on either side of the road. "And how much do you wanna bet that Grandma will throw me out of her kitchen . . . chocolateless."

Savannah didn't have to be told that this time she should go to the back door of the mansion rather than the front. Knocking on the front door was an honor that only free agents were afforded. Since this afternoon, she had joined the unhappy rank of servants at Chateau Eleanor. So much for things like respect or courtesy.

And she wasn't surprised when no one answered her knock,

other than the dreaded threesome, whom she could hear growling and yipping on the other side of the door. Their tiny toenails scraped as they clawed at the woodwork while snuffling along the edges of the door, trying to get her scent.

"Watch it, hairballs," she muttered. "You don't know who you're messing with."

Determined to get inside despite the ravaging canines, she tried the knob and was both relieved and concerned when the door opened.

Why hire a bodyguard if you don't bother to lock your doors at night? she thought as she stepped into a small room that served as a utility room and pantry. In an instant, the dogs were upon her, the bolder of them burying his fangs in the toe of her loafer, which he had perforated earlier in the afternoon.

She reached down and snatched him off the floor, holding him by the scruff of the neck. The bit of fluff snarled and snapped as he dangled from her hand. Holding him only inches from her face, she looked straight into his beady little bugged eyes and said, "The next time you bite me, you foul creature, I'm going to smack you with the Sunday edition of the *L.A. Times*, and you'll be flatter than a fritter."

To emphasize her point she tightened her grip and gave him a slight shake, like a mother dog would give a naughty pup. Instantly, the terrier realized he had been demoted from alpha dog, and he seemed to deflate in her hand. At her feet, the other two appeared to sense the shift of power, and their growls changed to whimpers.

Gently, she placed him on the floor at her feet and gave him a soothing scratch behind his ear. "There, there . . . now you're not such a bad boy after all," she told him as she knelt and stroked first one, then the other of his companions. "And neither are you. You fellas just need to be reminded that you aren't rottweilers or Dobies, that's all."

When she stood, she glanced up and saw Eleanor Maxwell standing in the door that led to the kitchen, watching her with a slightly amused look on her face and a large glass of red wine in

her hand. For once, the hard nastiness was gone from her face, and Savannah caught a glimpse of a woman she could actually like. Then she decided the warmth on Eleanor's face was nothing more than a drunk, sappy grin. Savannah had seen the expression many times on her own mother's face, a mother who had spent most of her days—and nights—perched on a bar stool.

"You like dogs?" Eleanor asked. "You look like an animal lover."

"Some of my best friends have been cats and dogs," she replied. "They're kinder than most people. They listen better, and are a helluva lot more loyal and faithful."

"More faithful . . . that's for sure."

Savannah heard it: that distinct note of pain in Eleanor's voice. She had been recently betrayed, and judging from the tears that sprang to her eyes, deeply hurt.

Savannah reminded herself to check out the circumstances of Eleanor's divorce. Another woman, maybe? A woman who, even though she had won the first round of the matrimonial battle, might have chosen to send a few death threats to the ex-wife?

"Come have a glass of wine with me," Eleanor said, turning around and walking back into the kitchen without waiting for an answer.

Savannah glanced down at the dogs and thought, You guys aren't the only ones around here who are accustomed to having the upper hand.

She followed Eleanor through the kitchen and out to the patio on the sea side of the house. Two chaise lounges had been pulled out to the edge of the patio, overlooking the moonlit ocean. The area was dimly lit by the glow of several ship's lanterns that hung from the branches of a nearby olive tree.

On a small wrought-iron table sat a bottle of wine that was more than half empty. Beside the bottle was a second glass. Apparently, Lady Eleanor had been expecting company. Savannah wondered if the anticipated arrival was her.

Eleanor sat on one of the chaises, uncorked the bottle, and began to fill the other glass.

"I don't drink when I'm working," Savannah said. "But I'll be happy to sit with you for a spell."

As she lowered herself on the other lounge chair, she saw that Eleanor was still pouring.

"I don't want somebody to sit with," she said, holding the glass out to Savannah. "I want somebody to drink with."

Savannah gave her a cool half-smile. "Then you'd better offer me an iced tea or a Pepsi," she said softly but firmly.

Eleanor Maxwell returned the chilly smile without blinking. "I'm not as easily intimidated as Killer is," she said. "You'll have to do a lot more than pick me up and shake me to get the best of this old girl."

"I wouldn't dream of trying to best you, Lady Eleanor. That's not my job. I'm here to protect you, remember?"

"Yeah, right. Protect me. It's a sorry day when somebody's got to seek protection from their so-called loved ones." She drained the last swig from her own wineglass, set it on the table, and settled back with the one she had poured for Savannah.

"So, you think it's one of your friends or family who sent you the letters?"

"Probably. Who else would want to upset me? They love to torment me, the whole bunch of them. They're jealous, you know, because I'm trailer trash who's made good."

Savannah blinked, taken aback by her candor. Few people she knew—or had ever known—would have given themselves such a distasteful label.

"People don't mind so much if you're born with money," Eleanor continued, "but it really irks them when you rise above your circumstances."

Stretching her legs out in front of her, Savannah felt a wave of fatigue roll through her from head to toe. It had been a long, stressful day . . . though, come to think of it, not that long, and she had certainly experienced worse days. Again, she wondered if she was somehow past her prime. Or maybe she was coming down with something.

"On your list of jealous loved ones," she said, pulling herself

back to the duties at hand, "who would you put at the top of the page under 'Irked'?"

Eleanor took another long drink from her glass and gazed out at the dark sea a few moments before answering. "There are at least three people who all have to share the number one spot on the list," she finally said. "My daughter . . . who blames me for every damned thing that's ever gone wrong in her empty, ridiculous life; my ex-husband . . . who's bitter that I dumped him after he 'made me the success I am today;' and Kaitlin . . . for the same reason. To hear them tell it, she and Maxwell are responsible for all of this." She waved her hand, indicating the house and gardens.

Savannah wondered if their claims might have a basis in fact, but decided that Eleanor wasn't the one to objectively answer that question. So she swallowed her curiosity and allowed her to continue.

"When I met Burt, he was a traveling insurance salesman and I was a short-order cook at a truckstop. He stopped in one day when I was making my Christmas fudge for my favorite customers and—well, as they say, the rest is history. Burt could sell anything to anybody. He sold the idea of 'Lady Eleanor, Queen of Chocolate' to Kaitlin, an agent/promoter kid he'd met in L.A. She added the whole Victorian image bit, and I've been wearing those damned wigs and corsets ever since."

"And the candy stores? Were those her idea, too?"

"No. Burt pushed for that. Personally, I don't give a hoot about having stores in every mall on the West Coast, but . . . nobody thought to ask me whether I wanted them."

Savannah watched as yet another wall of her fantasy castle in the clouds crumbled before her eyes. Lady Eleanor didn't care about her own shops? The ladies in their long dresses, serving bits of heaven in tiny pink bags or shiny silver and gold boxes?

"What about the Raspberry Delights or the Lemon Crème Parfaits?" Savannah said, trying to keep her voice from trembling. "Aren't those, you know, your own creations?"

"Oh, please. Burt hired some pipsqueak kid from a New York City gourmet cooking school to come up with that crap. But, of course, if you repeat any of what I'm saying, I'll deny it and sue you."

"Of course. Don't worry; I'm discreet." Devastated, she thought, but discreet. "How about the recipes on your cooking show?" She was almost afraid to ask.

"Naw, those are mine. The only thing that's mine anymore. That and my granddaughter, Gilly. But it's just a matter of time until that rotten mother of hers turns her against me, too."

Eleanor sighed and closed her eyes for a moment. In the dim light of the lanterns, Savannah wasn't sure, but she thought she saw a tear sparkling on the woman's cheek.

"Those times in my kitchen," she continued, "when I can just cook, and Gilly's sitting there on her stool, tasting the things I make, telling me all about her school friends and chattering on about silliness . . . those are the only good times I have anymore. They're all that makes it worth . . . going on."

Yes, there were definitely tears on Lady Eleanor's cheeks. Savannah wasn't sure how seriously to take this mood downturn. Was it deep, heartfelt sorrow, or was the woman simply entering the crying-jag period of her drinking routine?

Either way, Savannah didn't like what she was hearing. It had been her personal experience that when people grew genuinely, truly tired of living, they were in danger of checking out—one way or the other.

"Maybe you should talk to somebody, Eleanor," she suggested as gently as possible. Such suggestions were seldom met with enthusiastic agreement.

"To hell with you. I don't need a shrink."

"O-kay. How about a spiritual counselor, a minister or rabbi or—"

"I don't need God, either. He turned his back on me a long, long time ago."

At least half a dozen of Savannah's grandmother's admonitions

about the Almighty's abiding love came to her mind, but she decided not to share those words of wisdom. Lady Eleanor didn't appear to be in a receptive mood.

Another one of Granny Reid's observations rang a mental bell as well: "If somebody's done made up their mind to be ornery, ain't much you can say to talk 'em outta it. Just save your breath and steer clear of 'em."

Savannah decided maybe it was time to steer clear of Eleanor Maxwell. At least until she was a bit more sober.

"I'm concerned about your lack of security measures around here," Savannah said. "Your back door was unlocked. If I could just walk in, so could anybody else. You need to—"

"Nobody's coming into this house without me knowing it. That's what the dogs are for."

"Those dogs, noisy as they are, won't stop an intruder who's intent on doing you harm."

"That's what the shotgun's for."

"What shotgun?"

"The one in the broom closet right beside the pantry door, loaded and ready to rock and roll."

Savannah shuddered. "We should talk about that, too. Tomorrow afternoon, I need some time to discuss all these matters with you and—"

"I'm busy tomorrow. We're going to be shooting a commercial for the shops in the afternoon."

"Eleanor, I know you're a busy lady, but if I'm going to provide you with any kind of effective protection, I have to be here. I'm going to pack a bag and stay here with you, at least for a few days until I can assess your—"

"What you have to do is find out who's writing me those stinking letters. That's all you've got to do. That, and stay out of my hair. You're not here to tell me what to do. I tell you what's what, not the other way around. Now get out of here and leave me alone. It's time for me to start cooking."

Slowly, Savannah stood, feeling the chill of the ocean's night breeze as it swept over her skin. She paused beside Eleanor's

chair, studying the woman who was burying her nose inside her wineglass, a bitter and sad soul who needed far more from her fellow humans than she would ever admit. And if she continued to act as she was, she would most surely never receive what she needed.

"Good night, Mrs. Maxwell," she said. "I'll be back tomorrow afternoon . . . with my suitcase. In a house this size, I'm sure you can find room for me. And we will talk about the measures we need to take to keep you safe. Be well till then. Lock your doors and turn on your alarm system before you go to bed."

Eleanor shot her a poisoned look but, for once, didn't talk back. Savannah considered that a point for her side. She also decided to leave while she was ahead.

She walked away, around the side of the house to where her Mustang was parked. She was eager to leave, more than happy to put this sad world behind her for the day.

But she paused, her key in her car door as an uneasiness crept over her and a trickle of apprehension skittered down the back of her neck. Was someone watching her from the shadows, just there, near the garage where the limousine was parked? Had she actually seen something from the corner of her eye? Heard someone moving in the bushes? Or was she just feeling the heebie-jeebies from her unpleasant contact with Eleanor?

Maybe it was one of the coyotes Gilly had mentioned, hunting rabbits or chasing birds in the underbrush.

But Savannah didn't think so. The hair on the nape of her neck didn't prickle at coyotes or birds. The only kind of varmints who raised her hackles were humans. The two-legged kind were the ones you had to watch out for.

She opened her car door, twisted her key in the ignition, then flipped on her headlights.

The beams lit the area but revealed nothing unusual . . . if you didn't consider a black Jaguar roughly the size of a house unusual.

But still, those cold fingers of caution were tickling the back of her neck.

"I know you're there," she said to the darkness . . . just in case. "Not only that: I know who you are and what you're up to."

Okay, so I don't know diddly-squat, she thought, but they don't have to know that.

"All I've got to say is, what you're figuring on doing . . . you'd just better not, 'cause you won't get away with it."

She could have sworn the silence grew heavier, the dark shadows darker. But, as she had expected, nobody replied and nothing moved.

Finally, she got into her car, started the engine, and drove away. Ah, well, she thought as she passed through the gates and headed toward the warmth of hearth and home. I don't know if that was enough to stop whomever from doing whatever, but it'll give 'em something to think about. Oh, man, I need a hot bath and a couple of friendly, furry faces that don't bite.

Chapter 4

After a restless eight hours of nightmares, populated by monstrous chocolate-coated queens chasing her with an ax and screaming, "Off with her head! Off with her head!" Savannah woke to a pounding on her front door. The cats leapt off the foot of her bed and headed for cover under the dresser, their usual hiding place when someone visited.

"Some watchcats you two are," she muttered as she hauled her tired body out of bed and slipped on her favorite blue terrycloth robe. "It's probably Tammy . . . lost her key again."

The moment she stood, it hit her: the dizziness and a throbbing pain across her forehead. She swallowed and felt as though she had just taken a gulp of prickly pear cactus juice—with the prickles.

The loud pounding on the door seemed to shoot into her ears and through her body, causing her aches to ache and her hurts to hurt. She was sore in places she hadn't known she had.

"Oh, great, a cold," she grumbled in a voice that was half an octave lower than usual. "Just what I need."

On the way to the door, she grabbed a handful of tissues from a box on the coffee table and blew into them. She was still blowing when she opened the door and found Dirk on her front porch.

"Oh, now that's appealing," he said as he brushed by her and walked into the living room. "What's the matter, you sick or something?"

"Yeah, I think I've got a cold, and I should give it to you, waking me up like that. Why are you here so early?" She reconsidered. "Why are you here at all?"

She followed him as he continued on into the kitchen.

"I came over for breakfast," he said. "Remember, the other morning? We were gonna have breakfast together and then you made me go to the bank and—"

"Boy, you've got some nerve," she said, sinking onto a chair at the kitchen table. She propped her elbows on the table and her face in her hands. "I feel like death warmed over, and you come here expecting me to cook for you. Why I oughta—*ach-oo!*"

"Bless you."

"Eh, bite me. What have you got there?"

She noticed for the first time that he was carrying something with him—something pink—and now he was setting it on the kitchen counter.

A rustling of paper . . . and the smell of cinnamon and coffee filled the room, penetrating even her stuffed-up nasal passages.

"You brought me Pastry Palace cinnamon rolls?" Suddenly the world seemed bright; perhaps life was worth living, after all. "And coffee? Oh, Dirk, you're the best."

From the depths of the hot pink paper bag he pulled two giant Styrofoam cups. With great aplomb he set one of them in front of her and pulled off the plastic lid. "With extra cream, not milk, and two sugars, just the way you like it."

She took a sip, and the hot sweetness soothed her angry throat. "Dirk, darlin', I adore you."

He grinned. "And here we have . . . an extra goopy, super cinnamon roll with cream cheese frosting." He opened a small cardboard box and waved the pastry under her nose. "For this, you should volunteer to be my sex slave. After you get over that cold, that is. I don't want you givin' me cooties."

"I ain't giving you nothing, boy, with or without cooties. But, oh, this is so-o-o-o good! It warms the cockles of my little heart."

He grunted as he plopped down onto the seat next to hers and unwrapped his own breakfast. "I hate to think how long it's been since I had my . . . ah . . . cockles . . . warmed."

"Do you mind? Person eating here."

They munched and sipped in blissful silence for several minutes. Savannah could feel the infusion of sugar and caffeine jump-starting her groggy system. And along with enhanced consciousness came suspicion.

"Why did you really come over here," she said, "bearing coffee and goodies? I mean, not that you aren't the soul of generosity, but—"

He gave her a wounded look, then bit off a mouthful of roll. "You're sure a cynical old broad, you know that?"

"Cynical middle-aged broad. Let's just say that I know you. And if you'd just intended to be sweet, you would have dropped by Joe's Donuts, gotten a free dozen, and come over with that. But this—" She waved a hand at the bounty. "You actually opened your wallet and shelled out cold, hard cash for this spread. You want something. No doubt about it."

His lower lip protruded like that of a petulant kindergartner. The pout looked ridiculous on a fight-scarred, streetworn, forty-something face. "You really know how to hurt a guy. I was just—"

"You wanna come over to watch football tonight on my big screen?"

"No, geez, you're—"

"Is there a fight on HBO? You've really got to get your own cable, you know. Your antenna with the sheets of tinfoil hanging from it is a disgrace. What do you get, two channels?"

"Three, and—"

"Or do you want me to go on that worthless ATM stroll again with you, wear that stupid old-lady garb and . . ."

He coughed and took a quick sip of coffee. But she had seen it—the gleam of hope in his eyes.

She nodded knowingly. “Yep, that’s it. You want me to do the decoy bit with you again. No way, José. It ain’t happening. This girl’s got a paying gig.”

“The thing that John set you up with? That chocolate gal?”

“The very one. I spent the day at her mansion yesterday, and I’m going back this afternoon. In fact, I’ll be living there in the lap of luxury, in the land of milk and chocolate, earning megabucks, while you—”

“The gig sucks, huh?”

“Big time.” She reached into her robe pocket, pulled out a fresh tissue and dabbed at her nose. “The so-called ‘Lady’ Eleanor isn’t. She wants to know who’s been sending her hate mail so that she can blow them away with the shotgun she keeps in her broom closet.”

“Do you have anybody you like for it?”

“Oh, I like them all for it. Everybody around her hates her, and if you spent two minutes with her, you’d see why. She’s a miserable person, and she’s determined that everyone around share her misery.”

“Have you seen the letters?”

She nodded, and sneezed.

“Do you think they’re serious?”

She shrugged. “Who knows? But either way, you have to operate on the assumption that they are. Better safe than sorry and all that.”

“So, you’re gonna stay over there for a while?”

He actually looked disappointed. If she hadn’t felt so rotten, she might have been flattered that he would miss her. But in her present state of mind, she decided it was the free food and big-screen TV that he was grieving.

“I’m taking a suitcase,” she said. “She’s already told me she doesn’t want me to stay, but . . .”

“But you’ve never been one to worry about whether you’re wanted or not.”

She gave him a searching look over her tissue. “Gee, thanks . . . I guess.”

"No problem. Hey, are you gonna eat the rest of your roll? You didn't get any sneeze cooties on that half, right?"

This time when Savannah stepped out of her car in the Maxwell driveway, she was well-prepared. "Hey, you sweet things," she mumbled as she pulled a plastic sandwich bag from her purse and unzipped it. At her feet, the silkies snarled, but with only a fraction of the ferocity they had displayed the day before. And no one sank his fangs into her living tissues. Definitely an improvement.

"Look at what Auntie Savannah brought you."

She tried to ignore the added pain in her sinuses when she bent over to feed them the tidbits of fried chicken livers seasoned with garlic powder. "Don't think this is because I particularly like you," she said as they gobbled down the offering. "But I figure things will go much more smoothly around here if you and I are friends."

They ate every smidgen and even licked her fingers clean. Tails wagging gaily, they sat up and begged for more. She had to admit that with doggy smiles on their furry faces, they were pretty darned cute. "All right," she said, "I like you a little bit."

"My mother will scream at you if she catches you feeding her dogs," a female voice said from the region of the garage. Savannah turned to see an attractive blonde in a skimpy bikini watching her, a beach towel dangling from one hand, a pair of sunglasses in the other. Her suit was wet, as well as the towel. Savannah assumed she had just been to the beach.

"So, what is it?" the woman asked, pointing to the bag in Savannah's hand. "Arsenic?"

"Chicken livers and garlic. Dogs love it. At least, my granny's bloodhound in Georgia does. Figured it was worth a try."

"Lace it with rat poison next time. Do us all a favor."

Savannah folded the plastic bag and placed it back into her purse. "Your mother? You must be Louise, Gilly's mom."

"You know my kid?"

"I met her last night just before midnight. She was sitting in

the gazebo alone . . . crying. I spent a few minutes with her, seeing if she was all right."

Savannah hoped Louise Maxwell could hear the heavy subtext in her words, but although she was extremely attractive in her Hawaiian print bikini with her golden, shoulder-length hair and perfect tan, she didn't appear particularly intelligent or perceptive and only mildly concerned.

"Well, was she . . . all right?"

"She was pretty upset, but we talked, and I think she felt better afterward."

"Good," she said flatly, not looking particularly grateful or even interested. Then a sudden look of anger crossed her face, giving her a flush of passion that took Savannah by surprise. "Crying, huh? Just before midnight? That's about the time she goes down to hang out with my mother. I'll bet the bitch said something rotten to her again."

Savannah's eyes narrowed. "Yeah, it's sad when a child hears harsh, ugly things. It wounds their spirits."

Again, her pointed barb seemed to sail over Louise's head. Most unfulfilling, she thought, and decided not to waste her breath. One of Granny Reid's favorite sayings came to mind: "Don't try to teach a pig to sing. It's a waste of your time, and it irritates the pig."

Nothing she could say here and now would improve Louise Maxwell's parenting skills.

"Wait a minute," Louise said, taking a few steps toward her, "I know who you are. You're the private detective that Eleanor hired to protect her."

On closer examination, Savannah decided that Louise had spent too many years in the California sun without serious sunblock. While she appeared to be in her twenties from a distance, she looked older up close, due to the webwork of squint wrinkles around her eyes that could no longer be classified as "fine." And the skin on her abundant cleavage had turned mottled and leathery.

"That's right," Savannah said. "I'm here to watch out for your mom. Do you know anyone who might want to hurt her?"

"Well, duh . . ." Louise replied, rolling her eyes like an adolescent. "Who wouldn't? She treats everybody like crap and has for years."

"Even you?"

A more astute person than Louise Maxwell might have seen the suspicious glimmer in Savannah's icy blues, but the blonde prattled on, clueless.

"Oh, especially me! Can you imagine having a drunken witch like that for a mother? She messed me up good. I mean, I have major issues because of her."

"Did you send her those threatening letters, maybe as a means of working through some of your issues?"

That time even Louise got it. She crossed her arms over her chest and lifted her chin a couple of notches. "I did not. I haven't said a word to my mother—or written anything to her either—for three years. And I won't, until she apologizes for messing me up so bad. And, of course, we all know that won't happen because Lady Eleanor doesn't apologize for anything to anyone. She's much too high and mighty for that."

"It must be pretty stressful, living here on her estate and not speaking to her."

"Not really. We've learned how to avoid each other."

"And meanwhile, your mother supports you and your daughter?" Savannah asked evenly.

Louise's nostrils flared. Savannah thought she might start snorting fire any minute. "That's the least she can do, considering what she's done to me! The very least! My shrink bills alone are $3,500 a month, not to mention my rebirthing therapy and my herbal detoxing wraps and acupuncture remedies. She made me sick; she can pick up the tab while I'm healing from her years of abuse."

Savannah said nothing for a moment, just stood there, quietly observing and absorbing. "Okay," she finally said, "whatever.

But if you actually knew who was threatening your mother's life, you'd let me know, right? I mean . . . if she croaked, who'd pay all those bills?"

Louise's eyes narrowed, accenting the squint lines. "I don't think I like you very much," she said. "You've got a smart mouth and a lousy attitude."

Savannah chuckled. "You aren't the first to express that sentiment. And you probably won't be the last. But, then, I don't really give a fiddler's fart, because I'm not here to make friends. My job is to keep your mom safe, and I intend to do that." Turning away, she added, "Good luck with your assorted therapies. I hope you heal soon, for your sake and for Gilly's."

As she walked across the driveway toward the house, she heard Louise muttering behind her back. Savannah was pretty sure it was something like, "Good luck to you, too, bitch. You'll need it."

Fine, she said to herself. Fine and dandy. You, lady—and I use the term loosely—just got moved to the top of my shit list.

Savannah walked in the front door and through the house without seeing a soul. The pile of dirty dishes in the kitchen sink gave her a clue that it might be Marie's day off. The door leading to the ocean side of the house was open, and she thought she could hear voices on the lawn.

She shuddered at the thought of watching Eleanor Maxwell gobbling her breakfast again. But sooner or later, she would have to face the lady of the house, grisly as that prospect might be. So she headed in that direction.

Just before she reached the door, she heard a sound coming from the library, a small but cozy room off the dining room. She recalled hearing Marie refer to it as the "office." Perhaps Eleanor was attending to business and would be more amenable to being interrupted than when she was eating.

She walked to the door of the library and looked inside. Standing at the desk in the far corner of the room was a fiftyish white-haired man in a pinstriped suit with a bright blue paisley

tie and a pink shirt. The last guy she had seen who was dressed that badly was trying to sell her steak knives at a county fair.

But she was less concerned about his fashion blunders than by the fact that he was reading a letter that he was holding. By the tan color of the paper, she was pretty sure she recognized it as one of the threatening messages Eleanor had received.

So engrossed was he in what he was reading that he didn't notice her until she cleared her throat and said, "Hello."

He jumped as if someone had shoved a hot wire down the back of his ugly pink shirt. Fumbling with the paper, he shoved it first behind him, then dropped it onto the desk. "Yeah," he said. "Who are you?"

Quickly Savannah walked across the room, her hand outstretched. "Savannah Reid. I'm working for Mrs. Maxwell. And you are . . . ?"

"Martin Streck, her manager and accountant. If you're working for her, why haven't I heard of you?"

A certain arrogant gleam in his close-set gray eyes told Savannah that Martin Streck was a man who prided himself on knowing just about everything and anything worth knowing.

She gave him a saccharine smile and batted her eyelashes. "Well, I don't know, Mr. Streck. Maybe little ol' me wasn't worth botherin' you with. I'm sure Eleanor would have gotten around to telling you about me sooner or later."

He looked her up and down with eyes that took in every detail. "What sort of work do you do for Eleanor?"

Again, she gave him the eyelash routine. "Why, sir . . . I believe that's confidential. In fact, maybe that's why you didn't know about me. Maybe I'm one of Eleanor's secrets."

She could feel him cringe as she walked over to the desk and looked quite deliberately down at the paper he had dropped. Yes, it was one of the letters she had seen the day before.

"But, then," she said, "I thought those letters were a bit of a secret, too. And it looks like everybody and their dog's brother's cousin is getting to read them and handle them. Not a good idea."

"I'm not just anybody, Miss Reid. I'm Eleanor's accountant and I—"

"Ms."

"What?"

"I said, Ms. Ms. Reid."

Usually, she didn't really give a flip what she was called, but a guy like Streck brought out the feminist in her.

He took a deep, exasperated breath. "Okay, Ms. Reid . . . I've worked for Eleanor Maxwell and her husband for ten years. I'm been involved in the most intimate details of their lives. They don't keep secrets from me."

She nodded agreeably. "Except for me."

"What?"

"You need to get your hearing checked, darlin'. I said, 'Except for me.' Or maybe she just forgot to mention me the last time y'all talked over those intimate details."

Casually, she opened her purse and pulled out a pair of surgical gloves and a clean plastic bag . . . just a couple of basics she had been carrying, along with a tube of lipstick, since she had become a detective on the force years ago.

She put on the gloves, lifted the letter by its corner and slipped it into the plastic bag. "The fewer people who see this, let alone handle it, the better," she told him as she placed the bag, then the gloves, back into her purse. "I told Mrs. Maxwell as much yesterday, but—"

"What—what do you think you're doing there?" he sputtered.

She gave him a big grin as she sashayed across the room to the door. "Just earning my keep." Another eyelash flutter . . . and she was gone.

Even if she hadn't heard voices on the patio, Savannah would have headed outside for some fresh air. She found herself hungry for the company of somebody who didn't give her the creeps, and those wholesome souls seemed to be few and far between at the castle that chocolate built.

A dolphin swimming by would be good, but even a seagull would do. Anything with a friendly face.

The scene she found on the patio was even more whimsical than she could have hoped.

A formal tea party. Attended by Gilly and Eleanor, a life-sized baby doll, and a teddy bear. All were elegantly attired for the occasion. The doll wore a long, lacy christening gown, the bear a red plaid vest and black top hat, while Gilly and her grandmother were decked out in enormous sun hats festooned with feathers and silk flowers. Copious amounts of gaudy jewelry were draped about their necks and wrists, dripping from their ears and sparkling on every finger. Gilly's tiny body was almost completely cocooned in a pink feather boa, while Eleanor wore a bright purple and red kimono.

"Lord have mercy," Savannah said, her hand shielding her eyes. "I'm nearly blinded by all this splendor. Whatever are you fine ladies doing out here this afternoon?"

"We're having tea," Gilly said in an aristocratic English accent that rivaled her grandma's TV persona. "High tea, that is. Would you care to join us?" She dropped the accent and turned to her grandmother. "She can play with us, too, huh, Nana? I like her. She's a friend of mine."

Eleanor looked up at Savannah with a gentler, kinder face than Savannah had ever seen her wear before. Gilly seemed to have a positive, calming effect on her grandmother.

"I suppose she can, if she wants to," Eleanor said. "But where will she sit?"

Gilly climbed off her own chair, getting momentarily tangled in her boa. "Teddy can sit over here with Marjorie, and Savannah can have his seat."

Having rearranged the toys, Gilly grabbed Savannah's hand and pulled her to the empty chair.

"Are you sure Teddy and Marjorie won't mind?" Savannah asked Gilly.

"Oh no. They like sitting together. They're very good friends."

Gilly returned to her own seat, adjusted the wide-brimmed hat on her tiny head and tossed one end of the boa over her shoulder with the panache of a silver screen glamorpuss. "Now, we have to get you some tea and—" She looked across the table at Savannah, and her smile disappeared. "Have you been crying?"

Savannah was touched by the girl's depth of concern, though a bit confused. "No, why do you ask?"

"Your nose is all red, and your eyes are poofy."

"Poofy? Oh . . . no, I haven't been crying. I woke up this morning with a bit of a cold."

"And you brought it over here?" Eleanor snapped, suddenly alert. "I hired you to protect me, not infect me!"

"I'll be very careful to cover my mouth when I sneeze," Savannah told her with an exaggerated patience that she didn't feel. "And you've already warned me about breathing down your neck, so . . ."

Eleanor glared at her for a few seconds, and Savannah could practically hear her mental cogs spinning; she was debating whether to kick her and her cold germs off the property or to let it slide for the moment.

Apparently the lady was in a mellow frame of mind. Instead of ejecting Savannah from her chair she turned toward the house and gave an unceremonious whistle, like a New Yorker signaling a cab.

A second later the kitchen door opened, and a man in a tuxedo appeared. Hurrying over to the table, a snowy linen towel draped over his left forearm, he said a bit breathlessly, "Yes, ma'am. More tea? Crumpets? Sandwiches?"

"Yes, more of everything." Eleanor waved an airy hand, signifying the whole spread, which Savannah had just noticed was quite impressive. Crumpets with lemon curd and raspberry jam, tiny sandwiches that had been cut into the shapes of hearts and diamonds, adorned with thin slices of cucumber and the occasional dot of red caviar.

Suddenly, Dirk's coffee and cinnamon roll seemed hours away.

"And my friend is joining us," Gilly said, spreading on the accent thick. "Will you please bring her a spot of tea, too, Sydney?"

The formally attired fellow with the white towel nodded his head graciously. "Certainly, Miss Gilly. Right away."

So, this was Sydney, the chauffeur and occasional teatime butler. Savannah decided that he was about her age but looked a bit older due to his salt-and-pepper hair, which he still had in abundance. Dirk would have been jealous.

He was taller than six feet, but his shoulders were badly hunched as though he had carried a heavy burden most of his life . . . or maybe just the past few years. Savannah imagined that working for Eleanor Maxwell could cause one to age prematurely.

But she had to like a man who smiled so warmly at a child and scurried away to do her bidding. She remembered that Gilly had mentioned him the night before as one of the people in her life who "liked" her.

"Do you two have tea often?" Savannah asked, addressing her question more to Gilly than Eleanor, who seemed a bit on the sullen side of the street this afternoon.

"The four of us," Gilly whispered, nodding discreetly toward the doll and bear.

"Oh, of course. The four of you."

"Just when I stay home sick from school."

Sydney appeared with a silver tray that was laden with reinforcements for the half-empty plates of goodies. As he set Savannah's teacup in front of her, she noticed that he lacked the grace and dignity of a professional butler. But he seemed to be doing his best—for a guy who was usually a chauffeur and handyman.

"Will there be anything else, miss?" he asked Gilly.

"That will be all for now, Sydney," the child replied with a graceful, dismissive wave of her hand.

"Hang around," Eleanor added. "I'll yell if we need some-

thing. Go work on the kitchen. It's a mess. That damned Marie . . . just had to go see her mother in L.A. Never mind whether she's needed around here or not."

Sydney gave a slight bow in Gilly's direction and turned on his heel to leave. But a split second before he walked away, Savannah saw him shoot a quick look at Eleanor Maxwell that radiated pure hatred.

And although Savannah could hardly blame him, she was surprised how completely that look changed his otherwise pleasant face. She didn't envy Eleanor, who seemed to have a knack for bringing out the worst in everyone around her.

"Those are my favorites, right there," Gilly said, pointing to a crystal plate holding pink, yellow, and white petit fours. "The pink ones have strawberry jam in the middle. The yellow ones are lemon. Marie puts roses on the top of them, just for me, 'cause she knows I like roses."

"And"—Eleanor interjected as she shoved one of the cakes into her mouth and chewed—"because Grandma tells her to."

Gilly looked down at the plate of sweets and shrugged. "Yeah," she said, the sparkle gone from her voice. "Everybody does what Grandma tells them to . . . if they know what's good for them."

Eleanor smiled broadly.

Savannah took a sip of her tea and tried not to hate Eleanor Maxwell. It was a personal policy of hers: Don't hate the people who are paying your bills. At least, not so that they can tell.

Chapter 5

Savannah chased Eleanor throughout the afternoon, trying to finagle a moment of quality time with her uncooperative client. But Eleanor was too busy barking orders on the phone, then taking a long, leisurely bath and an even longer nap to discuss something as mundane as personal safety.

"Just find out who sent me those damned letters and leave me alone!" she screamed when Savannah attempted to present her with a list of suggestions to enhance security at the house and studio.

Standing at the recently slammed bedroom door, list in hand, Savannah resisted the urge to kick it open and throttle the wicked queen.

"I've just about had my can full of this," she muttered to herself as she walked downstairs to the kitchen, where Sydney was loading dishes into the dishwasher. He had shed his tuxedo jacket, which was hanging on the pantry door, and his sleeves were rolled up to the elbow.

At his feet, the three terriers pranced about on tiptoes, their toenails clicking on the highly polished oak floor. They were watching his every movement, hoping some food tidbit might drop. One of them was even sitting up and begging quite beguilingly.

But Sydney didn't appear to be beguilable. His face looked as glum as Savannah felt.

"There's gotta be an easier way to make a buck, Syd, my man," she said, feeling an instant companionship with anyone in Eleanor's employ.

He chuckled and scraped some leftover petit fours into the garbage compactor. The dogs yipped and ran in circles around him, but they might have been invisible for all the attention he gave them. "I was just thinking the same thing myself," he said as he shook some powdered soap into the washer's dispenser. Just the flowery smell of the detergent made Savannah's nose tickle, but she pushed down the urge to sneeze. Her head ached enough already.

"How long have you worked for Eleanor?" she asked

"Seems like my whole life, but it's really only been about seven or eight years."

"Time flies when you're having fun, right?"

"Yeah, really. It's been a blast." He laughed again, but there was no humor in the sound.

"So, why do you stay?"

He looked at her with eyes that were deeply tired, reflecting a spirit whose life force was ebbing low. He shrugged. "You get used to a place, you know, and the people."

"And the way they treat you?"

He paused, then shook his head. "No, I don't think anybody really gets used to that."

"What exactly do you do here, when you aren't playing butler for Gilly?"

He smiled and for a moment Savannah could see that he would have been handsome when he was younger. And less tired. He took one of the leftover chicken salad sandwiches, pulled it into three parts, and gave one to each terrier. They attacked the tidbits like famished wolfhounds. And once they had licked even the smallest crumb from the floor, they left the room, tails wagging.

"Gilly's the nicest part about being here," he said. "She's a sweet kid. Louise needs to take better care of her."

Savannah bit her tongue and simply nodded her agreement.

As he wiped down the marble counters with a wad of paper towels, he gave her a list of his assorted duties. "I'm supposed to be Eleanor's driver—I live in the chauffeur's apartment over the garage and have for years—but I don't take her out much, because she's agora . . . agro . . . something that makes you afraid to leave home."

"Agoraphobic?"

"Yeah, that's it. She hardly ever leaves the property. Has everybody and everything brought to her. So, I keep the cars in good shape, plant her precious lilies, prune her roses, string gobs of lights all over the house at Christmas until it looks like a Las Vegas casino. But I don't know why we bother. She doesn't throw parties anymore. She doesn't like having anybody in the house but us—you know, people she knows really well."

Savannah locked eyes with him. "And does she know all of you . . . really well?"

He returned her pointed look, then threw back his head and gave a hearty laugh that filled the house. It echoed eerily, as though the sound were foreign within those walls. "No, I don't suppose she does," he said. "If she knew half of what any of us say or think about her, she'd send us all packing."

Savannah laughed with him. Then she decided to let him have it, verbally, in the diaphragm, just to see what he would do.

"Who's sending Eleanor those hate letters, Sydney? Do you know?"

He stopped laughing abruptly and stared at her, slightly open-mouthed for a moment. Then he walked over to the garbage compactor and tossed his handful of paper towels into it. "Could be anybody, right?" he finally said, " Like a crazy fan or . . ."

"She thinks it's somebody she knows. Somebody here."

He sighed and leaned against the butcher-block island. "Could be one of us."

"Us?"

"Somebody who works for her: Marie, Kaitlin, Martin, a member of the film crew, one of the gardeners."

"How about family?"

"She doesn't have that much family. She and Burt are split up and now she's just got Louise and Gilly . . . and her sister, Elizabeth."

"Sister?"

He nodded. "Yeah, Liz and Eleanor are twins. But Elizabeth's a lot nicer and better looking than Eleanor. Beauty is as beauty does and all that."

Ah, Savannah thought, there's something to my evil-twin theory after all.

"Are they close?"

"They're identical twins, but Liz doesn't come around here much. They've had a falling out. Eleanor's pretty much on the outs with everybody."

"So I gathered." She paused, thinking of the woman locked inside this magnificent prison, with herself as the warden. "She must be terribly lonely."

But Sydney didn't seem to share her momentary pang of compassion. He shrugged and wiped his hands on a dish towel. "If Eleanor's alone and lonely, she deserves to be. She's worked really hard at it." Grabbing his tux jacket off the pantry doorknob, he said, "Sorry, but I have to change the oil in the Jag and then separate some lily bulbs. Catch you later."

"Sure. Later."

Savannah stood in the kitchen, thinking for a minute or two, evaluating their conversation. She liked Sydney, but she didn't completely trust him. When she had asked him if he knew who was sending the letters, he hadn't answered her directly. And she had learned long ago not to trust people who answered your questions with a question of their own.

Sydney knew more than he was telling her; she was sure of it. And why wouldn't he? When you did things as intimate for

someone as emptying their garbage and doing their dishes, you learned all sorts of things.

Of course, if you wanted to remain employed, you also learned to keep such things to yourself.

She took the list she had made for Eleanor out of her pocket and scanned it:

√ Reset security code on house alarm system and activate it every night.
√ Same with entry gates.
√ Make sure all doors and windows are secure before retiring.
√ Get the shotgun out of the broom closet and stow it someplace safe.
√ Install better lighting around house and some motion detectors.
√ Repair holes in property perimeter fencing.

As Savannah's eyes scanned the page, she realized that Lady Eleanor wasn't likely to do any of these things, let alone all of them.

Like many egocentric people, Eleanor didn't really believe that she was mortal, that someone could actually do her harm.

For so long she had surrounded herself with people who only obeyed. It was beyond her mental grasp to think that someone might kill her without her express permission.

And Savannah herself didn't really believe that the woman's life was in danger. After all, many people wrote nasty letters to people they didn't like, especially celebrities. An anonymous note was a coward's way of venting hostility without taking any personal risk. If you didn't have a personal standard that prevented you from acting like a jackass and a chickenshit, you could make an enemy crazy for the price of a stamp.

It was a long, long way from writing threatening words on a piece of paper to actually committing the act of murder.

But . . . when you were talking about the taking of human life,

you didn't think in terms of "What usually happens is . . ." You took all possibilities under consideration.

And dammit, Savannah thought, she's got to be a little more careful. Queens have been assassinated for centuries. Some of them even deserved it.

But, of course, whether they derserved it or not didn't matter. No queen—noble or wicked—died on her watch. No way. She wouldn't allow it.

So why was a little voice in her head saying something nasty like, Famous last words, girl. Famous last words.

"Oh, shut up," she told her inner demons as she headed upstairs to what would be certain rejection. "What do you know about anything?"

But she felt sort of sick inside, and it had nothing to do with the cold she was catching. It was a tightness in her stomach, and she knew the cause. It was because she had learned long ago . . . those little devils were usually right.

Savannah stood in the shadows at the edge of the set, watching the evening taping of the Lady Eleanor, Queen of Chocolate, show. At her elbow stood a positively giddy Tammy, so excited that she was about to dance out of her cargo shorts.

What was it about TV shows, any TV show, that piqued people's curiosity and inspired them to adore even the least adorable?

With her nose running like a faucet and her head throbbing like it was being hit by John Henry's hammer, she wasn't in the mood to idolize anybody, let alone Eleanor the Crab. The so-called lady had already snapped at two of her hapless crew and outright screamed at another one, and still, Tammy gazed at her as though she were true royalty.

"This is just too cool," Tammy whispered. "I'm so psyched that you invited me to see it."

"It wasn't exactly an invitation. I need you. I want you to work."

"Oh, I know. But it's just so fun to see it all happening right before your eyes."

Savannah felt another sneeze rising to the surface. She pressed her finger under her nose but half of it escaped. "*Ach*—"

"Sh-h-h," Kaitlin warned them as she walked by, wearing her headphones and carrying her ubiquitous notebook.

"Sorry." Savannah nudged Tammy and led her out of the converted barn with its hot lights and into the cool night air.

"Ah, it's better out here anyway," she said as they walked away from the crew's parked cars and up the driveway toward the gates and the main road.

Savannah reached into her purse and pulled out several plastic bags that contained the letters Eleanor had received. "I want you to take these to Dirk and ask him to get somebody to dust them for prints. They're probably covered, because they've been passing them around here like hot potatoes, but it's worth a try."

"Okay, if I have to."

Not a lot of love was lost between Dirk and Tammy, and Savannah didn't have to question Tammy's reluctance.

"Yes, you have to. And"—she pulled another list out of her purse—"here are the names of the people who work here and miscellaneous family members. Ask him to run them, see if anybody comes up with a record."

"Oh, he's going to just love that. Can't I ask Ryan?"

Like most females who weren't dead, Tammy was madly infatuated with Ryan Stone and refused to believe he was a lost romantic cause. She never missed an opportunity to see, speak to, or touch him in hopes that his sexual orientation might be reversed by the sheer power of her feminine wiles.

"No, you can't ask Ryan. He and John aren't actually in the bureau anymore, and we ask them for enough favors as it is. Dirk owes me one."

"Dirk owes you a million."

"True, but we have to collect one at a time so as not to shock his system." She looked back toward the studio and sniffed the air. "Do you smell that?"

"What?"

"I could swear I smell chocolate. The recipe Eleanor's doing

tonight is a cake called Death by Chocolate. If we go in and keep quiet like good little girls, maybe they'll give us a bite."

When they reentered the studio, Savannah saw to her delight that their timing was perfect. Lady Eleanor was indeed dishing up pieces of a decadently rich dark chocolate cake to members of the crew.

At first Savannah was surprised with the grace and generosity she was displaying as she served up her creation. Then she saw that the cameras were still rolling. This "feeding of the hungry multitudes" was just part of the act.

Deciding to be one of those fed, Savannah jostled her way to the front and nabbed a plate.

In a display of utter selflessness, she offered it to Tammy, who was standing behind her. Tammy graciously declined, as Savannah had known she would—otherwise she never would have risked it.

This chance of a lifetime. This opportunity to sample, firsthand, the creation of a chocolate goddess. To sink her teeth into—

It was awful.

Savannah stood there, her mouth full of dry, bitter, nasty cake and nowhere to spit it, except back on the plate—which Granny Reid had distinctly taught her was a no-no under any circumstances. Repressing a shudder, she swallowed and wished in vain for a glass of anything—even quinine—to rinse it down with.

She glanced around and saw that no one, except for Lady Eleanor herself, was actually eating any of theirs. Kaitlin Dover was watching her from the other side of the set, a knowing grin on her face.

Apparently the crew had wised up long ago and knew a secret that the world had yet to learn: Lady Eleanor, Queen of Chocolate, was a rotten cook.

No wonder the recipes Savannah had tried at home had failed miserably. They were lousy recipes!

Following the lead of those around her, she discretely stashed

her still-full plate on top of a piece of equipment . . . any equipment . . . and casually watched the rest of Eleanor's performance.

"Now, dear viewers, be sure not to overbake this delicate confection," she was saying to the camera, "or you'll lose its subtle flavor."

Overbake it? Savannah thought. You couldn't burn that brickbat with a blowtorch.

And as for the subtle flavor, she had never personally chewed on a burned truck tire, but she would expect it to have the same delicate piquant.

"Good?" Tammy whispered in her ear.

"Delicious," she replied dryly.

"Yeah, I had a feeling."

Tammy chuckled and Savannah elbowed her in the ribs. "Shush, or they'll kick us out again and—"

The words left Savannah's brain as she turned to see why Lady Eleanor had abruptly stopped speaking. The cameras were still rolling, but the star of the show was frozen, standing still, eyes and mouth wide open, her face turning an alarming shade of purple beneath her auburn wig.

"What's wrong with her?" Tammy whispered. "Is she choking?"

Half a dozen possibilities raced through Savannah's mind as she hurried toward her client, her heart pounding, no longer concerned about whether or not she interrupted the taping.

By the time she reached Eleanor's side behind the faux kitchen counter, she had narrowed it down to a stroke or heart attack.

Eleanor was leaning on the range in front of her, sweat pouring down her face, her hands clutched over her chest.

Savannah grabbed her by the shoulders and eased her to a sitting position on the floor. Instantly they were surrounded by a tight circle of crew members, including Kaitlin.

"What is it?" the producer was shouting. "What's wrong?"

"Back up and give us some air," Savannah said as she loosened

the buttons of Eleanor's high-necked lace blouse. She glanced up and saw Tammy beside Kaitlin, her cell phone already in her hand. She was punching 911.

"Can you talk to me, Eleanor?" Savannah asked. "Can you tell me what's wrong?"

Eleanor shook her head, then gasped out the words, "Hurts . . . can't breathe."

"Are you choking?"

She shook her head no and pointed to her chest.

Her purple complexion had changed to an ashen gray and rivulets of sweat streamed down her face.

"Just try to relax and take deep breaths," Savannah told her as she continued to remove her upper clothes. Beneath the blouse was a tightly laced long-line bra—a constricting foundation for the genteel-lady costume.

Savannah fumbled with the laces for a moment, then had them free. "There you go, now breathe slowly. Like this—in . . . fill up your tummy . . . and slowly out. Come on. You'll be okay. An ambulance will be here in just a minute or two. Everything's going to be okay."

But Savannah knew it wasn't going to be okay. More than once she had held a dying person in her arms. She knew the look.

Eleanor's eyes locked with hers for a moment, and she saw that Eleanor knew, too.

"Tell Gilly . . ." she said, barely whispering the words. "Tell Louise . . ."

"Yes, of course." Savannah lowered her back onto the floor. Someone handed her a bunch of towels and she shoved them under Eleanor's head. Then she grasped both of her hands tightly. "What do you want me to tell Gilly and Louise?"

"That I love . . ." She gasped and shivered. Savannah squeezed her hands and prayed that an ambulance with paramedics might appear out of thin air. But although it seemed far longer, less than a minute had passed since Tammy had made the call.

"I understand, Eleanor," she told her, leaning forward, her face close to the woman's. "I'll tell them you love them."

Tears flooded Eleanor's eyes and she choked back a sob. "I do. Really."

"I know, sweetie, I know. I'll tell them, I promise. You just rest now."

Savannah's words seemed to have a soothing effect, because the hands that were gripping hers relaxed, and Eleanor's face took on a peaceful expression.

"Not . . . so . . . bad," the woman whispered. "Not so bad . . . now."

As though from far away, Savannah could hear someone—she thought it was Kaitlin—asking, "What can we do?"

"Send somebody out to the main road to make sure the ambulance gets in the gates," Savannah replied. "Bring them in here as soon as they arrive."

She looked up and saw that it was Kaitlin leaning over them, her face stricken as she stared down at Eleanor.

"Is she . . . ?" Kaitlin nudged Savannah's shoulder. "Is she going to . . . ?"

Savannah didn't want her to say the words aloud. Maybe if nobody actually said it—

"Just tell them to hurry." Savannah emphasized the urgency of her message with her eyes and the gravity in her voice. Her own pulse was racing, her hands shaking. Her legs felt like jelly.

Kaitlin nodded. "I will. I'll make sure they understand." Then she disappeared.

Savannah released one of Eleanor's hands and placed her fingertips to the woman's jugular vein. She felt a pulse there, but it was faint and erratic. Eleanor's breaths were more even than before, but shallow. Her eyes were closing.

"Wake up, darlin'," Savannah said, gently jostling her. "Keep those eyes open for me. Look right up here at me, okay? Help's going to be here any second now. Just relax."

Tammy knelt beside them on the floor and reached out to pull the hot, heavy wig off Eleanor's head. Her own hair was matted to her scalp, and she looked like a ewe who had been badly shorn.

"Her pulse?" Tammy whispered.

"Thin. Thready."

Savannah looked up at the crew members who stood around them, watching, saying absolutely nothing, frozen by fear and uncertainty. The silence in the studio was deadly, the air thick with dread.

"Did they give you an ETA?" Savannah asked.

"Seven minutes," Tammy replied.

"Okay, that was about two minutes ago. Five more to go."

She reached down and wiped the sweat off Eleanor's face, but Eleanor's open eyes had ceased to focus. She stared over Savannah's shoulder, seeing nothing.

Savannah put her fingertips to her throat again. "No pulse," she said.

Tammy bent over and placed her ear to her nose. "No breath."

"CPR," Savannah said, positioning herself over Eleanor, her hands on her chest. "Let's go."

"Savannah," Tammy said, "she's dead."

"No. She's not dead . . . not until she's pronounced. Do what I tell you, girl! Tilt her head back, pinch off her nose and blow after five! Here we go: one, two three, four . . ."

Chapter 6

"I've probably been more bummed than I am right now at some time in my life," Savannah observed as she watched the county coroner's van pull away with her latest client. "But I don't rightly recall when."

Tammy put her arm around Savannah's shoulder and gave her a sideways hug. "It wasn't your fault. Dr. Liu said it was probably a heart attack. We did the CPR. It was just her time."

Savannah walked across the lawn to the gazebo where she had talked to Gilly only the night before. Now it seemed like ten years ago.

Savannah pulled her sweater more tightly around her and shivered, although the night air was decidedly warm. Her head ached, and every muscle in her body cried out for a hot bath and a bed. She wasn't sure how much of her misery was due to her cold and how much to having a client die in her arms.

"That poor little Gilly," she said. "Her grandmother may have been a drunk, but she cared about the kid. I had a tea party with them just this after—"

Savannah's throat started to close up as a sob rose to the surface. She quickly swallowed it. If she started to cry now, she'd fall to pieces. And that was another one of her professional standards: never come unglued on the job. Wait until you're home, and

make sure you have several pints of Ben & Jerry's Chunky Monkey in the freezer. Then slip into your comfy robe, grab a box of tissues and a large spoon . . . and let 'er rip.

But at the moment she was a long ways from the freezer or her blue terry-cloth robe. So she sucked it inside and pushed it down—to explode another time.

Dirk exited the studio, a roll of yellow perimeter tape in one hand. He looked around and, spotting them in the gazebo, walked their way.

"I'm glad you caught the case," Savannah said as he approached.

"Well, I'm not," he grumbled. "Did you get a load of those camera crews lined up outside the gate? This is gonna be a media circus. Hell, you'd think Martha Stewart or Emeril kicked the bucket, not some two-bit hustler like that old broad was."

Savannah bristled. "Excuse me. The poor woman's dead."

"Then she won't mind what I say about her, will she." He sighed and sank down onto the cushioned bench beside Savannah. "Anyway, how come she's a 'poor woman' now? You called her a bitch this morning, right there at the breakfast table. I heard you."

"Oh, shut up, Dirko," Tammy snapped. "Sometimes you've got the sensitivity of an armadillo."

"A what?"

"Never mind, just watch what you say. Savannah's feeling bad about this."

Dirk actually seemed surprised. "Really? Why? She was fat, she was old, and she croaked. It happens all the time."

Savannah sprang to her feet and stepped back a few feet to put a safe distance between herself and Dirk before she did him serious physical harm.

"One of these days, Dirk, I'm going to slap you stupid and it won't take long. In the first place, Eleanor was only a few years older than we are, buddy, and secondly, she wasn't fat, she was . . . a lady of abundant proportions."

"Well, excuse me," he said with a sniff. "I don't always keep

up on the most current p.c. terms."

"Oh, screw p.c. and screw you, Coulter. It's a matter of having the sense to understand that everybody doesn't come in one size or shape. Women's bodies are beautiful, and that goes for the big ones as well as the smaller ones. It's believing that any human body that's walking around—seeing, hearing, speaking, feeling, functioning—is a miracle of nature and worthy of respect. And so is the person who inhabits that body."

The emotions that she had shoved down came boiling to the surface and choked off the rest of her speech. She dissolved in wracking sobs.

So much for not coming unglued while on duty.

"Savannah!" Dirk was standing . . . walking toward her, his arms outstretched. "What's the matter with you, Van?"

A moment later he was holding her and she was crying all over the front of his shirt. Tammy was patting her back and murmuring, "There, there."

"What is it, hon? Why are you crying like that?" he said, stroking her hair.

Tammy supplied the answer. "She thinks she killed Eleanor, you idiot."

"What? Why?"

Dirk wasn't always the most perceptive, but Savannah decided to forgive him, because it felt so good to have his big, strong arms wrapped around her. And his shirt smelled good . . . like him. Insensitive but dependable ol' Dirk.

"Eleanor hired her to protect her," Tammy explained, as if he were a mentally retarded cocker spaniel. "Eleanor died. Savannah feels responsible."

"Ah, hell . . . you didn't kill her," he said. "And if you could've stopped it, you would've. That's all there is to it."

Savannah pushed herself away, out of his arms. "It's not that simple."

"I hate to admit it," Tammy interjected, "but it really is that simple. Dirk's right this time."

"What do you mean this time?" he wanted to know.

"Oh, get over yourself, Dirk." Tammy squeezed Savannah around the waist. "Come on. Let's take you home. I'll draw you a bubble bath, and Dirk can pour you a stiff drink."

Savannah pulled some tissues out of her pants pocket and blew into them. "As tempting as that offer is, I'll have to take a rain check." She looked up at the gatekeeper's cottage, where she had seen Louise go, moments after Kaitlin Dover had told her the news about her mother. "There's something I have to do first."

"Are you sure?" Dirk said. "Are you all right?"

"Yeah, I'm all right. And yes, I'm very sure."

"So, is that supposed to make me feel better?" Louise Maxwell lit up a cigarette and tossed her pack and lighter onto the glass-topped coffee table. She was sitting on a leather sofa that had seen better days in a room that was cluttered with magazines, empty pizza boxes, and plastic soda bottles.

Gilly sat, crying softly, on the sofa beside her mother.

Savannah was standing. She hadn't been invited to take a seat.

"I was hoping it might make you feel a little better," Savannah said, "both of you."

Louise tapped her cigarette tip on an overflowing tray and ran her fingers through her blond hair. "Sorry, but it's much too little too late. My mother waits until she's friggin' dying to tell me that she loves me? How messed up is that?"

For just a moment, Savannah allowed herself to reflect on the fact that she had never heard her own mother speak any words of affection or praise. Did it hurt? Sure. Did she let herself dwell on it? Not anymore. She didn't have time to hate. Or the energy either, for that matter. Life was too short.

"I believe she really meant it." Savannah turned to Gilly, who seemed to be absorbing her words more than her mother. "They say that the words of a person who's . . . dying . . . are always true. She asked me twice to tell you both that she really loved you. I'm sure she did, in her own way."

"That's why she had tea parties with me," Gilly offered.

"That's exactly right. And that's why she made sure that Marie put roses on your petit fours."

Louise stood, walked over to the cottage door, and opened it wide. "I think I've heard about all the comforting words I want to hear from you tonight. If you'll just leave me and my daughter to grieve in peace."

Savannah looked over at Gilly. "Are you going to be all right, sweetpea?"

The girl nodded. Savannah could see in her eyes, sad though they were, that the child was strong. She'd make it, in spite of her circumstances.

Some kids grew and thrived in the rockiest of gardens. Savannah had grown into a pretty sturdy weed herself in some less than perfect soil.

"Good night," she told them both as she left. "And I'm very sorry for your loss."

She walked out of the cottage and found Dirk and Tammy waiting for her, ready to take her home. God bless good friends, she thought. God, bless 'em good.

An hour later, Savannah emerged from her steamy, rose-scented bathroom wearing her blue robe and a more relaxed look on her face.

"Well, you look better . . . red nose and all," Tammy told her when she came down the stairs and entered the living room.

Tammy was sitting on the sofa, a serving tray on the coffee table in front of her. Savannah eyed the steaming mug on the tray with a mixture of anticipation and suspicion.

"You didn't make me an herbal something or the other, did you?" she asked. "Not that I don't love your cooking but . . ."

"Oh, please. You hate my cooking."

"That's not true. Except for when you try to sneak that carob-wannabe-chocolate crap into my chocolate chip cookies. And I'm not big on your miso soup or your celery soy shakes." She sighed

and collapsed onto the sofa next to Tammy. "Come to think of it, golden girl . . . I guess I'm not a big fan of your cooking. But as talented and beautiful as you are, who needs to cook, too."

"Good save." She picked up the mug from the tray and held it out to Savannah. "Here, this will fix whatever ails you."

Savannah lifted one eyebrow. "What is it? Not essence of octopus, or ginseng wheat-grass juice, right?"

"Oh, stop. It's a hot toddy. Dirk made it for you. And since he was raiding your liquor cabinet to make it, I'm sure he was generous with the booze."

Savannah took the mug and peeked inside. A slice of fresh orange and another one of lemon floated on the top, studded with whole cloves. The citrus-scented steam filled her stuffy nasal passages with the promise of good Irish whiskey.

She took a drink, held it in her mouth for a moment to savor the spices, and then swallowed. It flowed through her like warm, liquid flame, soothing as it went.

"Ah, that's too good. And you're right; he didn't spare the booze."

"I've heard that a good Irish toddy will cure a cold in twelve hours."

"I don't know if it will cure it, but a few sips and you won't mind being sick half so much."

Diamante jumped into Savannah's lap and began rubbing her face against the front of her robe. Cleopatra joined her, vying for attention.

Savannah looked around. "Where is Dirk, anyway? I thought he'd still be here when I got out of the tub."

"No, he left as soon as you went into the bathroom."

All of a sudden, Tammy wasn't looking her in the eye. That wasn't a good sign.

Savannah took another swig of the toddy. She had a feeling she was going to need it. "Where did he go?"

Tammy reached over and petted Cleopatra, buying time before she finally said, "Ah, you know . . . back."

"Back? You mean to Eleanor's place?"

"Mmmm . . . yeah."

Savannah glanced at her mantel clock. "It's almost two A.M. Why is he going back there now?"

"I don't know. Maybe he left something. You know how Dirk is. He'd forget his head if it weren't attached."

Savannah stared at her, then nudged her with her elbow. "Spill it, kid. What exactly did he say he was going back there for?"

Tammy shrugged and cleared her throat. "He might have said something about finishing up . . . processing the scene."

"Processing? Is he going back with the Crime Scene Unit?"

"I think they might already be there. I think they might have got there right after we left."

"Oh, you think so, huh?"

Savannah set her mug back on the tray and brushed the cats off her lap. "He does think it's a murder scene. He thinks somebody killed her somehow or he wouldn't be treating the place like a crime scene."

"He's just being thorough. You know, erring on the side of caution and all that."

"Bullshit. Dirk doesn't err at two in the morning. He's a hard-working cop, but he's not that conscientious unless he's got strong suspicions. I've gotta go back there. And you have to drive me."

Savannah stood and headed for the stairs. But the effects of the long, traumatic day, the hot bath, and Dirk's toddy hit her legs, and she had to grab the banister to keep her balance.

Tammy hurried to her and offered a shoulder to lean on. "You aren't going anywhere, young lady," she said, "except straight to bed. Dirk told me not to tell you he was going back, because he knew what you'd do. And he told me that if you showed up there, he was going to hold me personally responsible."

"I should help him process that scene. It was my responsibility and . . . *ah-h-h-chew!*"

"Go." Tammy pushed her from behind. "Up the stairs and into bed right now."

Savannah wanted to resist, but it was a clear case of the spirit

being willing and the flesh being weak. “All right,” she said, “but only because you called me a young lady. And only if you’ll bring me the rest of that toddy.”

“You got it. I’ll tell Dirk that you took three sips and were dead to the world. He’ll be so proud.”

Obediently, Savannah trudged up the stairs, her friend right behind her. “Yes, Dirk is easily impressed.”

Tammy nodded. “Especially with himself.”

Chapter 7

As Savannah drove to the San Carmelita police station the next morning, she experienced one of those brief but precious moments when she was truly grateful to be alive. The foothill road that she took from her house to the station passed a number of orange and lemon groves. The smell of the sun-warmed fruit reminded her of the previous evening's treat, and she marveled once again at its healing properties.

When she had awakened in the morning, her head had been completely clear, and other than a nagging sadness and an ache of guilt, she was happy to be in the land of the living.

In the distance, the sun sparkled on the blue of the Pacific, and she could see the palm-lined streets leading to some of the most beautiful beaches on the West Coast.

The station was centrally located in town, on the older, more picturesque Main Street. Like most of the mission-founded towns along the coastline, San Carmelita had begun at an old adobe church a hundred or so years before. The town had grown gracefully, filling the space from the ocean to the foothills with first citrus groves, then stores and houses. From the tiny white bungalows with red-tiled roofs crowded side by side on the beach to multimillion-dollar mansions perched on the hillsides, the town had a lazy, gentle feel about it. And in the years that it

had been her home, Savannah had done all she could as a cop and an investigator to keep it that way.

The older she got, the more she realized the intrinsic value of "lazy" and "gentle."

The thought that someone might have been "less than gentle" with her most recent client was so disturbing that she put the idea aside with an effort and promised herself not to worry about it until she knew more.

She needed information. And the police station—specifically, Dirk's desk—was the place to start.

Every time she pulled into the station-house parking lot, she felt a tug of nostalgia, a twinge of resentment. She had worked hard at being a cop. She had been a damned good one. But years ago she had investigated some people in high places and toppled a couple of political icons and had been kicked off the force for her efforts.

The whole fiasco had been horribly unfair. But she wasn't bitter, and the resentment was only a twinge. She loved her present life as a private detective, and if she hadn't gotten the boot, she'd still be on the force, answering to the schmucks who'd unjustly fired her.

Through the glass front of the building, she could see that the front desk was occupied by one of her least favorite cops, Kenny Bates, a stud-muffin, at least in his own opinion. Kenny didn't seem to notice that for a womanizer, he led a fairly female-free existence. Gals weren't exactly lining up to take a bite out of his cupcake. Savannah strongly suspected that Kenny Boy hadn't had a nibble or even a sniff in years.

The last time she had seen him, he had been working the front desk at the coroner's office. He must have been promoted—or, considering it was Kenny, demoted.

"Hey, hey, hey, Savannah baby!" he proclaimed as she walked through the door. "Just couldn't stay away, huh?"

She glanced at the too-thick, slightly askew toupee, the uniform that was two sizes too small, causing his buttons to strain across his ample belly. She caught the fairly pungent odor of

nacho cheese chips on his breath as he slid the clipboard across the counter for her to sign.

"Oh, yeah . . . Bates. I live for these moments together." She scrawled "Daisy Duck" on the ledger and passed it back to him. She had been signing in with assorted cartoon character names since she had been canned . . . and the vigilant Kenneth Bates had never even noticed.

Ken lit up at her words. She shook her head. Dissing him was just too easy, hardly any challenge at all.

"Really? Me too," he gushed. "Hey, why don't you come over to my place tonight, and we can watch TV together. I've got that new 'adult' channel—it's channel sixty-nine! Get it? Sixty-nine!" He guffawed at his own joke, reminding her of a buck-toothed donkey she once knew in Georgia. "Maybe we can get us some ideas from watching it, huh?"

She shoved the clipboard back at him and took off down the hall, eager to breathe fresh, non-nacho-scented air. "Eat dirt and die, Bates, you friggin' maggot," she said over her shoulder.

"Yeah, well, if you change your mind, give me a ring," he called after her.

She found Dirk at his desk in the squad room. As usual, he was fighting with his computer. Dirk had never recovered from the shock of having to upgrade from his Underwood typewriter to a computer keyboard and mouse.

"Damned thing," he swore as she walked up behind him and leaned over his shoulder. "It ate my document again. I hit one button—I don't even know which one—and poof! It's gone. I hate it when that happens. Stupid piece of crap."

She reached over him, scrolled to the bottom of the page, and hit the "restore" icon. His form instantly materialized.

"It's not the machine's fault. It's operator error," she said, pulling a chair from a nearby empty desk and setting it next to his.

"Tell me something new," he grumbled. "What I really hate is when the darned thing freezes up on me and I have to turn it off the old-fashioned way, you know—with the on/off button—and

then when I turn it on again it yells at me for not closing it down properly."

"That is aggravating, it's true." She looked around the room at the empty desks. Other than one guy whom she didn't even recognize standing at a filing cabinet on the other side of a partition, Dirk was the only one in sight. "Where is everybody?"

"What do you mean everybody? I told you, the cutbacks are wicked. We're down to three detectives. That's it. Ray took his retirement last year, and Bruce went out this year, and they haven't replaced either one of them."

"No wonder you're always asking me to go on stakeouts with you. You're lonely, Coulter."

"Lonely, my butt. I'm just keeping you off the streets and outta the pool halls."

She reached across him and nabbed his coffee cup.

"Hey, don't drink outta that!" He tried to snatch it back, but she was too quick. "You'll give me your cold."

It was room temperature. She grimaced and gave it back to him. "Lukewarm . . . yum. I don't have my cold anymore. That toddy you made last night cured me."

"Completely?"

"My nose is dry, and I haven't sneezed or coughed once since I woke up."

"Wow! I've discovered the cure for the common cold."

"I think the Irish discovered it long, long ago." She studied the form he was filling out on the screen. The words "Eleanor Maxwell" caught her eye. "What're you working on?"

"Nothing," he said, too quickly. "Just the usual crap."

"Did you get any sleep, or did you stay up all night processing the scene?"

He frowned. "Bimbo-head wasn't supposed to tell you about that."

"I pried it out of her—threaten her with mutilation and she caves every time. What have you got?"

"Nothing. Really." He closed the screen and switched off the computer.

"Where's the body?"

"Dr. Liu's got it."

"When is she going to do the autopsy?"

He shrugged. "Don't know for sure. Could be today, tomorrow. Depends on how many bodies she's got piling up down there."

She gave him a piercing look. "Is she doing it right now, Dirk?"

"Yeah. She's probably just about done." He sighed. "And I suppose you want to come with me to the morgue."

She nodded, reached over and ruffled his hair. He hated that. It would take him five minutes to get those precious few strands combed just right to cover the thin spots. "You betcha. Let's go. Now's as good a time as any for good news . . . or bad."

At the coroner's office Savannah and Dirk found Officer Rosa Ortez manning the front desk. Her smile was bright, her manner professional as she asked them to sign in.

"So, you're Kenny's replacement, huh?" Savannah asked as she wrote her own name, not Minnie Mouse's, on the sheet.

"Yes," Rosa replied. "As of Monday."

"How'd that happen?"

Rosa grinned broadly. "He pinched my butt; I took his job."

Dirk laughed. "Sounds fair to me. But now I have to look at his ugly mug over at the station every morning. You were a lot easier on the eyes."

She shrugged. "Sorry. This is a lot closer to my baby-sitter. And Kenny hates working at the station, where there's actually something to do. Unlike here." She waved her hand, indicating the relatively silent and empty building. "Deadly quiet."

"Oo-o-o-o, bad one." Savannah placed the pen back in its holder and waved good-bye. "Keep a stiff upper lip."

"Oh, like that's any better," Rosa replied as they left the reception area and walked down the tiled hallway toward the coroner's autopsy suite in the back of the building.

There was no point in stopping at Dr. Jennifer Liu's office

halfway down the hall. She was hardly ever behind a desk. The swinging double doors that opened into the rooms where autopsies were performed were both closed. That usually meant a procedure was underway.

Savannah steeled her nerves before opening the door. It was never particularly pleasant to watch an autopsy performed, but she found it much harder when the body had belonged to someone she knew. When she swung it open and looked inside, she was relieved to see that the corpse on the table had already been wrapped in a white shroud and was ready for the funeral home's collection. From its general height and shape, she figured it was the remains of Eleanor Maxwell.

Dirk followed close behind her. "Dr. Liu?" he called. "Anybody home?"

A moment later, the county coroner walked out of a back room and joined them beside the body on the stainless-steel table. An exquisitely lovely, petite and slender Asian woman, Dr. Jennifer Liu could have been cast as a runway model, a martial arts expert, or a ballerina. But most people who met her would not have guessed she was a medical examiner.

Her long, glossy hair was tied back with a blue paisley scarf, and she wore green surgical scrubs and disposable paper booties over her sneakers. The scrubs were bloodstained.

"Is this Maxwell?" Dirk asked, nodding toward the body.

"That's her." She turned to Savannah. "Hey, girlfriend. How's it going? Haven't seen you for a while."

Savannah decided not to mention that fact that she considered rare visits to the coroner's office a good thing. Not that she didn't like Dr. Jen, but . . . "Things have been pretty quiet with me," she replied, then added, "Until this, that is."

Dr. Liu nodded. "Yeah, Dirk told me you were her bodyguard or something like that."

"Apparently, I was more 'something' than guard."

The doctor gave her a warm, comforting smile. "There's no reason to suspect foul play at this point," she said. "She died of a

heart attack, and she was being treated for a heart condition. Natural causes."

"Oh yeah?" Dirk said. "That's good news, huh, Van?"

"I guess."

Dr. Liu walked over to a nearby table and picked up a manila folder. Opening it, she studied the papers inside. "I talked to her physician, a Dr. Raymond Hynson, and he said she was suffering from advanced heart disease."

"Was she taking meds for it?" Dirk asked.

"Dr. Hynson had prescribed metosorbide for her. And once you inventory the contents of her medicine chest at home, and I get the lab tests back, I'll let you know if she was taking what he'd prescribed."

"She drank quite a lot," Savannah offered. "Isn't that a no-no for people taking metosorbide?"

"Yes, it is." Dr. Liu shook her head and closed the folder. "What a shame. Some people just don't realize what they're doing to themselves."

Savannah remembered sitting on the patio, gazing out at the dark sea with Eleanor Maxwell—the tears on her cheeks, her comments about how little joy there was in her life.

"Maybe she did realize it," Savannah said. "There's more than one way to commit suicide."

"Was Lady Eleanor, Queen of Chocolate, that unhappy?" Dr. Liu asked, looking at the bundled body on her table.

"Oh yeah," Savannah said. "Definitely that unhappy. No doubt about it."

Chapter 8

"So, it looks like you're off the hook," Dirk said as he drove Savannah home. "Natural causes. Would have happened no matter what you did, short of keeping her from drinking and lowering her cholesterol."

Savannah watched the neighborhood whiz by the car window, but she wasn't seeing it. Her thoughts were elsewhere—on the plastic bags she had given to Tammy the night before.

"Hey, I'm not just talking to hear my own head rattle, you know?" he said, nudging her.

"What? Oh, yeah, right. I'm off the hook. Except . . ."

"Except what? There isn't anything else you can do for her."

"I still haven't done what she hired me to do."

"What are you talking about? She doesn't need protection anymore, she's—"

"I know." Savannah sighed. "But she didn't hire me to protect her. She made that abundantly clear. In fact, she was downright rude about it. All she wanted me to do was find out who was writing her those threatening letters so that she could kill them."

"Is that what she said?" Dirk was instantly alert. "She was going to kill them?"

"I think she was speaking figuratively."

"Well, I certainly hope so."

"And I still need to do my job."

Dirk shook his head. "Savannah, that's dumb. Your client croaked."

"Yeah, but she paid me in advance. I think she'd still want to know who it was."

Abruptly, he pulled the Buick over to the side of the road and turned to face her. "Look," he said, "the gal's dead. She ain't ever gonna know nothin', so—"

"Granny Reid says the moment we pass over we instantly have all knowledge. It's like a veil being lifted, and once we leave the physical world and join the spiritual one, we see everything clearly."

"Then you don't have to find out anything for her. According to your grandma, she already knows everything, right?"

Savannah turned and gave him a long, hard look. "Okay, smarty-pants. Maybe I want to know for myself."

He threw the car into drive and pulled back into traffic. "Well, hell, girl, why didn't you just say so in the first place? Let's go back to the mansion and check out that medicine chest."

"And her dresser drawers, and her desk and her closets and—"

"Anybody ever tell you you're a nosy old broad?"

"Yeah. It's a gift. And I keep telling you, boy . . . I'm middle-aged."

Dirk knocked at the front door of the mansion, but when nobody answered, Savannah reached across him and tried the knob. Just as she had suspected it would, it opened easily.

"They didn't bother to lock it before," she said. "Not much reason to bother now."

The tripping of tiny toenails across the hardwood floors announced the arrival of the terrible threesome.

"Meet my buddies," she told Dirk as she knelt on one knee and began petting first one, then the other. "They're named Satan, Killer, and the little runt one is Hitler."

"Are you serious?" Dirk offered his hand, but Satan snarled. "Stupid names for some barking rats."

"Are you guys hungry?" she asked. Then she noticed the bits of dog food in Killer's tiny beard. Satan's whiskers were wet, so they had water. And they weren't rushing out the door to go doggy-wee-wee, so she assumed Marie must still be on duty.

"They look fine to me," Dirk said, dismissing them with a wave of his hand. It occurred to Savannah that nothing short of a German shepherd or rottweiler was a "real" dog to Dirk. But then, he hadn't been bitten by one of these little ones, either. She still had a bandage on her forefinger.

"Anybody here?" he shouted, his deep voice echoing through the house.

The answering silence seemed heavy and thick, as though the house itself knew that something had changed.

Looking around at the antiques, the heavy drapes, the dark fabrics, Savannah said, "I don't think I'd want to be here after midnight . . . in the middle of a thunderstorm—"

"With a psycho ax-murderer on the loose from a local nut-house . . . yeah, yeah, yeah. You've got some imagination, Van. It's just your average, run-of-the-mill mansion."

"With a carousel horse and a suit of armor in the living room?"

"Exactly. I've got the same sorta stuff in my trailer."

"Oh, yeah . . . with your TV-tray coffee table and your orange-crate bookshelves." Savannah started up the stairs. "Come on, I've been dying to see the master suite."

When Savannah opened the door to Eleanor's bedroom and looked inside, her first thought was, Somebody beat us to it. It's already been searched.

The canopied bed was topsy-turvy, a tumble of blankets, sheets, and pillows, some of it spilling onto the carpet. Half of the dresser's drawers were open, clothes hanging out. The closet door stood ajar, the heel of a rhinestone-studded pump stuck beneath it.

Every horizontal surface was littered with food wrappers, empty booze bottles, jewelry and makeup and assorted items of clothing, some clean but more dirty.

The room had a stale odor about it, as though it badly needed a breath of fresh air.

"She really was depressed," Savannah said.

"Why didn't the maid straighten up in here?" Dirk shook his head as he looked around, taking in the mess. "Hell, this is worse than my trailer. At least I keep all of my dirty clothes in one pile."

"Yeah, you're quite the Suzy Homemaker. I suspect that Eleanor wouldn't let the maid—or anybody, for that matter—in here. This was her cave, where she hid from the world."

Dirk walked over to the closet, pushed the door open, and looked inside. "What do ya suppose she was hiding?"

"The fact that she wasn't Lady Eleanor . . . queen of anything. She was living in a world not of her own design. A lot of women do."

"What?"

"Never mind. You get the bathroom, and I'll see what I can find in here."

Savannah rummaged through the dresser drawers but found only the expected brightly colored, plus-sized muumuus, housedresses, and nightgowns. Judging from the amount of loungewear, Eleanor spent more time lolling around than dressing up.

Not that Savannah would judge her for that. Why not live in pj's if you could? If you had to pour yourself into one of those Victorian corsets and put on a heavy, hot wig every evening . . . kick back the rest of the time.

The miscellaneous candy wrappers, empty cookie boxes, and potato chip bags scattered about revealed a diet that was relatively nutrient-free. Not the ideal for anybody, let alone a heart patient. And Savannah counted at least half a dozen empty fifths of hard booze.

She could hear Dirk rummaging around in the adjoining bathroom. "What did you find?" she called out to him.

"All kinds of crap she was taking," he said. "I've got a dozen prescriptions here at least . . . from several different doctors."

"Are you bringing them with you?"

"Oh, yeah. How about you?"

"Nothing interesting." She walked over to the nightstand, which was covered with movie magazines and romance novels as well as the ever present junk-food wrappers.

Opening the top drawer of the stand, she saw a clutter of reading glasses, old *TV Guides*, and more gaudy costume jewelry. Her practiced eye scanned the mundane contents, looking for the unusual or the informative.

She found it: a journal, leather-bound with loose-leaf pages. A purple felt-tipped pen was tucked between the pages, and the writing throughout was in bold purple ink. The handwriting was large with plenty of curly flourishes, and although the entire book was obviously written by the same hand, the penmanship varied from neat and formal to almost illegible.

Savannah didn't have to read more than a page or two to realize it was Eleanor Maxwell's.

"Bingo," she said. "Diary."

Dirk poked his head around the corner. "Really? Hers?"

"Yep. Could make interesting reading, you know, if . . ." She didn't want to speak the words aloud. "If we find out she was murdered."

"Exactly," he replied.

He disappeared back into the bathroom, and she continued to search the remaining drawers. But the journal was the only thing of interest she uncovered.

"Are you about done in here?" Dirk asked as he exited the bathroom, a paper bag in his hand containing the medications he had found.

"Yes. I peaked with the diary. Let's go."

They were just leaving the master suite and entering the upstairs hall when they heard a noise on the lower level.

"That's too loud to be the mutts," Dirk whispered.

Savannah listened to the heavy footsteps. "Definitely a two-footed critter. Maybe Marie."

"Let's see."

The thick Oriental rugs cushioned their steps as they made

their way quietly down the hall. When they reached the top of the staircase, they could see down into the foyer. Savannah recognized the thick white hair and the pinstriped suit. This time Martin Streck was wearing a purple shirt with an olive tie. She decided he must be color-blind and single. No wife would let her man leave the house dressed like that.

The accountant was holding a large file box, and from the way he was carrying it, the thing was full and heavy.

"Hey," Dirk called as he passed Savannah on the stairs and hurried the rest of the way down. "Whatcha got there, buddy?"

Streck hugged the box closer to his chest and lifted his nose a few notches. "Who are you, and what are you doing here?"

Dirk reached into his pocket, pulled out his badge, and flipped it open, displaying the gold shield. "Detective Sergeant Coulter. I'm conducting an investigation. So I'll ask you again: What have you got in the box?"

One glance at Dirk's face told Savannah that he had exhausted his supply of "nice" and was entering "cranky." Dirk never bothered to stock a lot of "nice" on his personality shelf, and he was frequently running out.

"I'm Martin Streck, the late Mrs. Maxwell's accountant. I need these files to settle her estate." He turned to Savannah. "What have you got to do with this?"

She smiled and shrugged. "I'm just hanging out with what's-his-face here."

"Put the box down," Dirk said.

Streck stuck out his chin. "I will not. These belong to my client and—"

"Belonged . . . belonged to your client," Dirk interjected. "She's dead, and those files are part of my crime scene. Put 'em down. Now."

"Crime scene? What crime has been committed?" A fine sprinkling of sweat popped out on Streck's forehead, and his breathing sounded as if he had just run a hundred-yard sprint.

"The one I'm investigating, and that's all you need to know."

Dirk handed the bag of medications to Savannah, walked over and snatched the box out of Streck's hands. "And you need to leave before you interfere with my investigation."

Streck sputtered a few seconds, then said, "I'm going to have a talk with your superior, Detective. This is most improper. I—"

"You are irritating me," Dirk told him, shoving his face close to the other man's, "and that's damned close to interfering with me and my investigation."

"Yeah, you'd better make some tracks," Savannah added. "Coulter here is very irritable. Almost as irritable as he is irritating, and that's saying something."

"You haven't heard the last of this." Streck huffed and snorted as he stomped across the foyer to the door and jerked it open. "You have no right to keep me from fulfilling my duties to my client. I've never seen such a . . ."

He left, slamming the door behind him.

Savannah and Dirk both looked down at the box in his arms. "He didn't waste any time getting over here and removing those files," she said.

"He sure didn't. All the more reason for me to take a look at them."

Savannah walked over to the window and watched as Streck peeled out of the driveway, screeching his Lexus's tires as he left.

"He's plenty hot and bothered," she said.

"Yeah." Dirk grinned. "And that's why we're going to give these files a long, thorough look."

Chapter 9

Savannah sat in her favorite chair, an overstuffed, wingbacked monstrosity covered in a cabbage-rose chintz. A matching ottoman supported her feet and a sleeping Diamante. Cleopatra stood on the arm of the chair, batting at the fringe on the shade of the floorlamp that supplied reading light for the person relaxing there.

Dirk, Tammy, Ryan, and John sat around her dining-room table in the next room, the files that Dirk had confiscated that day spread out before them. Chatting among themselves, sipping tea and coffee, and nibbling the chocolate chip cookies she had baked for them, they made a cozy picture.

It was a sight that would have normally warmed Savannah's heart. Usually, she would have been there with them, sipping, nibbling, and chatting . . . her favorite pastimes. But her job for the evening was to read the journal she had found in Eleanor's nightstand. And the more she read, the sadder she felt.

Eleanor's writings had been anything but eloquent. In the simplest and sometimes terse language she had described her daily torments.

Written in that large, flowing hand with purple ink, her words touched Savannah, giving her a greater appreciation for the woman than she had held before. No wonder Eleanor Maxwell

had been difficult: she was terribly unhappy and almost completely alone.

A couple of passages impressed Savannah as being particularly honest and poignant.

> *My kid hates me. My only child wishes I were dead. What does that say about me? She says I messed her up, that it's my fault she's miserable. I guess it is. But I didn't know I was being such a rotten mother. I thought I was doing okay at the time, or I would have done something different. The last thing any mother would want to do is mess up her kid. Make her child hate her. She acts like I did it on purpose. Out of spite. Who would ever deliberately do something like that?*

And other passages relating to the breakup with her husband described the pain of betrayal.

> *I know he's in love with someone else. I remember when he loved me, so I recognize the signs. I keep thinking about them together. Picturing him making love to her, saying sweet things to her like he used to say to me. But I can't see her face. I wonder, is she a stranger, someone I've never met, someone who's a member of his world and not mine? Or is she a friend, somebody I see every day, someone who looks me right in the eye and knows? And knows that I don't know. And secretly laughs at me.*
>
> *He lies to me. He says, "I'm going here, I'm doing that." And I know he isn't. I call him a liar and he says I'm crazy, I'm imagining things. I don't know which is the worst, the cruelest. Being unfaithful to me or trying to make me think I'm crazy. I hate him. I may kill him. And when I find out who she is, I might kill her, too. Especially if she's a so-called friend.*

"Are you okay, Savannah?"

Savannah jumped, startled out of her reverie, and looked up to see John Gibson standing in front of her chair, watching her with soft, compassionate eyes.

"What? Oh . . ." She looked down at the open diary on her lap. "Yes, I'm all right. Just depressing reading, this journal. Eleanor's life wasn't pretty."

With the consummate grace that was John Gibson, he sat on the end of the sofa close to her, reached for her hand and folded it between his own. "I have to tell you, love," he said, "I wish I had never given you this referral. It has obviously cost you much more in sorrow than it would ever have paid."

"That isn't your fault, and you have nothing to feel bad about. Anytime I take a job, I know that it could end up badly. It's the nature of the work."

He patted her hand. "But not this badly."

"True. My clients usually survive my services."

"And Mrs. Maxwell would have, too, but for her health problems. I'm sure you'll feel much better when you get those laboratory results and know, once and for all, that she died of natural causes."

Savannah glanced at her mantel clock. "It's after seven. Dr. Liu would have gone home by now. We won't hear from her until tomorrow morning at the earliest."

As though taking some perverse cue, the phone on the end table next to Savannah's chair rang.

She gave John a quick, nervous look. "Or maybe not," she said, picking it up. "Hello?"

A voice with a thicker Southern accent than her own answered, "Hey, Savannah, it's Cordele."

Cordele, one of her many sisters in Georgia, was the one least likely of her eight siblings to ever call. Savannah's mouth went dry as she considered all the tragic possibilities, starting with her octogenarian grandmother. "Cordele, what is it? Is Gran—"

"Everybody's fine. Gran sends her love."

"Oh, good." She placed her hand over her chest and could feel her heart pounding. John was looking at her with concern. "Everybody's fine," she repeated, nodding to John. "So, what's up?"

"Me . . . in a few hours. I'm flying out there to see you."

Mixed emotions flooded Savannah's system. She loved all of

her siblings dearly, but they weren't the easiest people on earth to entertain. And without much notice, and in the middle of a case . . .

"I don't know if this is the best time, darlin'," she said as gently as she could. "We're pretty crazy around here right now and—" My nerves are shot to hell and back, she added silently. "I don't know if it's a good time for a visit."

"I knew you'd say that," Cordele replied, "that's why I went ahead and paid for the flight. Nonrefundable, nontransferable . . . all that."

Savannah felt her nostrils flaring slightly. They always did that when she felt she was being grossly manipulated by a member of her own family.

"You really should have called first," she said as evenly as she could manage. "I would have—"

"You would have told me not to come," Cordele supplied. "And that's why I didn't call you first. It's very important that you and I talk. We have some issues we need to work through."

Those last few words caused a trickle of ice to shiver down Savannah's back. A psychology major in college, Cordele could be a pain in the ass with her "issue solving." She seemed to have a never-ending supply of issues.

"Really, Cordele," Savannah said, trying not to let her voice shake, trying not to start screaming, "this isn't a good time for—"

"There's never a good time to work through family problems, Savannah, but it absolutely must be done."

Savannah's hackles rose. Her sister's authoritative, self-righteous tone made Savannah want to box her ears soundly with a frying pan.

"Cordele, if you want to come out here and go to Disneyland or hang out on the beaches, fine, but I'm not in the mood for—"

Beep.

Her "call waiting" had cut in. She glanced at the caller I.D. and saw it was from the coroner's office.

"Cordele, I'm getting another call, and I have to take it. It's very important and—"

"So are the things I have to discuss with you."

"I know, but—"

Beep.

"I'll see you tomorrow morning at LAX, nine forty-five," Cordele continued. "I'm coming in on Sunrise International, flight three ninety-six from Atlanta. Pick me up. Bye."

"Cordele, I don't know what I'll be doing tomorrow, I—"

Beep.

"Damnation!" Savannah punched the FLASH button. "Hello, Dr. Liu."

"Hi, Savannah," came a calm, quiet voice of reason. "Did I call at a bad time?"

"Oh, only a little worse than usual. What's up?"

"Is Dirk there?"

Not only was Dirk there, he was breathing down her neck and had been since she had uttered the words "Dr. Liu."

She handed him the phone.

Everyone had vacated the dining room and was standing around her chair, collectively holding their breath.

"Coulter here," he said. He listened, nodded, then frowned. "Are you sure?"

"What? What is it?" Savannah whispered.

"And would that cause a heart attack?" he continued, waving her off. "How much?"

"How much what?" Tammy wanted to know.

"Where would somebody get that?" he said.

"Get what?" Still sitting in her chair—but on the edge—Savannah reached out and tugged on the leg of Dirk's jeans.

Ryan and John said nothing, but watched anxiously.

"So what's your final word? What are you ruling it?" Dirk grimaced and gave Savannah a thumbs-down. "Okay, thanks . . . I guess."

He clicked the phone off and laid it on the end table before answering the flurry of "Who? What? When? How? Where?" he was getting from the circle of eager eavesdroppers around him.

"Poisoned," he said.

"What do you mean, poisoned?" Savannah asked, jumping to her feet. "You mean, like rat poison, cyanide, arsenic and lace?"

"Like phenylprophedrine, or something like that," he said. "Dr. Liu got the lab results back, and her bloodstream was full of it."

"Wait a minute," Tammy said. "I saw something about that drug a few weeks ago on the Internet. They were discontinuing it because several people had died."

"Yes." Ryan nodded. "I saw a news byte about that. I believe phenylprophedrine was being used to treat cold symptoms, but it interacted badly with some heart medications. Didn't a lady die in Florida and a man in Oregon?"

"Yes, I think that's what the article on the Internet said," Tammy agreed. "They were heart patients, and the drug interaction caused their blood pressure to soar and—"

Savannah held up both hands. "Wait! Everybody quiet!" She turned to Dirk. "So Eleanor died of a drug interaction?"

"Yep."

She sagged into her chair, her knees weak with relief. "Then it was an accidental death. Thank God."

"Not so fast," Dirk replied. "Dr. Liu says she had a lot in her system, way more than she would have taken if she'd just been treating a cold."

Everyone was silent, digesting this. Finally Tammy said, "So . . . maybe suicide?"

John pointed to the journal that Savannah had placed on the table next to the telephone. "You said the poor girl was dreadfully depressed. Do you suppose it's possible she took her own life?"

Savannah turned to Dirk. "Is that what Dr. Liu is ruling it? A suicide?"

Dirk stared at her for a long moment, as though trying to make up his mind about something.

"Come on," she said. "Just spit it out, for pete's sake."

"Naw, she thinks it's more likely a homicide. And I agree with her. I mean . . . that would be a stupid way for somebody to kill themselves . . . overdosing on cold medicine."

Savannah sat back in her chair and rubbed her throbbing temples with her fingertips. "Boy," she said. "You know it's bad when you're actually hoping for a suicide. How warped is that?"

"Well, I guess you know what this means, boys and girls," Ryan said.

"It means," Savannah replied, "that I let my client get murdered right under my nose."

"No, that's not what it means at all." Ryan sat down on the ottoman and placed a comforting hand on her knee. "It means we have a killer to catch. It's the least we can do for Lady Eleanor, Queen of Chocolate."

"Here, here," John said, patting Savannah's shoulder.

"Yeah, yeah, yeah. Whatever." Dirk turned and walked back into the kitchen. "But if I'm going to have to keep lookin' at these boring papers, I'm going to have to have some more of those cookies. Van, you wanna throw some in the oven."

Savannah thought of Cordele boarding a plane in a few hours and coming to California to work out some familial "issues." She thought of Lady Eleanor, dying in her arms of a fatal drug interaction . . . just as some cold-blooded killer had intended she would. She thought of her dear friend, Dirk, and his need for physical sustenance during these trying, difficult times.

"Eh," she said, "bite me."

At nine forty-five the next morning Savannah was standing outside the baggage-claim area in the Sunrise International terminal cursing herself for not having the chutzpah to just not show up as demanded. Let Miss Smarty-Pants Cordele find her own way from LAX to San Carmelita—or better yet, back to Georgia.

She had a lot of nerve, arriving out of the blue and expecting chauffeur service on top of room and board. Who did Cordele think she was, anyway, the Queen of Sheba, the Czarina of Timbuktu?

Savannah had sincerely entertained the thought of just letting her sister cool her heels awhile at the airport before coming to get

her. After all, she had work to do. Dirk was at the mansion, investigating, as he should be, and she should be there, too. But no, she had gotten roped into baby-sitting her almost-thirty-year-old sister.

Having worked herself into a pretty good lather by the time the plane landed, Savannah had a speech all rehearsed. It had to do with feeling that her boundaries hadn't been respected, nor her preferences taken into account, that her territory had been invaded without her permission, etc., etc.

But the moment the passengers of Flight 396 from Atlanta began to disembark, she felt a sense of excitement. A member of her immediate family, her own flesh and blood, had traveled across the country to see her. She really should feel honored and pleased.

She *did* feel honored and pleased. Having decided that she should, she did. Maybe it would be a great visit, a bonding experience between siblings.

But the instant she set eyes on her sister, the recently generated warm and fuzzy feelings disappeared.

It wasn't the fact that Cordele had the straightest posture of absolutely everybody getting off the plane—including a couple of Marines. It wasn't that her white blouse was buttoned up tightly under her chin or that she was probably the only person in America under the age of thirty who actually wore a brooch pinned at her throat. It wasn't the baggy navy blue skirt or the conservative black loafers that were modest to the point of dowdy. It wasn't the lift to her chin that conveyed what a truly superior human being she felt herself to be. It wasn't the way she walked—as if she had sat on a steel rod that now extended from her rear end to her tonsils.

No. It was the combination of all of the above. And the fact that Sissy Cordele hadn't changed one iota. She was still an uptight snob.

And . . . she had cut her hair. Really, really short.

Savannah decided that was the safest conversation-opening topic.

She hurried to her and gave her sister a hearty hug. Cordele returned it with a weak, one-handed pat on Savannah's back.

"Hi, darlin'," Savannah said, trying to summon some degree of enthusiasm. "You look great. You ah . . . you cut your hair."

Cordele reached up and smoothed the slickly gelled hair back, though it had so much goop on it that it probably wouldn't have moved in an eighty-mile-an-hour hurricane. "Yes," she said, "I decided it was time to liberate myself, to come out from behind the veil of my hair and reveal the true me to the world."

"Oh. Okay."

Cordele tossed her head in what might have been a devil-may-care gesture if it hadn't been for that perfectly stiff posture. For a moment, Savannah thought she might have dislocated her neck.

"You really should cut yours." Cordele fell into step beside Savannah as they approached the luggage carousel. "If you can find the courage to do it, you'll discover that it's very freeing. But of course, you have to give up your security blanket that you hide behind. You have to be willing to come out and reveal the real you."

"Uh-huh." Savannah scanned the thin trickle of suitcases that was beginning to spill down the chute and onto the carousel.

"Really. You should cut off all those split ends," Cordele continued. "I can do it for you when we get back to your place and—"

"Thanks but no thanks," Savannah interjected. "My hair and I are pretty good as is. Really."

Cordele shrugged and gave her sister a slightly wounded but terribly patient smile. "I understand. Not everybody can do it. I had to grow to the point where I could truly let go."

Savannah felt her guts growling deep inside. This was going to be a long, long . . . how long did she say she was staying?

"How long did you say you're staying?" she asked.

Again, Cordele gave her the "patient smile." The smile of a highly evolved soul tolerating the less enlightened. "As long as it takes, Savannah. As long as it takes." She turned back toward the carousel and watched the parade of luggage passing by.

Savannah sighed. "O-o-okay. Whatever."

Cordele's saintly smile evaporated, and she turned to face Savannah. The sisters were practically nose to nose.

"I have to tell you right now," Cordele said, "that having someone say, 'whatever' to me pushes one of my major emotional buttons. I mean, I feel like I've just been disrespected and my opinion dismissed when someone says that. It really, really, deeply upsets me, and I think you should know that."

Savannah stared at her sister. Bit her tongue. Counted to ten. But it didn't help. She still said it: "Okay. Whatever."

"Don't take this wrong, Savannah," Tammy whispered, "but I can't stand your sister."

Savannah stood in her living room, strapping on her shoulder holster. She glanced quickly toward the kitchen, where Cordele was eating some of Tammy's yogurt, having found nothing else in Savannah's refrigerator that was "fit for human consumption" as she had not so tactfully worded it.

"Don't feel bad. I don't know anybody except Gran who does."

"Your grandmother likes her?"

"Well, I don't know if she actually *likes* her, but she loves her. She has to; she's her grandmother. It's like a grandma rule."

Tammy smirked. "Isn't there a sister rule like that, too?"

"Nope. No such law on the books."

Savannah opened the coat closet door and reached up to the top shelf for her Beretta.

Tammy tugged at her sleeve. "You're not really going to leave me here with her all day, are you? Entertaining your nutso relatives is just so-o-o not a part of my job description."

"Take off. Go on over to the Maxwell estate and wait for me outside by the gate. I'll be along shortly and you can help me help Dirk."

"Really?" A look of relief flooded her face. "Oh, that would be so great!"

"Go."

Tammy nodded toward the kitchen. "Does she know you're leaving her to go to work?"

"Nope. Haven't broken the news to her yet. She thinks we're going to spend the afternoon rehashing old family grievances."

"Are you going to tell her now?"

Savannah drew a deep breath of resolve. "Yep."

"Then I'm outta here, right now."

Savannah watched as Tammy hightailed it out the front door. "Chickenshit," she mumbled after her.

She strolled into the kitchen, where Cordele was scraping the bottom of her yogurt cup. "Is that enough lunch for you?" she asked. "I'd be happy to make you a sandwich, warm up some soup, or . . ."

"No, this is plenty for me." Cordele gave Savannah's figure a quick glance up and down. "I worked through my food issues long ago. I no longer use it as an anesthetic to dull the pain of my childhood woundings. It's nothing more than fuel to me now."

Bully for you, Savannah thought, but she smiled and said, "That's lovely, dear. Then I won't feel obliged to rush home and make fried chicken and mashed potatoes for dinner. I'll just throw together a salad and pick up a quart of brown rice from the local Chinese takeout."

Cordele scowled. Then her scowl deepened. "What do you mean 'rush home'? Where are you going?"

"To work."

"When?" She seemed to notice the Beretta in its holster for the first time. "Now?"

"Yes." Savannah fought to keep the anger out of her voice but wasn't at all successful. "I should have been working this morning, but I wasn't. So I may be out until late tonight. I hope you don't mind entertaining yourself while I'm—"

"*Entertaining* myself? Do you think I spent six hundred dollars for plane fare and came all the way out here for *entertainment?*"

Savannah walked over to the sink, grabbed a tumbler out of the cabinet, and poured herself a glassful of water from the re-

frigerator. Meanwhile, she warned herself to speak kindly, gently, tactfully. Treat your sister as you'd want to be treated yourself, Savannah girl, she could hear her grandmother saying.

She drank the water slowly, giving herself time to carefully compose her words, while her sister stood there, glaring at her, hands on her hips.

Finally, she set the glass on the counter, turned to Cordele, and said, "To be honest, I don't really know why you came to see me. All I do know is that my own life is very complicated right now. I'm working on something that's very important and—"

"More important than me? More important than your relationship with your own flesh and blood?"

"No-o-o. My family is more important to me than my work. But right now, I need you, my family, to understand my situation. A woman was murdered . . . a woman who hired me to protect her. And now I have to find out who killed her. I have to find out so that they won't kill anybody else. I have to find out so that the people who loved the victim can have closure."

"Revenge, you mean. You're not a cop anymore, but you've still got that vengeance mentality. Look at you, standing there with a gun strapped on your body. The person who killed her is probably a tormented soul who needs help and compassion more than punishment, but you don't see that. You're only interested in catching them and having them locked up—or worse."

Savannah stared at her sister and shook her head. "Don't you lecture me about vengeance, young lady. You don't know squat about it. Unless you've had someone that you love murdered, ripped away from you by some no-good sonofabitch who thinks he's got the right to take somebody else's life, don't you shoot your mouth off about revenge. What you call vengeance is another person's justice. And don't you tell me that justice isn't important, because justice is what I *do!* As long as it's within the bounds of the law, justice is a righteous, necessary thing!"

Cordele looked shocked for a moment. Then angry. Then the scowl on her face gradually faded, replaced by a sappy, conde-

scending smile. "I can see that you're deeply upset by me expressing my opinion on this issue."

"Really? Go figure."

"That's understandable, considering where you're coming from."

"And where might that be?" Savannah asked, although she was fairly certain that Cordele's answer would make her want to feed her her teeth on a knuckle sandwich.

"You've always had a simplistic, black or white, plus or minus, view of the world . . . the good guys versus the bad guys. And of course you see yourself as one of the good guys."

Savannah's eyes narrowed. "When it comes to murder and the apprehension of murderers, I *am* one of the good guys. Believe me, I've seen plenty of the bad ones. You wouldn't want to run into them in a dark alley."

"So you see it." Cordele leaned back in her chair and folded her hands primly on the table in front of her. "Of course, in my studies in the science of psychology, I've learned that the human psyche is far more complicated than your elementary viewpoint. There are no bad people in this world, only misguided ones who—"

"Oh, can it, Cordele. What the hell do you learn about anything sitting in a classroom? I could show you crime-scene pictures that would make you puke. I could tell you things that your 'misguided' monsters have done to innocent people that would scar your soul. If you want to feel sorry for them, go right ahead. I'm going to go to work. I'm going to find out who poisoned a woman to death, and I'm going to stick their ass in a sling and wring 'em dry. And if that offends your enlightened sensibilities, tough."

Savannah turned on her heel and stomped out of the kitchen. She paused at the hall closet to grab her jacket.

Cordele was right behind her. "When are you coming home?" she demanded.

"I told you already. Late. Read a book, watch TV, and order yourself a pizza. There's some money in the cookie jar."

"I don't eat pizza. It's junk food."

Savannah snatched her purse and keys off the table by the door. "Then check the fridge. I think there's a head of lettuce in there and some carrots. You can—" She paused at the door, debated whether to finish her statement, and decided not to. She left before telling her sister what she could do with the vegetables in question.

Granny Reid would have been so proud.

Chapter 10

When Savannah arrived at the gates of the Maxwell estate, Tammy was sitting in her Volkswagen bug parked right across the road. Savannah waited for her to run across the highway and get into the passenger's seat before she drove up to the key pad and punched in the security code.

"I didn't know you had that," Tammy said. "When did they give you the combination?"

"They didn't. I saw it written on a piece of paper and taped to the inside of the pantry door. Discreet, huh?"

The gates swung open, and she drove the Mustang through.

"Not very. Gee . . . anybody could have seen it there."

"Exactly. Doesn't narrow down our list of who might have been on the property lately."

Tammy thought for a moment. "And with the murder weapon being something she ate, it could have been planted almost anytime."

"Please don't remind me. I'm depressed enough as it is."

Savannah drove past the barn-converted-studio and saw Dirk's battered Buick parked behind the building.

"Let's start here," she said. "We'll see how far Dirk's gotten on his own this morning."

* * *

"Where the hell have you been?" was the cry that greeted them when they walked through the studio doors. On the far side of the cavernous room, Dirk was on his hands and knees behind a partition, sifting through what appeared to be a pile of garbage. "You said you were going to give me a hand, and I've been working my tail off all morning by myself with no help from anybody."

"And you haven't come up with anything," Savannah replied as they walked across the room to join him.

"How do you know I haven't?"

"Because you're crankier than usual. If you'd found anything good, you'd be more cordial."

She knelt on the floor beside him and saw that it was indeed the studio garbage that he was searching. The trash consisted mostly of paper, but enough coffee, sodas, and chocolate cake had been added to the mix to make it a disgusting mess. He was wearing a pair of surgical gloves. Though he had no hygienic standards about sifting through garbage with his bare hands, she knew he was concerned about contaminating anything he might find in the way of evidence.

She dug in her purse for a pair of gloves for Tammy and another for herself. They both slipped them on and began to rummage with him. He appeared to be collecting bits of chocolate cake and stashing them in an evidence bag.

"I had to go to the airport to pick up my sister," she reminded him, as she tossed a coffee-soggy piece into his bag.

Tammy knelt on the other side of Dirk and wrinkled her nose at the smell of the garbage. "Yeah, and hanging out with Cordele isn't exactly fun."

"Oh yeah." Dirk nodded thoughtfully. "I remember that one. Met her in Georgia when we were there last year. She's the one with the stick up her—"

"Yep, that's Cordele, all right," Savannah replied. "And she's come to visit me for an undetermined length of time."

"Lucky you." Dirk picked up another hunk and dropped it into the bag.

"Yeah, lucky me," Savannah said. "I've got a homicide to in-

vestigate and don't have to hang around the house and get my head shrunk."

"She's a shrink?" He folded the bag closed, took a black marker from his pocket, and began to scribble pertinent information on an orange label, which he then affixed to the bag, sealing it.

"No. She's studying to be one." Savannah continued to sift through the mess, but saw no more cake fragments. "She's just learned enough to be dangerous—to herself, that is. Someday she's going to tell the wrong person that they're passive-aggressive and they'll forget all about being passive, if you know what I mean."

"I can understand how she might bring out the worst in a person." He stood and brushed the remnants of garbage from the front of his jeans. "Why don't you put her on a plane and send her home?"

"Easier said than done," Tammy muttered. "She's a Reid, and they don't obey very well."

"What's that?" Savannah said.

"Nothing." Tammy looked around at the empty, relatively dark studio. "Where's your Crime Scene Unit? Why aren't they helping you today?"

"More budget cuts from our dear mayor." Dirk walked over to a box he had stowed near the stage and dropped the bag into it. "We've only got three guys on it—actually, one's a broad—and they're on the other side of town, dusting for prints at a house burglary."

"Since when does a burglary take a backseat to a homicide?" Savannah wanted to know.

"When it's the mayor's sister-in-law who got burgled."

"Oh." Savannah peeled off her gloves and tossed them into the trash heap. "So, you figure it was the cake?"

"That's the last thing she ate." Dirk walked onto the set with its green marble counters and cozy, stained-glass cupboards. "That redhead producer—"

"Kaitlin Dover?" Savannah followed him reluctantly onto the

set. Only hours ago she had been kneeling right there—in that spot between the counter and the oven—holding Eleanor Maxwell, watching her die.

"Yeah, Kaitlin." Dirk produced another bag from inside his jacket and took the remainder of the cake, plate and all, that was sitting on the counter, and shoved it into the bag. "She was by earlier, and I had her show me the film—the one they were taping when it happened."

Tammy joined them on the set. "Could you tell anything from looking at the tape?"

"Just that she made the cake, took a few bites, got sick, and kicked the bucket."

"Wait a minute." Savannah tapped her fingers on the marble. "A bunch of us had a bite of that cake. I ate some myself, and I didn't get sick."

"You aren't on heart medications," Dirk reminded her. "It was the interaction that did her in, not the stuff itself."

"But I should have had some sort of symptoms if it was that concentrated in the cake." Savannah turned to Tammy. "What would the symptoms be? Do you remember from that Internet article you read?"

"I don't think it said anything about overdose symptoms, but I remember it was used for colds, to clear congestion and . . ."

Savannah raised one eyebrow and poked Dirk in the chest with her forefinger. "Hot toddy, my hind end. You didn't cure me, big boy. I'll bet you a plug nickel it was that bite of cake that dried me out."

Dirk sniffed. "Well, that's appreciation. See if I ever make another one of my special toddies for you."

"I didn't say I didn't like it. I said it wasn't what dried up my nose. You wait till they run some tests on that cake and you'll see that it's full of that stuff."

Dirk looked around the kitchen. "Well, just in case it isn't, I've gotta take everything else that I can find around here in for tests, too. Anything remotely edible."

Savannah began opening cupboards, but most were empty.

"Why do I get the feeling they didn't actually do much cooking here in this kitchen?"

"They didn't," Dirk replied. "I already talked to Kaitlin about that. She said that Eleanor put most of the stuff together down at the house and brought it up here after it was cooked."

"Sure, that makes sense." Savannah found some pots and pans, but they were dusty and obviously hadn't been moved recently. She closed the door and kept looking as Dirk and Tammy did the same. "You know . . . I'll bet the cake we ate wasn't even the one she mixed up here on the show."

"What do you mean?" Dirk said, his head in the refrigerator.

"I mean . . . she mixes up one here on camera to demonstrate how it's done to her audience, but when she puts it in the oven to 'bake,' she takes out the one that's already been baked and serves it."

Tammy nodded. "Sure. You can't wait for it to bake on a TV show."

Dirk had donned another pair of gloves and was placing the items from the refrigerator into yet another evidence box. "Well, that may be true, but we still have to take all this crap in and have it checked, just in case."

"And all the stuff from the kitchen in the house," Savannah said. "They're just gonna love you at the lab."

Dirk growled, "If we can drag it all down there, the least they can do is run the lousy tests."

Savannah grinned. "Yeah, you be sure to put it to 'em just like that. There's nothing like that Coulter charm to ensure cooperation."

This time when Savannah stepped onto the mansion's verandah with Dirk and Tammy in tow, the three mini-hounds from hell didn't even bother to get up from their comfortable chairs where they were having their early afternoon snooze. Killer simply opened one eye, blinked lazily, and closed it, then shoved his nose under one paw.

"Vicious creatures," Tammy said. "Until they get to know you.

Then they'd lead you straight to the family heirloom silver and help you carry it out of the house."

"It was the garlic-flavored chicken livers that brought them around," Savannah told her. "One sandwich bag of that spread three ways and they're in my power forever."

"Food . . ." Dirk opened the front door, which was unlocked, and walked inside. "That's how you control all of us."

"Ah, yes, the power of fried chicken, mashed potatoes, and cream gravy." Savannah grinned.

Ordinarily, she would have added chocolate cake to the end of that list, but for the moment, she was turned off to the whole idea—a definite first for her. She didn't know if she could ever eat chocolate cake again. This murderer was going to get caught and pay the price for that alone . . . if not for Lady Eleanor's demise.

"Hello," Dirk called. "Anybody here?"

"In here," came a voice from the kitchen.

"Damn," he muttered. "We're gonna have to string some tape around this house and seal the doors. Now that we know it was a murder, we can't have people running around disturbing things."

"I'll do it if you want," Tammy offered.

Dirk looked surprised, then rummaged in his jeans pocket and pulled out his keys. He tossed them to her. "The tape's in my kit in the trunk. Thanks, kid."

"You're welcome . . . Dirko," she replied. She bounced away, long blond ponytail swinging.

"Better watch out," Savannah told him. "You two might actually start liking each other if you aren't careful."

"Naw. It'll never happen."

She followed him into the kitchen, where they found Marie unloading the dishwasher.

"Good afternoon," the maid said, stopping to dry her hands on a towel. "May I get you something to drink? A cappuccino or . . . ?"

"No, thank you," Savannah said. "This is Detective-Sergeant Coulter from the San Carmelita Police Department. Dirk, this is Marie, Eleanor's housekeeper."

Dirk shook Marie's hand and nodded graciously. "Glad to meet you. But I'm going to have to ask you to leave this house here right away and don't come back in until we clear it."

"But, but I work here," Marie sputtered. "I don't understand. We'll be having Mrs. Maxwell's memorial service tomorrow and we're expecting a lot of people. I have to get things ready."

"No, you don't." Dirk took her by the elbow and gently led her toward the back door. "You have to vacate the premises—at least the house itself. It's a crime scene."

"What?" Marie's jaw dropped. "What do you mean, a crime?"

Savannah stepped forward. "Dirk, she doesn't . . . you know."

"Oh, yeah." Dirk let go of her arm and put on his gentler face. "I'm sorry to inform you that after receiving the results of the coroner's autopsy, we're investigating Mrs. Maxwell's death as a possible homicide. So that means—"

"A homicide?" The maid leaned her hand against the pantry door for support. "Someone killed her?"

"We don't know yet for sure," Savannah said, rushing to her side. "That's why we have to continue to investigate. And that's why no one can come into the house until we're finished."

"But . . . but . . ." The maid looked around as though seeing her surroundings for the first time. "What will I do?"

"You live in the servants' quarters, right?" Savannah asked.

Marie nodded.

"And where's that?" Dirk asked.

"In the gardener's cottage behind the garage."

Savannah reached out and placed a comforting hand on the woman's shoulder. "So, why don't you go back there for now, maybe lie down awhile? I know this must be disturbing news to hear."

"It is. *Very* disturbing," Marie said, her voice shaking. "Mrs. Maxwell murdered! What a terrible thing."

Savannah could feel her trembling. She led her gently to the back door and opened it for her. "Try not to worry," she said. "I'm sure we'll have this all straightened out soon."

Savannah and Dirk watched through the open door as the

maid walked away on unsteady legs. "I'll come by and check on you later," Savannah called after her. "Just try to get some rest."

They continued to watch until she disappeared behind the garage. "You're gonna check on her, huh?" Dirk finally said. "Maybe you can squeeze something outta her. Maids know everything that's going on in the house they work in. She's probably got some juicy stuff to tell."

Savannah gave him a sideways look and a nudge in the ribs. "Squeeze her? Please. The woman's obviously distraught. I was just going to offer her a shoulder to cry on if she needed it."

She closed the door and walked back to the kitchen. "Of course," she added, "if I get the opportunity to squeeze her a bit while she's crying, so be it. You know, housekeepers are a fount of information . . . not to mention good ol'-fashioned gossip."

By the time Tammy joined them in the kitchen, Savannah and Dirk had already collected several boxes of staples from the kitchen cupboards and pantry.

"We found the recipe for the Death by Chocolate Cake," Savannah told her, "and we're taking what's left of the ingredients, like flour, sugar, baking powder, salt, cocoa, and so on."

"That way you can tell which one was contaminated?" Tammy pulled on a pair of gloves before looking through the items in the boxes.

"That's right, kiddo," Dirk told her. "If there's phenylprophedrine in the cake itself, it probably came from one of those ingredients."

"You figure the killer knew what she was going to be baking and put it into one of these?"

"That's what I'd do," Savannah said. "It would be a lot easier than trying to contaminate the actual batter when she was baking it."

"That's the problem with poisoning. . . ." Dirk began to put each item into its own bag and affix the orange evidence labels to seal them. "Unlike a shooting or stabbing, or even a strangling, the killer doesn't have to be present at that actual moment of

death. Conceivably, they could plant the stuff weeks before. Although I don't think that happened in this case."

"Why not?" Tammy asked.

"Because," he replied, "according to Kaitlin Dover, the show's producer, Eleanor didn't announce what dish she was going to cook until just a day or less before the show."

Savannah walked over to the broom closet and pulled out the loaded shotgun that Eleanor had mentioned. "Whoever it was," she said, "had to know what ingredients she'd be using ahead of time to contaminate one or more of them."

"What's that doing there?" Tammy asked, pointing to the gun.

"Just your standard, double-barreled, twelve-gauge home protection device," Savannah replied, cracking the breech and removing the shells. "With a child on the premises—not to mention possibly a killer—we don't really need to have this thing loaded."

She popped the shells into her pocket. Searching a nearby shelf, she found a box full of ammo next to some corn flakes. She removed those, too, and replaced the gun.

"So, are we about done here?" she asked Dirk.

He looked around the kitchen, down at the boxes filled with their bags of potential evidence, and nodded. "Yeah, I think this should be enough to send the boys and girls at the lab into a tizzy. They hate this much work anytime, let alone on a Friday afternoon, when they're all looking forward to starting their weekend."

"Too bad," Savannah said. "If I have to work on the weekend, why shouldn't they?"

"Were you planning on working this weekend?" Tammy asked as they each took a box and started for the door.

"Heck yeah," she replied. "What do you think I'm going to do? Sit around the house with Cordele and rehash old family grievances?"

Dirk nodded. "I see your point. Investigating a homicide is a lot more fun than that rehashing family crap."

"Much more fun," Savannah agreed. "But then, so is getting a triple root canal . . . a Pap smear . . . a mammogram. . . ."

* * *

They were loading the boxes into the trunk and backseat of Dirk's Buick when they saw Louise Maxwell walking down the driveway toward them. She was wearing bright red short-shorts and matching cropped tee that showed several inches of bare midriff. She walked with a definite sashay to her hips that south of the Mason-Dixon Line might have branded her as a loose woman.

"Oh, goody gumdrop," Savannah said. "Just the person I wanted to see."

"Who's she?" Tammy asked.

"The daughter, Louise. Otherwise known as the person least likely to grieve Eleanor's passing and the most likely to benefit from her demise."

Dirk perked up. "Oh yeah? Well, I think we should get acquainted."

Savannah noted Louise's purposeful stride and said, "I think that's a given."

"What the hell are you people doing on my property?" Louise demanded.

At that moment, three furry mini-missiles flew off the verandah and streaked toward Louise, barking, growling, snarling, and showing their tiny incisors.

"Oh, shut up, you stupid mutts," she said, kicking out at them. "You're all going to the pound; you just wait and see."

As though understanding her words, the dogs backed off. One returned to his chair on the verandah, and the others soon followed. Savannah was impressed. Louise had quailed the terrors without garlic chicken livers.

Dirk was already on his way up the driveway, his badge out, his grimmest and most officious face on. "I'm Detective Coulter, SCPD, I'm investigating your mother's death. First, I'd like to say I'm sorry for your loss."

"Yeah, right." Louise looked over his shoulder. "What are *they* doing here?" She pointed an accusing finger at Savannah. "You have no business being here anymore. Get off this property. And

if she's with you"—she nodded toward Tammy—"she goes, too."

Savannah walked over to Louise and forced herself to smile, at least a little. "Your mother hired me to find out who was sending her those threatening letters. She paid me up front. I have to finish the job."

"You don't have to finish anything! She's dead, and I'm in charge now. You're out of here."

Dirk cleared his throat. "Well, technically, Ms. Maxwell . . . you *aren't* in charge. At least, not yet. If your mother left you this property in her will, you'll get it once the estate is settled, but for right now, everything's still pretty much up in the air."

Louise glanced over toward the house and noticed the bright yellow crime-scene tape that Tammy had strung around it. "What's that!"

Dirk stepped closer to her, his eyes watching every nuance of emotion on her face. "It's a police barricade," he said, "to keep anyone from entering the residence for the time being."

Savannah, too, was watching Louise carefully. You could read so much into those first moments when someone was informed.

"Ms. Maxwell, you have to prepare yourself for some hard news," he said.

Her face turned pale behind her suntan. "And what news is that?"

"We have reason to believe," he continued, "that your mother's death wasn't from natural causes."

Her mouth opened and closed several times, as if she were gasping for air. "What are you talking about? It was a heart attack. I heard it was a heart attack. She had a bad heart. She was on medicine for it."

"I know," he said. "But we believe that the heart attack was induced."

"Induced?"

"Caused by something . . . someone."

"Like what? Who?"

Savannah was watching closely, evaluating. And she had to say

that Louise seemed more nervous and scared than upset. Most people were upset when they found out that a relative had been murdered.

Interesting.

"That's what we're investigating," Dirk replied. "I'm sorry, I can't tell you much more right now."

Savannah decided to take a verbal stab at it. She stepped forward. "But I'm absolutely sure that we'll find out who did it," she said evenly. "We almost always do."

A flash of fear, then anger, crossed Louise's face. Then her expression went as blank as a freshly erased chalkboard.

But Savannah had seen it. And Savannah knew that Louise knew that she had seen it. Savannah looked at Dirk. He had seen it, too.

"And when we do find out," Savannah added, just for good measure, "you'll probably be one of the first to know."

Louise seethed for a moment, her fists clenched at her sides. For a few seconds, Savannah thought she might come at her, and she briefly enjoyed the mental image of throwing Ms. Louise Prissy Short-Shorts on her butt with a karate takedown.

But just as she was getting into the idea, the sound of running footsteps caused them all to turn toward the garage. Sydney was racing toward them, a stricken look on his face. "Is it true?" he asked breathlessly when he reached them. "I was just talking to Marie, and she says that Miss Eleanor was murdered. Was she?"

"I'm afraid it's a possibility," Dirk said. "And you are . . . ?"

"This is Sydney Linton," Savannah said, "Mrs. Maxwell's driver and handyman. Sydney, meet Detective Coulter, SCPD."

Dirk extended his hand, but Sydney seemed too distraught to notice the gesture.

"But how? Who? I mean . . . who could do something like that?" Sydney covered his eyes with his hands for a moment and shuddered. "I know Miss Eleanor was a difficult person, but . . . to kill her? It's got to be some sort of mistake."

"We aren't really sure of anything yet," Savannah told him.

"That's why Detective Coulter here is conducting an investigation."

"But the question is," Louise interjected, "why are *you* here? I want you out of here."

"We're not going through that again," Dirk told her. "I think you'd better turn around and march back to your cottage, find some of your own business, and mind it."

Louise turned, but said over her shoulder, "I'm going to call my attorney and tell him—"

"Ah, you don't need to do that," Savannah said. "At least, not until . . . I mean . . . not unless you're under arrest."

Louise shot her a look that could barbecue a rare steak to well-done in a minute, but she left. And not too soon for Savannah.

Savannah watched her for a moment, and when she returned her attention to those around her, she saw that they were all staring at her: Dirk, Tammy, and even Sydney.

"What?" she said.

"You don't think . . ." Sydney sputtered, "that Louise would have . . . ?"

Dirk gave a slight shake of his head, and she knew she needed to cool her dislike for Louise. It wasn't smart to flash too much of your hand in front of anybody, let alone *everybody.*

"We don't know anything yet," Dirk replied. "Really. We're just checking a few things."

Sydney seemed to calm down a bit. He raked his fingers through his thick hair, and the thought crossed Savannah's mind that he wasn't at all hard on the eyes. Whether in his tuxedo, serving tea, or in his present jeans and denim shirt, he was well-built and had a certain boy-next-door appeal. She wondered if he and Marie had ever been an item. To her understanding, neither was married.

"Well, I'm glad you're here," he told Dirk. "I hope nothing like that happened to Miss Eleanor. I hope that her death was from natural causes. But if it wasn't, I want you to catch whoever did it."

He glanced quickly up the hill at Louise's retreating figure. Savannah took note of the look, and so did Dirk and Tammy. They all three exchanged knowing glances.

"Is there anyone in particular you can think of who might have wanted to hurt Mrs. Maxwell?" Dirk asked him.

Again, another sideways look up the hill. "Well, not enough to kill her," he said. "Like I said, she was a difficult person. You saw that yourself, Savannah."

"Yes. I did. By the way, do you recall seeing anyone or anything suspicious around here the last few days? Anything out of the ordinary?"

He thought for a long moment before answering, "Not that I can think of. But if I do remember anything, I'll be sure to let you know."

"Thanks," Dirk said. "We appreciate it."

Sydney excused himself, and Savannah, Dirk, and Tammy finished placing the evidence parcels into the back of the Buick.

"You two wanna follow me over to the lab?" Dirk asked. "I'll take you out for a burger or something after we get done there."

Savannah nearly gasped. "Wow, free food! I never thought I'd hear those words out of—"

"Oh, shut up." His lower lip protruded. "That's what I get for trying to be a gentleman."

"Actually, I'm teaching a yoga class in about an hour," Tammy said, looking at her watch. "And then I've got some paperwork to do at the office. But thanks anyway."

Savannah looked over at the garage where Sydney had disappeared. Just beyond the garage she could see the corner of what she figured was probably the gardener's cottage where Marie lived.

"Tell ya what, guys," she told them. "You take off if you're done here, but before I leave, I think I'll go have a girl-to-girl talk with Marie. See if I can console her."

"Console her?" Dirk chuckled. "Yeah, right. I know you; you're gonna squeeze her."

Savannah grinned and shrugged. "Squeeze, console . . . whatever."

Chapter 11

Savannah sat in Marie's cozy apartment, sipping mint tea, eating fresh-out-of-the-oven oatmeal cookies, and feeling a little guilty that she had even considered "squeezing" this gracious lady.

"I love your place," she said sincerely as she looked around the apartment with its feminine floral fabrics, delicate lace doilies, fresh flowers in milk-glass vases, and sepia-toned family portraits in silver- and gold-leafed frames hanging in clusters on the walls.

Sitting in a rocking chair across from her, Marie was also drinking tea, a large yellow tabby cat curled in her lap. It was the first time Savannah had seen her wearing anything other than her black-and-white housekeeper's attire. She had changed into a soft pink fleece pullover and a pair of cream slacks. Her eyes were red and swollen, as though she had been crying, but when Savannah had knocked at the cottage door, Marie had warmly welcomed her inside and offered her refreshments. Having skipped lunch, Savannah welcomed the sugar boost.

"I still can't comprehend all that's happened," Marie was saying as she stroked the sleeping cat. "I couldn't even believe that Miss Eleanor had died, and now to hear that someone killed her . . ."

"We don't absolutely know that for sure," Savannah said. "Try to shield your heart from that grief until we find out what really happened. There's no point in suffering over something that may not be true."

Marie nodded and sniffed. "I understand." She hesitated, then added, "But at the moment, you think that's what happened?"

"Yes," she said gently. "We think it's a strong possibility."

Savannah watched the housekeeper over the rim of her cup as she sipped the fragrant tea. Marie had looked pale, even fragile, the first time she had met her. She seemed even more so now. Savannah guessed she was in her late thirties or early forties, but she looked as if her years had been hard ones. Deep lines in her face, a sallow complexion, and dark circles under her eyes gave the impression she wasn't terribly healthy. But she did radiate a certain quietness of spirit that led Savannah to believe she was content with her life.

Or at least that she had been, before Eleanor had died, changing everyone's world around her.

"What will you do now?" Savannah asked.

Marie shrugged her thin shoulders. "I'm not sure. I don't know if Louise will keep the house, or if she does, if she'll want me to stay on."

"Did you like working here?"

"Yes, actually, I did. Miss Eleanor could be demanding sometimes, but I love the house and I enjoyed keeping it."

"You did a good job. Everything was spotless. I've done enough housecleaning to appreciate what a lot of work it is."

She smiled. "Thank you."

"We searched Eleanor's bedroom suite . . ." Savannah paused, wondering how to word her question.

But Marie said it for her. "And you wondered why those rooms are such a mess."

"Something like that."

"Miss Eleanor would hardly ever allow me in there. Maybe once every few weeks to change the sheets and clean the bath-

room fixtures." She hesitated, as though considering how much she should divulge, then continued. "Miss Eleanor had problems, serious problems, with depression. Sometimes she found it difficult to function, and she would stay there in her room for days at a time. She'd pull the drapes and—"

"Eat and drink?"

Marie nodded. "Yes, mostly. Then she'd get it together and come out and tape her show and catch up on all her overdue business. But it didn't last long. A few days later, she'd hole up in there again. She would have me just leave the food—and bottles—on a tray outside her door."

"How did you communicate with her?"

"On the house phone."

"Do you know what she was so depressed about?"

Marie gave her a quick, guarded look, then went back to petting her sleeping tabby. "First one thing and then the other," she said. "Family problems. Everyone has them."

"True. But some are worse than others." Savannah broke one of her cookies in two and took a bite, chewing thoughtfully. "I understand that Eleanor and her husband were recently divorced."

Marie gazed out the window, not meeting Savannah's eyes. "That's right."

"I know you're a professional, Marie," she said, "and I'm sure you're a discreet employee. I hate to put you in a difficult position, asking you to reveal confidential matters. But I'm a professional, too, and my job is to find out what happened here."

"I understand." She took a deep breath. "Ask whatever you need to. I'll answer as best I can."

"Thank you." Savannah pulled a small notebook and pen from her purse. "Don't mind this. I just don't have the world's greatest memory and it helps me if I take notes. Is that okay?"

Marie nodded.

"Can you tell me who initiated the divorce, Eleanor or her husband?"

"She did. And I suppose you'd like to know why." The cat in Marie's lap woke, stretched, yawned, and jumped off her lap.

Savannah reached down to stroke him as he walked by her, on the way to the kitchen. "If you can tell me," she replied, "it might be helpful."

"They had a lot of problems, from what I could tell," Marie said. "But the last straw, I think, was that Eleanor discovered he was having an affair."

"Do we know with whom?"

"I have my suspicions, but I don't know for sure, so I'd rather not say."

Darn, Savannah thought. Gossipy, tell-everything-you-know-and-make-up-the-rest types were so much easier to interview than discreet people like Marie.

"Okay, I understand," she said, trying to sound more understanding than irked.

"Do you think that their divorce had anything to do with . . . you know . . . her dying?" Marie asked.

"I really don't know. At this point, I'm just gathering information." She took another bite of the cookie and jotted down a couple of notes on her pad. "Marie, this is strictly between you and me," she said, choosing her words carefully. "If you were conducting this investigation, who would you check out first?"

Marie hesitated, then reached over and warmed her tea from the pot on the tray in front of them. "I hate to point a finger at anyone, when it's such a terrible thing as murder, but . . ."

"It's okay. Nobody but you and me will ever know that you pointed anything at anyone. I'm just looking for a little guidance here. You know all of the people who come and go around here; I just met them. Please, help me help Eleanor."

Marie lifted the teacup to her lips with both hands, and Savannah saw that she was trembling. Her eyes registered her fear, like a raccoon in a tree with a brace of hounds baying right underneath him.

"Okay," she finally said. "Martin."

Savannah waited for elaboration. When none was forthcoming, she said, "Martin?"

"Yes. Start with Martin."

"Do you want to tell me why?"

She shook her head. "No."

Savannah searched the housekeeper's face, trying to read anything in her expression. But all she saw was fear . . . and maybe a little shame. Marie appeared to be one of those rare people who actually disliked saying negative things about her fellow humans.

People like Marie made wonderful friends, but they provided lousy interviews. Savannah realized she had gotten just about all of the juice out of the housekeeper that this "squeeze" was going to produce.

She stuck the rest of the cookie in her mouth and washed it down with the remainder of her tea.

Folding her notebook and putting it in her purse, she said, "Marie, thank you for your hospitality, and for telling me what you could. I apologize for putting you in a difficult position."

"I understand." Marie stood and walked her to the door. "You're just doing your job."

Savannah paused, her hand on the doorknob. "Marie . . . one more question. If you really knew who killed Eleanor Maxwell, would you tell me?"

She watched as the woman considered her answer. Savannah could tell that she was deciding whether to be completely honest or not.

"I guess that would depend," she said.

"On what?"

"On who it was."

"Okay. That's fair." Savannah offered her hand and Marie shook it. "But I should focus on Martin, huh?"

Something flickered in Marie's eyes. Savannah saw it, but it was too brief for her to analyze its significance before it was gone.

"Yes," Marie said quietly. "If I were you, I'd start with Martin."

Savannah checked her watch as she got into her car. Five-thirty. She debated about how to spend the rest of the evening, and her conscience got the better of her. With a sigh of resigna-

tion, she pulled her cell phone from her purse and punched in some numbers.

On the second ring, Tammy answered, "Moonlight Magnolia Detective Agency."

"You still there, huh?"

"Ye-e-e-es."

Savannah grinned. The kid sounded stressed. "Can you ta-a-alk?"

"No-o-o-o."

"Is she right there next to you, telling you her whole life story in depressing detail?"

"Absolutely."

Savannah laughed and made a mental note to treat Tammy to a facial or a massage. As a friend/employee she went way beyond the call of duty. "Go home," she told her.

"Really? Mother, may I?"

"Get. Now. Call me on your cell phone when you're outta sight."

Savannah was barely out of the gates and on the highway when her cell phone rang. It was a much relieved Tammy.

"Wow, that was a speedy escape," Savannah said.

"I resisted the temptation to run out of the house screaming," she replied. "I just walked . . . really fast!"

"I'm so proud. Driving you nuts, was she?"

"Good grief! She's really got some heavy problems. She was telling me about all these support groups she belongs to: Victims of This, Survivors of That, Ten Steps to Another Thing. She's got more support than Playtex!"

"Eh, Cordele's still searching."

"For what?"

"She's not sure. That's what makes it particularly challenging." Savannah turned off the highway and headed downtown. "Tell me something, kiddo . . . what exactly does somebody who only eats 'healthy' crap have for dinner?" She listened for a moment. "Yuck. All right, where do I buy some of that?"

* * *

About forty-five minutes later, Savannah walked into her house. She found Cordele curled in her big, cushy chair, the two cats on the ottoman next to her feet. She was deeply engrossed in a mystery novel from Savannah's bookshelves.

For a moment, Savannah thought of all the times she had seen her sister hunched over a book. It was her primary memory of Cordele as a child. Of the nine Reid siblings, Cordele had been the most avid reader, the best student in school, the quiet, somber one of a rowdy group.

Seeing her sister there in her own favorite chair, the cats warming her feet, the light from the lamp shining on the chestnut highlights in her hair—the same dark color as her own—Savannah felt a tug of familial connection and affection. She was glad she had made the decision to spend the evening with her rather than working on the case with Dirk.

She cleared her throat, and Cordele looked up from her book, startled. "Oh, I didn't hear you come in," she said.

Savannah smiled at her and was relieved when it was returned. "Have you eaten yet?" she asked.

"No. Have you?"

"Nope. Come on."

"Where are we going?"

"You'll see. Bring a sweater."

The sun was nearly setting when Savannah pulled the Mustang into the beach parking lot. The turquoise skies, streaked with clouds of coral, slate gray, and white, provided the perfect ambiance for a seaside picnic. The palm trees that lined the beach were black, stately silhouettes against the marbled sky. They dipped and swayed in the evening breeze, their dry fronds rustling as they danced.

"Wow, this is cool," Cordele said as they got out of the car. "A picnic at the beach! That's a great idea!"

See, big sisters can occasionally do something right, Savannah thought. But she said nothing as she reached into the backseat for an old army blanket she kept there and the bags of food she

had purchased at a local restaurant that catered to the "nutrition-conscious."

"What have you got there?" Cordele asked, trying to peek into the bags.

"Nothing. Here, you take the blanket and let's go before it gets any darker."

They settled on a stretch of sand where they could see the roller skaters on the boardwalk and some kids playing on a set of swings nearby.

Cordele spread the blanket, and they both plopped down on it. They slipped out of their shoes, and Cordele wriggled her toes into the sand.

"Let's see . . . what do we have here?" Savannah pulled out a wrapper and offered it to her sister. "I believe it's a whole-wheat pita stuffed with grilled chicken breast, avocado slices, alfalfa sprouts, tomato, and spinach."

Cordele's eyes widened. "Really? You got that special for me?"

"Well, I got one for myself, too." She rummaged around in the bag. "And here's some yogurt-based sauce for dipping, if you like. And some bottles of cranberry-apple juice. Isn't that one of your favorites?"

Cordele took the bottle and blinked rapidly a couple of times as though she had gotten a grain or two of sand in her eyes. "You remembered," she said.

"Of course I remember." She produced a couple of plastic wineglasses, filled both, and handed one to her sister. "Because it's a special occasion," she said. "Here's to the Reid girls."

Cordele toasted her, drank, and then pointed to the other bag. "What's in there?"

"Hot coffee with lots of cream and two big fat slices of chocolate-dipped cheesecake." She chuckled. "Woman does not live on alfalfa sprouts alone."

Laughing, Cordele shook her head. "I should have known."

They munched in contented silence for a while, then Savannah cleared her throat and said, "So, are we friends again?"

Cordele took a drink of her juice. "What do you mean?"

"I felt bad all day about this morning. I don't like it when my loved ones and I are on the outs."

When Cordele didn't reply, Savannah continued. "I'm sorry if I gave you the impression that I don't respect and appreciate the field of psychology. I truly do. And I think it's wonderful that you're pursuing a career where you'll be healing and helping people. I think you'll be really good at it."

Cordele swallowed hard. "Thanks."

"You've always been the smartest one in the family and the most dedicated when it comes to your education. I'm very proud of you."

Cordele's eyes filled with tears, and she nearly choked on her sandwich. Savannah found a clean napkin in the bag and handed it to her.

"I didn't mean to make you cry," she said. "That was supposed to make you feel better."

"It did."

"Those are happy tears?"

"Mostly."

Savannah was afraid to ask, but she knew it was expected. "So . . . why the unhappy ones?"

"Because, just once, just once in my whole miserable life, I'd like to hear my own mother say that she's proud of me. Or my dad. Your parents are the most influential people in a person's life and neither one of them has ever given me any validation. Do you know how much that hurts?" *Sniff.* "Do you?"

A couple of timeworn photos flashed across Savannah's memory: the blue ribbon from the spelling bee that had wound up in the trash rather than on the refrigerator door as she had hoped. The phone call to her mother telling her that she had graduated from the police academy with honors, that she was finally a cop—and her mother's drunken, lackluster reply. The equally dull response from her father when she had made detective first class.

"Yes, I think I do know how that feels," Savannah said.

"Do you remember that time when I was in the Christmas play and I got to be Mary . . . and Mom was too drunk to come see me, and Dad was out of town with his girlfriend?"

"Yes, I remember. You made a beautiful Mary, and you said all of your lines perfectly."

"But what good was it if nobody saw me?"

"I saw you. Gran was there, and the other kids."

"That doesn't count. I needed parental validation during my developmental years, and I didn't get it. I know you don't realize this, because you haven't studied psychology, like I have, but that sort of emotional abuse really damages a person's self-esteem."

"Well, actually, I am aware that it causes problems. And I—"

"No, you don't know. You have no idea the pain I've been through."

Savannah sighed. "You *have* mentioned it once or twice. In fact, that's pretty much the basis of most conversations you and I have had these past ten or twelve years."

"Well, you aren't very sympathetic."

Savannah bit her lower lip. "I believe I *was* sympathetic . . . say, the first eight or ten years. I've just run out of things to say about the topic of your unhappy childhood."

"What about your own miserable childhood?"

"I don't have much to say about that anymore, either."

Cordele stopped her sniffing and donned her all-seeing, all-knowing look. "That's because you're in denial about your upbringing. That's probably why you have food issues and haven't ever had a real relationship except whatever you've got with that Dirk guy and—"

"Cordele, stop!" Savannah held up her right hand in her best traffic-cop pose. "You wanna be a shrink, Godspeed. But you've got to learn not to shrink your friends, and especially not your family. Believe me, it's dangerous. Someday one of us is going to murder you, and it'll probably be me."

"But don't you want to know what's wrong with you? Don't you want the benefit of what I've learned?"

"Not really. I think I'd prefer to just wander around in the darkness of my ignorance and denial without your guiding light. Thanks anyway."

Cordele puffed up, reminding Savannah of some toads she'd seen in Georgia. "Well, if you don't want my help—"

"I don't. I want your love. For tonight, sitting here on this beautiful beach, I want your company. I want to just relax here with my sister and eat our dinner, and watch the sun go down, and I want to talk to you about absolutely *anything* other than the past. Please, can we do that?"

Cordele thought it over. "I suppose."

"Good." Savannah pointed across the water. "If you watch, really closely, you can sometimes see the beam from the lighthouse out there on Santa Lucia Island. Watch. There . . . did you see it?"

"Wow! That's neat. And the sailboats are pretty. Is that guy on what they call a waverunner?"

"That's right. If you like, we'll rent one while you're here and you can try it out."

"Cool." Her smile faded; storm clouds gathered on her brow. "You know, we were only about a three-, maybe four-hour drive to the Atlantic, but do you think our folks would take us to the beach even once—*once* in our entire rotten childhood?"

"Eah-h-h-h!"

When Savannah woke the next morning, she wasn't exactly bright-eyed and bushy-tailed. In fact, she was too tired to breathe. She lay in her bed, staring at the ceiling, wishing she could just mentally whisk herself away to some enchanted island paradise where there were no murdered TV chefs or disgruntled sisters.

And her cold was back with a vengeance. She sat up in bed and held her head in her hands, willing the throbbing in her sinuses to go away. It didn't. When she bent over to retrieve her house slippers from beneath the bed, she nearly blacked out.

"Oh, joy. Just what I need," she mumbled. She wondered if

there was any sort of rule against having whiskey hot toddies for breakfast. She could just imagine the joy Cordele would have tattling to teetotaling Granny Reid.

She could hear her now: I hate to have to tell you this, Gran, but Savannah has developed a substance addiction. Alcohol, I'm afraid. You know, I recently read an article in *Psychology Digest* about the likelihood of the children of alcohol-abusing parents developing addictions of their own. And since Savannah refuses to deal with her parental abandonment issues—like I've done, by cutting my hair off—it was only a matter of time till she became a boozer.

Yes, Savannah could picture it all.

So she decided to settle for coffee.

"Leave me alone. I feel like crap, and I hate the world right now," Savannah told Tammy when she tried to show her a website she had found. Savannah shuffled by the desk without even a glance in her assistant's direction and made her way to her cushy chair, coffee mug in hand.

As usual, Tammy's cheerful morning mood couldn't be dampened. It couldn't be dampened with a fire hose. She smiled brightly and said, "No problem. Sorry your cold came back. Can I get you something? Goldenseal or ginseng?"

"Peace and quiet?" she grumbled, sinking into her chair.

"You got it."

In less than three seconds, both cats had left their perches on the windowsill and were climbing all over her, begging to be petted.

"Get off me, you foul beasts. Just because Mommy makes a lap doesn't mean you have to use it. Scram."

"Boy," Tammy muttered, "you are in a bad mood."

"What did you say?"

"Nothing." Tammy left her chair at the desk and clapped her hands together and whistled. "Come here, Cleo. Atta girl, Di. Aunt Tammy will feed you. Mom's sick and grumpy this morning."

Savannah said nothing, but bared her teeth and growled.

Tammy chuckled as she led the cats into the kitchen . . . obviously terrified.

Savannah closed her eyes and held the coffee mug under her nose. She breathed deeply and could almost smell something through her stuffiness. Almost, but not quite. She took a drink and decided that coffee didn't taste like much if you couldn't smell it.

After enjoying less than two minutes of quiet, blissful solitude, she found her reverie interrupted when she heard the back door open and Cordele saying something to Tammy.

"Lord, help me," she whispered. "I've only got about one nerve left, and it's frazzled. If she gets on it, I might kill her."

Cordele came into the living room, dressed in a black leotard and tights. Savannah was shocked to see that beneath her usual costume of a baggy white blouse and a saggy dark skirt Cordele actually had a nice figure.

"Good morning," her sister said between sips from a water bottle. "Tammy says you're not feeling good this morning."

"I have a cold. I'm tired. It's been a tough week. That's all." She decided to stick her head out of her shell for a moment and attempt to be civil. "You look good in that getup. What are you doing?"

"My yoga. I do it every morning to calm my mind, to harmonize my spirit and my body."

Savannah tried to summon a modicum of enthusiasm. She couldn't find any, so she faked it. "That's good."

"It also helps with muscle toning and weight control. You should try it sometime."

Savannah glared at her with red, burning eyes. "I *have* tried yoga, Cordele. I live in southern California, for pete's sake. We've all tried everything at one time or another. We're very open-minded people."

"Obviously you didn't stick with it," Cordele replied, scanning up and down Savannah's body. "Discipline is the key."

"Eh . . ." Savannah mumbled, "go sit on a Lifesaver and tell me what flavor it is."

Cordele bristled like a banty hen. "What did you say?"

"Nothing. Never mind."

"No, I heard what you said. It was that obscene Lifesaver insult you used to say when we were kids. I remember the first time you ever said that to me. I was devastated."

"No!" Savannah held up one hand. "Don't you even start with me this morning, girl, or I swear I'll breathe on you. I'll cough on you and sneeze all over you, and give you this friggin' cold. You just aggravate me some more and see if I don't! Back off. I mean it!"

Tammy hurried into the living room, having overheard. She looked from one sister to the other, but they were locked in a glaring match.

"Cordele," she said. "Would you like to have some breakfast? I believe we have fresh strawberries and yogurt in the refrigerator. Some wheat germ to sprinkle on the top. What do you say?"

Eventually Cordele broke the glare standoff and stomped away into the kitchen.

"Thank you," Savannah mouthed to Tammy.

Tammy just smiled—her sunny good-morning smile. And Savannah thanked her stars above that she had a friend who was observant, perceptive, compassionate . . . and a morning person.

Chapter 12

No sooner had Savannah pulled into the parking lot at the station house than Dirk came bopping out of the back door. He hurried over to her Mustang and stuck his head in the open window on the passenger's side.

"Were you watching for me from the window?" she asked. "Or have you developed ESP in your old age?"

"I was watchin'. Hillquist is in the squad room, and I figured you'd just as soon avoid him if possible."

"Like creeping cruditis," she said.

Since Police Chief Norman Hillquist had fired her from the police force several years back, he had been her least favorite person on the planet. "Dirty, sucking, pond scum" was the way she usually referred to him. And that was to his face. Behind his back she was less kind.

"Thanks for sparing me," she said. "Get in, and I'll drive."

He hesitated. Like most men she had met, Dirk preferred to be the one behind the wheel. Usually she didn't care either way. But today she wanted at least the illusion of control over some part of her life.

"Get in," she said. "The lab's all the way across town. Just think how much gas money you'll save."

He opened the door and plopped himself inside. Giving her a

double sideways take, he said, "What's with your nose bein' all red? You got your cold back or somethin'?"

"No," she said. "I was putting on lipstick, and I missed."

"And your eyes are puffy, too. I hate to tell you this, but you look like shit, Van. You should be home, not running around with me."

"My sister is in my home."

He smirked. "So you prefer my company to hers, huh?"

"Yeah. Sorry state of affairs, no?"

They drove along in silence for a few minutes until they reached the industrial area of town. Savannah looked around at the endless rows of soulless gray buildings and asphalt parking lots.

"I remember when this was all orange groves and strawberry fields," she said. "Look at it now."

"Progress. It just keeps marching on. Pretty soon, San Carmelita will just be another part of L.A."

"Don't even say it."

She pulled into one of the lots and parked next to a dull gray building with an equally dull gray door. The only clue to its occupancy was the Great Seal of California and the county emblem next to the doorbell.

Dirk pushed the button, and a nearby intercom sputtered and crackled.

"Yeah?" asked a tired, harried-sounding voice.

"Coulter," Dirk replied, sounding equally droopy and irritable.

"Come in."

A buzzer beeped, and he pushed the heavy steel door open. Inside were the offices of the county's forensic laboratories where crime-scene evidence was processed.

Over the years Savannah and Dirk had brought everything here from hairs and fibers to chips of paint from cars and casts made of tire prints, bloodstained clothing, murder weapons . . . and a pet pygmy goat whom they'd suspected of eating a pair of rubber gloves that had been used in an armed robbery.

And Eileen Bradley and her team of technicians had handled it all. Not always gracefully or enthusiastically, but they had got-

ten the job done. A middle-aged woman, big-boned, with long gray hair that she wore in a braid down her back, Eileen wasn't somebody to mess with. Her subordinates were pretty much terrified of her, and that was just the way she liked it.

But she and Savannah had always gotten along. Even after Savannah left the force, she knew she was welcome to drop by the lab and chat. As long as she didn't get underfoot or touch any of the equipment.

"I told you not to come by before noon," Eileen barked at Dirk as she came out of her cubicle, which was about twice as big as the other three cubicles. All gray. But Eileen's had an Elvis calendar pinned to the partition wall.

"I was in the area," Dirk said. "I just thought I'd drop by and—"

"You're crowding me." Eileen walked up to Dirk and poked her finger at his chest. "You're being pushy, and I told you to knock that off. You can wait for your results, like everybody else."

Ordinarily, Dirk would have decked anybody who poked him in the chest, but in Eileen's presence, he wilted like a lettuce leaf in a frying pan.

"If you're not done yet," he said, "we can come back. No problem. I was just thinkin' that—"

"Yeah, yeah . . . I've heard it all before." Eileen looked over at Savannah, a faint twinkle in her eyes. "How do you put up with this guy?"

"Eh, he's not so bad. He buys me a Hershey bar every Valentine's Day and takes me out to Mickey D's on my birthday."

"What a catch. You'd better hang on to him."

"Okay, okay," Dirk interjected. "Is my stuff done or not?"

"It's done, but I don't think you're going to like what you've got." Eileen led them to the back of the room where several long tables were set up with beakers, microscopes, and assorted laboratory equipment that always reminded Savannah of her high school biology class.

"What have I got?" he asked, following her like an obedient

puppy. "Don't tell me there's nothing wrong in any of those samples I brought you."

"Are you kidding?" Eileen gave him a dirty look. "You brought me everything but the kitchen sink. I had to find something in those samples or you probably would have dragged that in next."

He brightened. "Then you *did* find something!"

Eileen strolled over to a pile of files that were lying on one of the tables and picked up the top one, a bright yellow folder. She flipped it open, taking her good old easy time.

Savannah suppressed a chuckle. Few people could get under Dirk's skin as efficiently as Eileen. And he didn't dare retaliate, because his lab results would take twice as long the next time.

"The cake contained high levels of phenylprophedrine," she said.

Dirk practically jumped out of his jeans. "I knew it! And I'll bet that it was in some of that stuff I brought in here, too—the sugar or the flour, or—"

"The cocoa." Eileen glanced down at the open folder in her hands. "The cocoa was absolutely full of it."

"I ate a bite of it," Savannah said, "and so did several others there that night. And obviously, we're all still kicking around. It must have not been a lethal dose."

"Not if a person only had a few bites of the cake, and if that person were healthy," Eileen said. "The most they would feel would probably be a dry mouth, an elevated pulse, maybe some anxiety or trembling."

"But if somebody had a bad heart and was on phenylprophedrine?" Dirk asked. "Could it cause a heart attack?"

"Sure. It could significantly raise the pulse rate and the blood pressure, which would put a strain on an already diseased heart. The combination could be fatal."

"But who would know something like that?" Dirk asked. "You'd have to be a doctor, or somebody in the medical profession, right?"

"Not necessarily." Eileen replaced the folder on the stack. "When phenylprophedrine was recalled, there were news stories

on TV and in the papers that warned people with heart conditions, especially people taking metosorbide, that it could be dangerous, even deadly."

"So," Savannah said. "We can narrow it down to a doctor, a nurse, or somebody who watches TV or reads the *Times*. That helps a lot."

Dirk shoved his hands into his jeans pockets and rattled his change—his "frustrated" gesture. "I don't suppose there were any prints on that cocoa box."

Eileen gave him one of her irritating smirks. "Now wouldn't that make it easy for you." She walked over to another table and another stack of files. This time she picked up a red folder. Opening it, she shoved it under his nose.

He looked it over before handing it back.

Savannah said, "Well?"

"The victim's," he replied.

"That's all?"

"Yep." He gave Eileen a "thanks for nothing" look. "After all, we wouldn't want to make it too easy, right?"

Half an hour later Savannah was dropping Dirk off in the police station parking lot.

"Sorry, buddy," she said. "But now we know for sure it's a homicide. All we've gotta do is find out who spiked the cocoa."

He replied with an inarticulate grumble.

"Cheer up," she added as he walked away. "It's barbecued pork chops and corn on the cob night at my house. Ryan and John will be there. Bring those papers of Streck's along, and we'll go over them again with you."

He just kept walking, head down, radiating gloom.

"Hey," she shouted after him, "at least you don't have to entertain my sister. You don't have a cold. You don't have to shave your legs or color your gray. You think you've got it rough? Boy, you don't know what rough is."

Chapter 13

"There's nothing on earth like a big, juicy pork chop to cheer that guy up," Savannah told Tammy as she threw a couple more pieces of meat on her backyard grill.

Tammy glanced over at Dirk, who was sprawled on a chaise lounge, a drowsy smile on his face, a beer in one hand, his empty plate in the other. He was past "satisfied" and was coming 'round the bend toward "sated." Another chop should do the trick.

With a pair of tongs, Savannah removed a few more ears of foil-wrapped corn from the coals and placed them on the platter that Tammy was holding. "Make sure John gets another one of those," she said. "Don't let Dirk have them all."

As Tammy walked away with the corn, Ryan left the picnic table where he had been sitting with John and walked over to the grill. He gave her a smile that gave her shivers, in spite of the warm evening and the proximity of the grill.

"You've outdone yourself, Savannah," he told her. "As usual, dinner was fantastic. One of these nights soon, you'll have to let us take you out to Chez Antoine. He makes an amazing chateaubriand, and his chocolate crème brûlée is orgasmic."

"I don't think I'll be free for awhile." Savannah gave a little nod in Cordele's direction. She was sitting by herself in a chair

under the arbor, staring into space, a bottle of Tammy's mineral water in her hand.

"Ah, that's all right. The more Reid girls, the merrier."

"Not necessarily," she muttered, brushing some sauce on the chops and stifling a sneeze and a sniffle.

Ryan studied Cordele thoughtfully for a moment. "Your sister does seem a bit depressed this evening," he whispered. "Is anything wrong?"

"Nothing out of the ordinary. For her, 'depressed' is more of a lifestyle than a mood."

"That's too bad. But still, John and I would love to take the two of you out for dinner. Heaven knows, we owe you some hospitality after all the great meals you've prepared for us recently."

"Are you kidding? You don't owe me diddly-squat. Dirk is out of his funk—that's worth a fortune right there."

Ryan shrugged. "I don't know how much we had to do with that."

"More than you think. Just knowing that he's going to get some help with this case perked him right up. Of course, he'd never admit that's the reason he's cheerful."

"He doesn't usually even admit to being cheerful."

"How true."

"So, when are we going to review what you've got on the case?"

"Right after the peach and blackberry cobbler."

"What? No chocolate cake?"

She made a face. "Please, I may never eat chocolate cake again. The phone's been ringing off the hook with reporters wanting to get a statement from me. Apparently, it was leaked that Eleanor, Queen of Chocolate, didn't die of natural causes, and they all want to talk to her so-called bodyguard who blew it."

"Ouch."

"Yeah, between losing a client and nursing a cold, I've had better weeks. But then, compared to Eleanor Maxwell's week . . ."

Dirk sauntered over to the grill, his empty plate in his hand and an expectant look on his face.

"Okay, okay, here you go." She plopped a couple more chops on his plate. "Don't ever say that we don't feed you around here."

"When I dish the dirt about you, Van, I never mention that."

She raised one eyebrow and shook her tongs at him. "Never say 'dirt' to somebody who prepares your food."

He gave his chops a suspicious look but walked back to his chaise and dug in anyway.

Savannah chuckled. "It takes a lot more than the fear of a little contamination to put Dirk Coulter off his chow," she said.

Later, as they gathered around the kitchen table to have dessert and coffee, Savannah slid a bowl of cobbler laden with vanilla ice cream in front of Cordele.

"You do still eat cobbler, don't you?" Savannah said. "It used to be your favorite. You always asked for that instead of a birthday cake, remember?"

A look of agony crossed Cordele's face as she wrestled with the decision on whether to indulge or refrain.

Tammy sat down beside her and picked up a spoon. "Ah, go ahead. A little refined sugar and flour once in a while won't hurt you. It's a special occasion."

Soon everyone had a bowl of warm cobbler à la mode and was happily munching away.

"Remember when we used to go picking blackberries by the roadsides in the fall?" Savannah said, trying to draw Cordele into some sort of meaningful social interaction with her friends. "That was fun, huh?"

Cordele didn't look up from her bowl. "Yeah, I remember. We used to get our arms all scratched up. It hurt something fierce."

Silence around the table. Everyone exchanged awkward glances, but nobody said anything.

"My brothers and I used to raid a neighbor's apple orchard," Ryan finally offered.

"Oh, that sounds like fun," Savannah said brightly.

Cordele took a deep breath. "Remember when we were picking berries on the side of the highway that time, and we found a

dead cat caught in the briars? I remember that like it was yesterday. That ol' cat was half-rotten and had flies buzzin' all over it."

Savannah sat, frozen, spoon halfway to her mouth, staring at her sister.

"I gotta tell you," Cordele continued. "It took the fun out of berry picking for me. Between finding that rotten cat and the briars scratching you all up, it just wasn't worth it."

Slowly Savannah stood and walked, trancelike, from the kitchen and into the living room. Tammy got up from her seat and followed her.

"Where are you going?" Tammy whispered, tugging at her sweater sleeve.

"To get a weapon," Savannah replied. "What do you figure would be best: a rope, a knife, a candlestick, or a gun?"

"That depends," Tammy said. "Are you talking homicide or suicide?"

"I figure I'll kill her first, then myself."

"I see. Well, in that case . . ." Tammy gave it several moments of serious thought. "Gun. Yeah, definitely the Beretta."

"Really? You think so? Why?"

"It would be too much work bludgeoning yourself to death with a candlestick."

She nodded. "Good point. Thanks."

"Anytime. What are friends for?"

With the dishes done, the cats fed, and Cordele in the living room reading her mystery novel, the Moonlight Magnolia team sat around the dining room table, studying the files that Dirk had confiscated from Martin Streck.

After comparing facts and figures for about an hour, they came to the same conclusion. "Streck's been embezzling from Eleanor for a long time," Tammy said.

"No kidding," Ryan replied. "He's just about bled her estate dry."

"And didn't you mention," John added, "that she and her husband had a recent parting of the ways, so to speak?"

"Their divorce became final about a month ago." Dirk shoved back from the table and stretched his arms.

"A lot of things come to light during a divorce," Tammy said. "Do you suppose either Eleanor or Burt figured out what Martin was up to?"

Savannah shook her head. "I guarantee you that Eleanor didn't know. She was the sort of gal that, if she had found out somebody was cheating her, she'd have chopped them up into paté and fed them to those hounds of hers."

"Maybe Streck hadn't yet been exposed, but was afraid he would be," Ryan suggested. "Perhaps he thought if he knocked off Eleanor, he could rig the books to hide his tampering from Burt."

"He *was* taking off with these files when we caught him," Dirk said. "And that maid, Marie, told you that we should be lookin' at him."

"Yes, but she wouldn't say why." Savannah took a blank sheet of paper and drew a small box at the top. "I suppose that if I'd been cashing in my client's CDs, selling off their stocks, and dipping into their bank accounts and skimming off their savings, I'd be pretty nervous about getting caught."

"Nervous enough to kill somebody?" Tammy said.

Savannah glanced into the living room, where Cordele was curled up in the big chair with her book. "Oh, sure," she said. "If there's fifty ways to leave a lover, there's gotta be a thousand reasons to commit murder."

She scribbled Martin Streck's name in the box at the top of the page. He had just been promoted to "Suspect Number One."

Chapter 14

Savannah had often wondered how Greenwoods Cemetery had gotten its name. Standing among the grave markers that lay flush with the earth was the occasional palmetto. But there wasn't a woods, or even a leafy tree, in sight. And since the drought-inspired water restrictions had required southern Californians to shower together, flush only when necessary, and water the lawns not at all, Greenwoods Cemetery wasn't looking particularly green, either.

Long ago, Savannah had decided that when she kicked the bucket, she wanted to be carted back to Georgia, where she could lie beneath the weeping willows near her beloved grandfather.

She had attended a depressing amount of funerals in this cemetery. And today's ceremonial burying was equally somber, as they laid Lady Eleanor Maxwell to rest.

Surveying the crowd that stretched from the open grave, surrounded by chairs across the beige lawns to the road, she wondered how many of the mourners had actually ever met Eleanor in the flesh and how many were simply groupie gourmets.

"Quite a crowd," Dirk remarked. "I'll bet there won't be anywhere near this many when I go toes-up."

"Unless it's in the line of duty, and then there'll be cops from here to San Diego," Savannah replied.

When he didn't answer, she turned and looked at him. He was just staring at her. "Don't even say that," he told her. "It's bad luck."

"Oh, pooh. Gran says that if you speak an evil out loud, it won't come true. Besides, you're too mean to die. You'll live to be a hundred and four and irritate us all the whole time."

He lowered his voice. "Nice theory, but it didn't work for her." He nodded toward the casket that hung on thick canvas straps over the grave.

"Sh-h-h." She glanced around, but the only one who had overheard was Tammy, who was standing on the other side of Dirk.

"Keep it down, Dirko," Tammy told him. "It's customary to only say nice things about people at their funerals."

"Yeah," Savannah added. "You keep the really juicy, nasty stuff to yourself and save it for the evening of the funeral, when everybody's comparing notes about who took it hard and who didn't seem to give a hoot."

Tammy's mouth dropped open. "I haven't been to a lot of funerals. Do people really do that?"

"Oh, absolutely," Savannah told her. "You can't win with the gossips. If you cry too much, they'll say you 'just plumb fell apart and made a spectacle of yourself,' and if you don't cry enough, they'll claim that you 'never did give a fig anyway' about the recently departed. You're damned if you do and if you don't."

"Wow." Tammy shook her head in disbelief. "I'd think that how someone grieves is a personal matter."

"Yeah, well, that's what you get for thinkin'," Dirk said. "And speaking of who's taking it hard and who ain't . . ." He nodded to the circle of Eleanor's immediate family and friends who were sitting in chairs at the gravesite.

Savannah's eyes went automatically to Gilly, who sat between her mother and Sydney Linton. The little girl seemed bewildered by all that was going on around her. Savannah's big-sister persona longed to hug the child, give her a glass of milk and

some chocolate chip cookies, and read her a story.

Louise had a dazed look on her face that Savannah suspected was pharmaceutically induced. Nerve pills, no doubt. She wasn't likely to do that cookie/story routine tonight, no matter how badly her daughter might need it.

But the chauffeur seemed to be concerned for Gilly. He was holding her hand and whispering to her from time to time. Whatever he was saying appeared to be helping. She would look up at him, nod, and smile just a little.

A minister appeared, walked to the head of the grave, and opened his prayer book. The crowd fell silent as the familiar "dust to dust" and "ashes to ashes" passage was read, followed by the Lord's Prayer.

Savannah watched Martin Streck, who stood behind Louise, his hand on her shoulder, trying to read his face and demeanor. It would have been nice to pick up a sense of guilt or fear from him, but she didn't. Other than a mild concern for Louise, he seemed pretty unaffected by the whole thing.

Marie sat on the other side of Sydney. She was the only one present—other than Gilly—who seemed to be genuinely distressed. Although she was wearing dark glasses, she was constantly wiping her eyes and nose with a lace handkerchief she held, knotted, in her hand. Her black dress made her seem even more pale and gaunt than usual.

Savannah didn't recognize the good-looking blond fellow who sat on Louise's other side. But from his age and the resemblance between him and Louise, Savannah assumed he was Louise's father, Burt Maxwell.

Eleanor's ex, she thought. Hm-m-m . . . definitely cuter than she had been.

Standing behind Burt was Kaitlin Dover and several others that Savannah recognized from the crew that had been taping in the studio barn.

They were all wearing long faces, and Savannah wondered if it was because Eleanor had died or because they had lost a steady gig. From what she had heard, jobs in Hollywood were few and

far between these days. Even a difficult boss like Eleanor Maxwell was better than no boss at all.

The minister had finished, and, one by one, they were filing past the closed coffin, each person dropping a single red rose onto the highly polished top.

Louise carelessly tossed her flower onto the casket, then turned to her daughter, whose rose was pale pink. "Go ahead," she told her.

Savannah's heart ached as she watched the little girl kiss the face of the flower, then gently place it on her grandmother's coffin.

Sydney laid his down next, then took Gilly by the hand and led her across the lawn after Louise. They made their way to the classic Jaguar parked nearby. Sydney opened the door, assisted mother and child inside, and took his place in the driver's seat.

Nearby, more than a dozen reporters' cameras clicked and whirred. Savannah saw at least three TV news crews filming the proceedings. Lady Eleanor was a hot story, especially now that word was out that she had been murdered.

They all focused on the Jaguar as it pulled away.

"It just occurred to me," Savannah said. "You know who's *not* here?"

"Who?" Tammy asked.

"Anybody who even looks remotely like Eleanor. And she's supposed to have an identical twin sister named Elizabeth."

Dirk shrugged. "Maybe she lives out of state and couldn't make it."

"Nope. She lives in Twin Oaks."

"That's only fifteen minutes down the freeway," Dirk said. "Wonder why she didn't show?"

"Maybe she didn't like her sister," Savannah suggested, trying not to think of Cordele at the moment she muttered the words.

"Or," Tammy said, "maybe she didn't want to show up and have everybody critique her manner of grieving. I sure wouldn't."

* * *

Against her better judgment, Savannah invited Cordele to go to the mall with her. Ordinarily, she would never have taken anyone but Tammy when she was hoping to do an interview. But Cordele's face had fallen when Savannah suggested that she might want to stay at home and finish her mystery. So she had caved and asked her to come along.

After the funeral, Dirk had said he was going to go after Burt Maxwell, to see if he could "squeeze him for a little juice about Martin Streck, or anybody else," as he had delicately put it. Savannah had offered to go to the mall restaurant where Eleanor's twin sister, Elizabeth, worked.

Savannah had meant well, inviting Cordele to come along, but now she was having second thoughts. It wasn't going to be easy, telling Cordele to get lost for a few minutes. She was bound to take it personally and be insulted. Cordele took it personally if it rained too hard in her vicinity.

"You don't mind, do you," Savannah said as they pulled into the parking lot next to the food court, "if I go into the restaurant alone at first and see if this gal's even working today? If she isn't, we'll both go to the nail salon and get a French manicure. How does that sound?"

The face fell . . . again.

"Come on, sugar," Savannah pleaded. "I really need to do this one little thing by myself, and then you and I can shop or get a Mrs. Fields cookie or . . . oh, right . . . you don't eat cookies. I'll buy you a frozen yogurt. With sprinkles or fruit on top. Whatever you want. How's that? Cordele?"

Cordele sat in the passenger's seat, staring out the side window, giving Savannah a fine view of the back of her head.

Savannah wanted to smack her. This was ridiculous, having to bribe a woman who was nearly thirty years old as if she were four and getting the cold-shoulder, silent treatment in return.

"Why did you even invite me if you were just going to get me here and then dump me?" Cordele finally said, still staring out the window.

"I told you when I asked you along that this would be a combination of business and pleasure. Let me take care of a little bit of business and then we'll have some fun. We'll go to Victoria's Secret and sample their new perfumes and maybe go play with some puppies in the pet store."

"No. I never go to pet stores."

Savannah was afraid to ask why. But she had a feeling she would find out anyway, so . . .

"Why don't you go into pet stores, Cordele?"

"Because it hurts too much. It reminds me that I never had a dog of my own when I was a kid. And I wanted a dog that—"

"What about Gulliver? We had that old sheep dog for ages. And Colonel Beauregard. He's the finest hound in the county."

"But they were the *family's* dogs, not my own personal pet. I wanted an animal that was just mine, that I didn't have to share with a thousand brothers and sisters. If I'd had a dog I would have taught him to fetch and to roll over and—"

"Meet you in twenty minutes at the fountain in front of Sears."

Savannah got out of the car and slammed the door behind her. "I wish I'd known that not having a pet of your own would scar you for life, Cordele," she muttered to herself as she walked across the lot to the mall entrance. "Hell, I would have gone out in the woods and trapped a skunk for you. That would've been fun . . . watching you teach a polecat to fetch and roll over. Gr-r-r-rr."

She was dimly aware that several people were watching her with looks that varied from curious to alarmed. Obviously they thought this angry woman who was talking to herself and growling under her breath might present a threat to society.

"Eh, screw 'em," she added at the end of her soliloquy. "If they had a sister like Cordele, they'd be nutty, too."

She located the restaurant on the mall map that was mounted just inside the entrance. Straight ahead and to her right. It had been years since she had visited the Twin Oaks Mall, and she was surprised at how much it had grown. They had added two

new wings, where specialty shops sold everything from gourmet coffees to stained-glass lamps, silk flower arrangements to high-tech sports equipment and video games.

Tucked between a bookstore and a candle shop was the Rain Forest Café. The restaurant was a bright and cheerful establishment with plenty of skylights, a profusion of green plants, and tropical-themed murals on the walls that gave it the ambiance of a South American jungle.

Not that the sounds of parrots and monkeys caused Savannah to think of food. And apparently, the décor had a similar effect on the other mall visitors. Other than a family in a booth in the back and a teenage couple at a table up front, the restaurant was empty except for the employees.

The bored waiters and waitresses wore khaki safari shirts and shorts with straw hats. The uniform looked almost cute on the younger ones, but ridiculous on the woman serving behind the bar—a middle-aged, heavyset woman who was a dead ringer for Eleanor Maxwell.

Savannah walked over to the bar, which served nothing but nonalcoholic smoothies, and waited for Elizabeth to come over. When she did, Savannah was greeted with a less than cordial, "Yeah . . . what can I get you?"

Hm-m-m, she thought, grumpy runs in the family.

"A pineapple-strawberry flip," she said.

Elizabeth trudged down to the other end of the bar, threw some fruit and ice into a blender, and pushed the button. The concoction was quickly whipped into a froth, which she poured into a tall soda-fountain glass.

Poking a straw into it, she shoved the drink under Savannah's nose. "That'll be five-fifty," she announced, drumming her fingers impatiently on the bar.

"Five-fifty? Wow!" Savannah said. "That's pricey for a milk shake with no milk in it."

Elizabeth reached out and seized the drink. "Do you want the smoothie or not, lady? I got work to do here."

Savannah made a point of looking deliberately up and down

the empty bar. Then she said, "I'll take it," and handed the woman a ten-dollar bill.

When Elizabeth brought her the change, Savannah decided to dive in . . . although she had a distinct feeling that the water would be deep and cold.

"I realize that you're . . . busy," she said with all the Dixie charm she could muster, "but could we talk for a couple of minutes? I'm—"

"No."

She went ahead and produced her investigator's license, flipping it open in Elizabeth's face. "My name is Savannah Reid and I'm a private investigator. I'm working on—"

"Oh, I know who you are. I heard about you on the news, and Louise told me about you when she called me about Eleanor. Some bodyguard you turned out to be. Not exactly Johnny-on-the-Spot, were you?"

Savannah's blue eyes went cold, and her recently summoned charm evaporated. In a voice that wasn't exactly oozing with sympathy, she said, "I'm very sorry for your loss. I attended your sister's funeral this afternoon and—"

"And you were wondering why I wasn't there."

Savannah took a deep breath. "I figured you had your reasons."

"You're damned right I did! Do you have any idea what it's like to have a famous sister . . . a rich sister . . . a famous, rich, *twin* sister . . . when you work in a friggin' restaurant, slinging hash for lousy tips?"

Savannah thought about suggesting that if she weren't such a vile person, she might get better tips, but she decided to say nothing except, "Nope. I guess I don't."

"Well, it's the pits."

"I'll bet it is."

"Do you know how many times a day somebody walks into this place and says, 'Hey, you know who you look like? No, really . . . you look just like . . .' It sucks. Especially when they say stu-

pid things like, 'If your sister's so rich, what are you doing waiting tables?' Boy, that's the one that really irks my butt big time."

"Yeah. I imagine that's pretty irritating."

"You don't know the half of it."

"Sounds like you weren't very fond of your sister," Savannah observed.

Elizabeth's eyes narrowed. "No, I wasn't. But I didn't kill her, if that's what you're getting at."

"Me? Getting at? Naw, I'm just sitting here shooting the breeze with you."

"If you want to investigate anybody, take a good, hard look at that lousy niece of mine, Louise. Now there's one who'd do about anything to get her hands on her mother's money. Eleanor spoiled her rotten, and look what she got: a daughter that wouldn't even talk to her. Did *she* come to the funeral?"

"Yes, she was there with her little girl."

Elizabeth's hard face softened. "Gilly's a little sweetheart. I miss her since I stopped going over there a few months ago."

"If you don't mind me asking, why did you estrange yourself from your sister?"

"You spent time with Eleanor and you ask me a question like that?"

"I just meant . . . was there some reason in particular a few months ago?"

"My sister and I had a blowout, okay? I offered her my opinion about . . . somebody . . . and she told me to leave. I did. And I didn't bother to go back."

Savannah leaned forward, her eyes locked with Elizabeth's. She could tell the woman wanted to say more. If she could just nudge her over the edge. . . .

"Did it have anything to do with Louise?" Savannah asked, taking a stab in the dark.

She had hit a bull's-eye. Elizabeth's face flushed with anger at the memory. "Yes. Louise and that snake accountant of Eleanor's—Martin something. It was a disgusting situation for that child to be growing up around."

"Louise and Martin?"

Unpleasant pictures floated through Savannah's brain. If there was anything more unappealing than Louise or Martin, it was the thought of the two of them together.

"Yeah, they were like a couple of dogs in heat, all over each other right in front of that little girl. Of course, Martin's just one in a long line for Louise, but with Gilly getting older, she needed to cut down on her shenanigans a bit, or at least keep it behind closed doors."

Louise and Martin. This opened up all sorts of possibilities, Savannah mused, sordid though they might be.

"And Eleanor didn't agree with you? About their relationship, I mean."

"Oh, I think she did. She couldn't have been happy about it either. But she didn't want to hear anything bad concerning Louise. Eleanor could talk trash about her own daughter, but heaven help you if you said a word about her."

"How long do you think it was going on—this affair?"

Elizabeth shrugged. "At least six months before I confronted Eleanor about it. I don't know if they ever broke it off. Could still be going on for all I know."

Savannah flashed back to earlier in the afternoon at the cemetery—Martin standing behind Louise, his hand on her shoulder. Had there been chemistry between them? In retrospect, very likely.

Savannah stood up and laid a three-dollar tip on the bar. She hadn't touched the smoothie. Even if she had wanted it before, the thought of Louise and Martin doing the grizzly bear hump had put her off her feed.

"Thank you, Elizabeth, for speaking with me. I'm really trying to do what I can for your sister, even if it is . . . after the fact, so to speak."

"Yeah, okay. No problem." Elizabeth gave her a grudging smile and quickly covered the dollar bills with her palm. "Thanks."

Savannah found Cordele sitting, as requested, on a bench beside the fountain in the center of the mall. Palmettos surrounded a blue-tiled pool where goldfish swam among myriad coins tossed there by well-wishers. A plume of water shot upward toward a skylight and fell, a spray of glittering iridescence, back into the pond.

Savannah steeled herself for another war of the words, but when Cordele looked her way, she smiled. Just a half-smile, really, but Savannah was happy even for that. Apparently she was over their last argument.

"Sorry—that took a little longer than I'd hoped," she said as she sat down on the bench beside her.

"It's okay. I was just sitting here, watching people go by." Cordele waved her hand, indicating the dozens of shoppers hurrying past them. "Folks sure do come in all shapes, sizes, and colors, don't they?"

"They certainly do. Sometimes I just sit in a public place and look at the passersby and think, not one out of fifty of these people is thin enough and young enough and attractive enough to be on the front cover of a fashion magazine. But they're all beautiful in their own way."

About that time, a woman in her seventies strolled by, wearing a turquoise pants suit, white patent leather shoes and purse, and large dangling earrings that nearly brushed her shoulders.

"Look at her," Savannah said. "A spring in her step and a sparkle in her eyes. You can just tell she's full of vinegar. She's lovely."

"That's because she's happy," Cordele observed. "And that's why I want to be a psychologist. I want to help people. I want them all to be happy. Or at least as many as possible."

Savannah reached over and put her arm around her sister's shoulders. "And that's why you're going to make a great psychologist. You'll make a real difference in the world, Cordele."

Savannah's sister looked at her with little-girl eyes. "Do you really think so?"

"Absolutely. No doubt about it. You'll be an instrument of healing and comfort to many, many people in the course of your career. You mark my words, darlin'."

Cordele blushed with pleasure, and Savannah gave her a squeeze. "How about that French manicure now? Maybe we'll splurge and get gorgeous toesies while we're at it."

"Okay." Cordele glanced around, as though afraid the Diet Police might be listening. "And then . . . if you still want to . . . a Mrs. Fields chocolate chip with macadamia nuts would be great, too."

"You got it."

As the two sisters walked down the mall to the beauty salon, Savannah was grateful for this peaceful interlude with her sibling. But she doubted whether even the sensual pleasures of a manicure, a pedicure, and a sugar fix could erase the thoughts of Eleanor Maxwell lying in her coffin, her supposed loved ones gathered around her. And among them, a killer—or killers—with evil secrets.

Yes, Savannah decided, she was very grateful for her own family. And at the moment, she was especially grateful for Cordele, warts and all.

Chapter 15

"Where's Miss Sunshine and Light?" Dirk asked Savannah as they sat together on the sofa, her largest mixing bowl full of popcorn between them. On the coffee table was his half-empty bottle of beer and her cup of Bailey's-enhanced coffee, along with a dozen folders, notebooks, and files pertaining to the case.

"Upstairs in the bathroom," Savannah replied. "I bought her a bottle of Victoria's Secret's new bath gel. She's blissfully soaking in a mountain of bubbles, just like I intend to do after you leave."

"Here's your hat; what's your hurry?"

"Something like that." She gave him a smile that diluted the insult. Not that he would have cared one way or the other. Dirk didn't really care what anyone thought of him and that made him difficult to offend.

"Tell me something," he said, lowering his voice conspiratorially. "Exactly what *is* Victoria's secret anyway?"

"That's for women to know, and men to find out only on very special occasions."

He gave her a sideways glance up and down her figure. "I guess you and I haven't had any occasions that were . . . special enough."

She sniffed and blew her nose on a tissue. "Nor are we likely to."

"Isn't that cold of yours getting any better?" he said with more genuine concern that she would have expected him to muster.

"Well . . . yes . . . actually I've noticed an improvement just today. Thanks for asking."

"Good. The sooner you get over it, the less likely you are to give it to me."

"Right." Picking up her notebook from the coffee table, she glanced over her list. "Did you go by the lab today?"

"Yeah. Eileen had taken the day off."

"A lot of people do that on Sunday. Don't take it personally."

"Anyway. That Mexican dude that works there on the weekends—"

"I believe her assistant is Honduran."

"Whatever. He said they didn't get any prints off the letter except for Eleanor's and one from Martin Streck."

Savannah took a handful of popcorn. "That doesn't surprise me. I already told you I caught him looking at one of the letters in her office. Was it that one—the most recent one?"

"Yep. That was it."

"And I don't suppose the county wants to spend the big bucks for a DNA test on the envelope seal unless we've got something substantial on somebody."

"Exactly. And it wouldn't be enough to just test the envelope. At this point, we'd have to swab and run tests on everybody there except maybe the dogs, and I haven't even ruled them out yet."

"Why do I have the feeling it would match either Louise or Martin? Maybe both."

"On the same envelope? Yuck."

"I'm kidding. Although, from what Eleanor's twin sister said, Louise and Martin have swapped more than just slobber."

"He's a lot older than she is. And not nearly as good-looking."

"Do you think she's good-looking?"

He shrugged and took a swig of his beer. "She's not exactly a dog. But a little skinny for my taste." He turned and gave her a

quick but searching glance. "Why? Do you think *he's* good-looking?"

"Eh, not particularly." She decided not to mention that Streck had nice thick hair. Dirk was particularly touchy on the topic of hair thickness or the lack thereof. It was his only form of vanity.

"Maybe the two of them are in cahoots," he suggested, stretching out his legs and propping his sneakers on the coffee table.

She reached over and swatted his leg. He lifted his feet as she slid one of the folders under his shoes. "Maybe so," she said. "Perhaps he robs Eleanor blind, and when he's finished draining the coffers, Louise knocks off Mommy Dearest."

"And if they're a couple, they get to share the money."

"Or maybe Martin's doing everything on his own."

"Or maybe Louise is. Or maybe it's somebody else."

"Did you get anything out of Burt Maxwell this afternoon?" she asked, sipping her coffee.

"Absolutely nada. I followed him to his house in Hollywood, where he told me in no uncertain terms that I was out of line trying to question him on the day that they buried his ex-wife. Slammed the door in my face."

"Well, he sorta had a point there. Not exactly great timing, but what can you do?"

"I'll go after him again tomorrow; that's what. And if he gives me any lip, I'll haul his butt to the station and stick him in the sweat box. See how he likes that."

The "sweat box" was the drab, gray interrogation room where the thermostat was always set at a comfortable 85, no matter what the weather was outside. About eight by ten feet with no windows, one door, one table, and two chairs, it was claustrophobic to say the least. Dirk swore by the sweat box—claimed he could get anybody to confess anything just to get out of there.

Savannah thought it was best used as a last resort, not a first line of offense. But then, she and Dirk had disagreed on a lot of things in the rocky course of their relationship.

"Maybe he'd talk to me," she suggested. "I mean . . . you've got a lot to do tomorrow, running down Streck. After all, he's our

hottest lead at the moment. It'll probably take you most of the day doing a background on him, huh?"

Dirk gave her a dubious look—the one he used when he had a feeling he was being worked. "Yeah, I guess."

"You don't mind if I take a shot at him, then?"

"No harm in trying," he replied. "But weren't you going to talk to Louise, too?"

"Yeah, I'll drop by there tomorrow morning. Mention to her that there's nothing left of the family fortune. That she's getting zippo as an inheritance. I should be able to tell by the look on her face whether that's news to her or not."

"But if you *can't* tell . . . and if Burt won't talk to you either . . . where does that leave us?"

Good old Dirk, she thought. Always walking on the sunny side of the street. She considered mentioning that if the sky fell in and the world came to an end during the night, they'd pretty much be out of luck, too. So why bother to live?

But she had spent too much of her life trying to teach Dirk the value of optimism. He was a lost cause. Instead, she thought for several long moments, then sighed and said, "If you don't find anything on Martin, and I don't get anything out of either Burt Maxwell or Louise, I'd say it pretty much leaves us where we are right now—up the proverbial, waste-polluted creek, paddle-free. Things can only get better."

An hour later, with Dirk gone and Cordele in bed, Savannah found the time to soak away some of the day's stress in her own jasmine-scented bubble bath. Having placed two votive candles on the edge of the tub by her feet and another two on top of the hamper nearby, she was savoring the simple pleasure of watching iridescent bubbles sparkle in the candlelight. They tickled deliciously as she scooped up mounds of the glistening, fragrant froth and let it glide down her arms and legs.

Savannah had always thoroughly enjoyed being female . . . but never so much as when she was taking a bath. Guys could have their showers; they didn't know what they were missing.

It was almost worth having to shave your legs.

Just as she was drifting into a delicious trancelike state, she heard—as though from far away—an unwelcome buzzing. It was coming from the cordless phone that she had left on the hamper next to the candles.

"I knew I shouldn't bring you in here," she told the phone as she dried her hands on a nearby towel and picked it up. "You seem to always know just when I—Hello."

A woman's voice with a sweet Southern drawl replied, "Hello yourself, Savannah girl."

"Gran." She smiled and settled back into the bath, the phone cradled against her shoulder. "You are the only one in the world I want to talk to right now."

"You must be taking one of your famous bubble baths."

"How did you know?"

"You sound relaxed and drowsy."

"Maybe I was in bed asleep."

A chuckle on the other end. "No, if I'd woke you up, you'd have been *crabby* and drowsy."

"That's true. I reckon you know me. How are you and everybody and everything back there?"

"Probably better than you." Gran laughed again, and the sound went through Savannah, more warming and comforting than any luxury bath. "How's it going with Cordele being there?"

"Oh, okay. We went to the mall today, did a little shopping."

"She didn't talk you into buying her a dog, did she?"

"We had the discussion, but no, I didn't."

"Good, 'cause I'd be the one who'd wind up taking care of it."

"You? Why would you . . . ?" Savannah thought it over, then the lightbulb came on in her head. "Gran, did Cordele move back in with you?"

"Sure she did. About a month ago. Didn't you know that?"

"No-o-o. She failed to mention that she's living with you again. Is she contributing any money for food or utilities or *anything?*"

The silence on the other end told Savannah more than she

wanted to know. Granny Reid was, once again, allowing her grandchildren to take advantage of her.

"Cordele's awful busy," Gran finally said. "She's always on the go. I hate to ask her to get a job while she's going to college and all."

"She's been going to college for the past ten years. She's making a career of it. The only problem is it doesn't pay. And speaking of money, are you footing the school bills, too?"

Again a heavy silence. Then, "Well, you know she got a scholarship, and that helped some. Cordele makes really good grades. She always has."

Savannah thought of her octogenarian grandmother struggling to make ends meet in that tiny, rural Georgia town. Her ramshackle, shotgun house that was cozy, but far too small for the Reid clan, especially now that some of the nine kids had acquired spouses and children of their own.

Gran had always been generous to a fault, opening her heart, her home, and her refrigerator to everyone who dropped by. And they did—several times a day.

"Gran, I thought you were through with letting those kids sponge off of you. You laid the law down and told them that—"

"I know. I know, and I've pretty much been stickin' by it. But I make an exception for Cordele. She's trying so hard to get her master's degree."

"She's not been trying *that* hard. Taking one class per semester isn't exactly working your tail off."

Gran sighed. "But she's got all those meetings she goes to. She calls them her support groups."

"How many does she go to?"

"Oh, she's out to one or the other 'most every night. I think she goes to a couple of them on Saturday."

"Maybe she could cut back on a few of those and get a part-time job at Wal-Mart. Then she could hand you a few dollars for groceries now and again."

"No. I don't reckon she could do without those meetings.

They're mighty important to her. Cordele's always been the nervous one of the bunch, you know."

Savannah growled under her breath, "Yeah . . . works out pretty good for her, too."

"What did you say?"

"Nothing."

There was a long and awkward lag in the conversation. Uncomfortable pauses frequently occurred when Savannah and her grandmother discussed the topic of her spoiling the grandchildren and the "greats," as she called their offspring.

"I was just worried about you, Savannah," Gran finally said. "When Cordele told me she was gonna surprise you with a visit, that she wanted to work out some—what did she call them—familial issues with you, I was afraid you and she were gonna have some trouble."

"Don't you worry about a thing, Gran."

"Promise me you won't fight with your sister."

"I won't make her bleed or break any of her bones. I promise. But I might tell her to get off her lazy backside and either get a job or get that degree, one or the other."

"Oh, mercy. That'll go over good. You'd better look out, Savannah girl, or you might be the one to end up bloody and broken. I'm here to tell you, there's more to Cordele than meets the eye. She ain't the tender buttercup she makes out to be."

Savannah grinned. "Don't worry, Gran. I'm bigger than Cordele, and I've got a gun. If she gets to aggravating me too much, I'll just pack her up and send her back to you."

"Those sound like famous last words if I ever heard some."

Savannah sighed and watched one of her votive candles flicker and go out. Her suds were about gone, too. "Yeah, don't they, though?"

By the time Savannah arrived at the Maxwell estate the next day, it was ten-thirty. She and Cordele had shared a fairly cordial breakfast and, reluctant to end a winning streak, short though it

might be, she had delayed leaving the house until absolutely necessary. Even then, Cordele had pouted, suggesting that if Savannah cared at all about confronting some long-standing family issues, she should hurry home—unless, of course, she cared more about catching society's misfits and putting them into dark, hopeless prisons where rehabilitation was a joke.

Savannah was terribly proud of herself. She hadn't growled at, bitten, or even snapped at her sister. She had simply smiled, nodded, quietly walked out of the house, got into her car . . . and peeled out of the driveway, leaving six months' worth of normal tire-tread wear on the pavement.

Yes, so far, it was a banner day. No one had bled. God was good.

At the Maxwell mansion, she found the gates wide open, so she didn't use her ill-gotten combination to break in. And as she passed the gatekeeper's cottage, she saw no activity at all.

No one seemed to be stirring at the studio; the yellow perimeter tape that surrounded the building appeared undisturbed. It wasn't until she arrived at the main house itself that the stillness started to give her the creeps. Things were too quiet. What was missing?

Oh, yes . . . she thought, the terrible threesome.

They hadn't bounded off the porch to attack her, as usual. And the cushioned chairs, where they usually napped when they weren't mauling someone, were empty.

While she couldn't say she particularly liked the terriers, she had grown accustomed to their shaggy little faces. And she had derived a certain satisfaction in knowing that—for a bagful of chicken livers—she had won them over. A feat accomplished by few.

She was beginning to think that no one was on the property when she heard a squeal coming from the ocean side of the house. Hurrying around the building, she found Gilly sitting on the lawn, playing with a tiny black pup. The squeal had been a cry of delight. She gave another one as the puppy nipped at her fingers, then jumped up and licked her chin.

"Hi, sweetcakes," Savannah said as she walked across the lawn and sat down on the grass beside them. "Who's your buddy?"

"This is Mona Lisa," Gilly said proudly. "We got her at the pound today. They said they think she's part lab and part German shepherd, so she's really just a mutt. But mutts are good dogs, too."

"Mutts are great dogs. You say you got her at the pound?" An unpleasant thought was forming in Savannah's brain, and she hoped she was wrong.

"Yeah. Mom took Killer and Satan and Hitler there today. She told me that the pound people would find new homes for them. But I heard her tell them that the dogs were mean and that they bite people. And the guy there said, 'Okay, lady, we'll take care of the dogs.' And he didn't say it nice, either."

Savannah winced. As an animal lover, she couldn't bear the thought of the three dogs taking the long walk down the green mile. It wasn't their fault that they hadn't been trained properly and were badly spoiled. She reminded herself to see if she couldn't remedy the situation later.

"But you got Mona here and brought her home. That's nice," she said, reaching down and stroking the dog's glossy coat. The pup was still very young, not particularly skilled at even walking. Wagging her tail a bit too hard caused her to topple sideways.

"Who named her Mona Lisa?"

"I did," she said proudly. "There's a song about a lady named that. It's a pretty song and she's a pretty dog. Don't you think?"

"I think she's gorgeous."

"Better than a husky or a poodle or a dalmatian from the pet store?"

"Every bit as good, that's for sure."

Gilly picked up a nearby plastic chew toy in the shape of a hot dog and squeaked it at the dog. She yelped and jumped back, growling a tiny puppy growl.

"She's full of vinegar," Savannah said. "That's for sure."

Gilly nodded. "My mommy said we could buy an expensive

dog from the pet store in the mall if we wanted to, because we're rich now that my grandma's dead. But I told her, no, that I wanted to take one from the pound and save its life."

"You did a noble thing," Savannah said. "I'm sure that Mona will love you very much and be a good friend to you for a long time."

Savannah looked back at the house and around the yard, but saw no one. "Where's your mom?" she asked the girl.

Gilly glanced around and shrugged. "I don't know. Maybe at the beach over there." She pointed down the hill to a stretch of sand that disappeared around a point. "She likes to go down there when she's feeling upset. She's been pretty upset."

Savannah stood and brushed the grass off her slacks. "I think I'll go talk to her awhile. You have fun with Mona."

"Okay. Will you come say good-bye before you leave?"

"I sure will. Later, punkin'."

Savannah headed down the path that led to the beach, but once she was out of earshot from Gilly, she stopped, reached into her purse, and produced her cell phone.

"Hi, Tam," she said. "Yeah, I'm over at the Maxwell place. Do me a favor, would you? Go online and see if you can find a local Silky Terrier Rescue group. I know they have one for dalmatians and for Boston terriers. And tell them to get down to the county pound right away."

She paused, listening, then added, "Yeah, you might not want to mention their names or their propensity for biting any hand that isn't feeding them. And if anybody asks, they just need a loving home and a bit of discipline, and their names are Moe, Larry, and Curly. Okay? Thanks, darlin'."

Chapter 16

Savannah found Louise Maxwell on the beach, as Gilly had suggested. But contrary to Gilly's other prediction, she didn't look at all upset to Savannah.

She was lying on an oversized beach towel, soaking up rays. And since her bikini was even more skimpy than the one she had been wearing previously, she was absorbing more than her share of California sunlight.

Before she saw Savannah she was gazing contentedly at some surfers farther down the beach and humming to herself. But the moment she noticed that she had company, Louise's pleasant—if somewhat dopey—smile disappeared.

"What are you doing back here?" she demanded, sitting up on her towel. "I thought I told you that you weren't welcome around here."

Savannah nodded. "Yes, that's what I thought you said, too. But fortunately I didn't take it to heart. I never worry that much about how welcome I am someplace."

Louise jumped to her feet, ripped off her sunglasses, and stood glaring at Savannah.

Savannah assumed this was meant to intimidate her into a speedy retreat. But Louise had no idea how many times Savannah had been glared at in the course of her professional ca-

reers as a cop and an investigator. And as long as the glarer wasn't holding a gun in their hand . . . she wasn't impressed.

"Listen, you," Louise said, taking a couple of steps toward her. "I've inherited all of this!" She waved her arm, indicating the house, property, and beach. "And you'd better not mess with me, or I'll have you arrested, or I'll sue you, or—"

"Don't you remember? You haven't officially inherited anything yet." Savannah weighed her next words carefully before speaking. She wanted to find out Louise's involvement in robbing from her mother, but she didn't want her to tip off Martin that Dirk was on to him. "And besides," she said, "when you do finally get your 'just dues' you may find out that it ain't nothin' much to crow about."

Louise's face went from enraged to confused the instant Savannah's words filtered into her brain. "What do you mean?"

She didn't know. Louise was as clueless as they came. Martin Streck might have been embezzling from her mother, but Louise wasn't part of the scheme.

Savannah felt slightly disappointed. It would have been fun to nail Miss Bikini Prissy Pot with something good.

"I said, 'What do you mean?'" Louise repeated. "You said my just dues wouldn't be much. What do you know about anything?"

"Who? Me? No, of course I wouldn't know anything about your personal business . . . your inheritance . . . anything like that. Don't worry about a thing, Ms. Maxwell. I'm sure everything's fine. I just like to run my mouth once in a while. It's a character flaw of mine that I'm working on."

She turned to walk away, to return to the house and say goodbye to Gilly. But before she did, she noticed with a deep sense of gratification that Louise Maxwell did indeed look upset. Quite upset.

Mission accomplished.

Savannah sat in her Mustang outside the brick office building on Sunset Boulevard and watched the front door. As always, the

famous boulevard was a bustle of activity, and since it was lunchtime, the traffic was bumper to bumper and the sidewalks were filled with pedestrians on their way to their favorite restaurants or bistros.

A thousand colorful signs screamed at passersby from every building front and rooftop, insisting that they drink a certain booze, smoke a particular cigarette, or visit a cabaret or comedy club. The visual clutter made Savannah grateful for San Carmelita's sign ordinances that wouldn't have tolerated such gaudiness.

But the building where Burton Maxwell had his offices, the corporate headquarters of all the Lady Eleanor enterprises, was relatively unremarkable. The only identifying marker was a small pink cameo-shaped sign with Eleanor's profile that adorned the front door of the three-story building.

It had taken Savannah half an hour to get a parking spot in view of the door. And now that it was one o'clock in the afternoon and she hadn't seen any sign of Burt Maxwell coming or going, she was beginning to doubt that this approach was going to work.

She called Dirk on her cell phone, leaned back in the bucket seat, and took a drink of the iced tea she had bought at a nearby McDonald's.

"Coulter here," he barked. He was in a bad mood . . . again.

"Reid here," she returned, just as tersely. "What's up?"

"I've been checking Streck out all morning. And I'm startin' to think he ain't our guy."

Ah, Savannah thought, the answer to Dirk's grouchiness. There was nothing quite like a dead end in an investigation to cause Dirk to plummet from his usual heights of mildly ill-tempered pissy to downright grump.

"Why not?" she asked, dreading any further conversation on the depressing topic.

"Because I've been going over these files here with the D.A. and some accountant dude she dragged in to look at 'em, too. They say that they can tell by looking at the way he was draining

off the money that he wasn't near done yet. They saw that if Eleanor hadn't died when she had, he could have milked her for a lot more and probably gotten away with it. Her getting killed when she did pretty much guaranteed that he'd be caught, because he hadn't gotten all his tracks covered yet."

"Are they going to charge him at least for the embezzling?"

"That's what they're talking about right now. I think we've got a pretty solid case against him for that, but you know how long it takes for these people to get the lead out and move."

"I hear ya, buddy." Savannah took a swig of her tea, her eyes on the still inactive front door of the building.

"Did you go talk to Louise?" he asked.

"Yep. She didn't know. Had no idea what I was talking about."

"You didn't actually mention Martin, did you?"

"No, of course not. Just hinted that she might not be rolling in as much dough as she thinks. By the way, she told her little girl that they're rich now. Nice, huh?"

She heard Dirk growl on the other end. "I think she's next on my list," he said. "You going to see Maxwell?"

"I'm sitting outside his office building even as we speak."

"You going in?"

"No, I figured I'd hang out awhile and see if he comes out for lunch. If he does, I'll follow him and approach him there. It's harder to throw somebody out of a public place than your own office."

"Yeah, and you like being in close proximity to food whenever possible."

"Hey, I think I hear Porky calling Petunia a pig here. What did you have for lunch?"

He laughed. "Nothin' yet, but I'm looking at a foot-long Italian sub and a pile of potato chips."

"Oink, oink."

Savannah glanced back at the building and saw the front door opening. "Hey, somebody's coming out."

Two young women in casual office attire strolled out, chatting

between themselves, and made their way down the street toward an outside Mexican restaurant with umbrella tables that advertised Dos Equis beer.

"False alarm," she said. But then the door opened again, and this time a tall blond man in a navy suit exited. "Bingo, it's him. Gotta go," she told Dirk.

"With any luck he'll go to a donut shop," Dirk replied, "and you can have your favorite lunch—custard-filled and chocolate-frosted."

"Cram it, Coulter. Your foot-long sub, that is."

She shoved the phone back into her purse and got out of the car. Following Burt from across the street, she had no problem blending into the crowd on the busy sidewalk. It looked like everybody and their dogs' uncles were going to lunch.

He passed a number of eating establishments before he finally ducked into a Starbucks.

"Nice choice," she mumbled as she started to walk across the street.

But the light was against her, and she had to wait for it to go through a lengthy cycle before she and the others waiting with her could cross. When it finally changed, they surged forward, en masse, and she lost sight of the coffee shop's door for a moment.

Emerging from the press of bodies, she glanced over at the store's entrance just in time to see a familiar face going in. She would have recognized that short-cropped bright red hair anywhere. Kaitlin Dover.

Bells chimed in her head and she felt her pulse quicken as she hurried to the glass windows at the front of the store. If Kaitlin's and Burt's meeting here was more than coincidental, she wanted to know. She also wanted to see how they greeted each other. Greetings said a lot.

She stopped at the edge of the window and, as discreetly as possible, peered inside. An old lady sitting at a table next to the glass gave her a questioning look, but Savannah ignored her.

She spotted Burt Maxwell right away, sitting at a bar against

the far wall, thankfully facing away from the front of the shop. And Kaitlin Dover had walked into the store, given a quick look around, and headed straight for him.

No chance meeting, Savannah thought, watching them closely.

Kaitlin walked up behind him and said something. Immediately he sprang up from his stool, turned around, and embraced her. He gave her a fairly fast peck on the lips, but his hands were too low on her hips for the hug to be one between casual friends.

"Hm-m-m . . ." Savannah murmured to herself.

For a moment she considered walking into the shop and confronting them. But then she decided against it. She had come to Sunset Boulevard to interview Burt Maxwell, hopefully to find a new piece to the puzzle. And this juicy revelation was better than anything she would have gotten from a chat, even if he had agreed to open up to her. Which wasn't likely.

Although, if she didn't go inside . . . she wouldn't be able to get one of those amazing caramel brownies.

Oh well, she thought, as she turned and walked back to her car. Sometimes in the line of duty you had to make sacrifices in order to call yourself a professional.

On her way home, she would pass by a dozen or so Starbucks. She'd stop at one of those and pick up some caramel brownies . . . and some chocolate-dipped biscotti, too.

Chapter 17

"You just got home! Are you going out again?" Cordele stood in front of the door, blocking the hallway and Savannah's way out of the house.

Savannah stood there, purse in one hand, car keys in the other. "Yes. I was going to run one more errand before we go out for dinner tonight. Is that all right with you?"

Cordele's face screwed into a petulant pout. "Not really. I was hoping you and I could talk awhile this afternoon."

Savannah wondered whether to ask or not, and decided there was no way around it. "Is something wrong?"

"Wrong? Wrong? Of course something's wrong. It's been wrong for years. We share a lot of past family history together that we need to deconstruct in order to work our way out of it. That's what I came to California for."

Savannah closed her eyes for a moment, then said, "I meant to say, is anything *new* wrong?"

"Well . . . not anything really new, but . . ."

"If it's waited this long, could it wait a little longer? I have something I really need to do."

"Business or personal?"

Either way, it's none of *your* personal business, she thought,

but she didn't say it. There was no point in making a bad situation miserable.

"Would you like to come with me?" she asked.

"Where are you going?"

"To juvenile hall."

"What for?"

"To talk to a social worker there. A friend of mine."

"About what?"

Savannah steeled herself and counted to five. "Cordele, darlin', would you like to come with me? Or do you want to stay here and read or whatever?"

Or would you prefer to swim to Hawaii? she added mentally. *I'd be happy to give you a ride to the pier and throw you off the end of it.*

"I finished the book this morning," she added in an accusing tone. "I didn't come all the way here just to sit around the house and be bored. I guess I'll come."

Savannah turned and walked to the door. "That's fine," she said with the enthusiasm of a bored convenience-store clerk. "Let's get going."

The offices of San Carmelita Youth Corrections were on the outskirts of town, where the warehouses and car repair shops gave way to orange groves and strawberry fields. Off the main highway, down a road lined with eucalyptus trees, sat a low, flat, and rambling building that looked like any other office complex until you noticed the heavy-gauge steel netting over the windows.

"Not a very cheerful place," Cordele remarked as they pulled into the parking lot and stopped in a space marked VISITORS.

"It's not supposed to be cheerful," Savannah told her. "The idea of winding up here really shouldn't be attractive. An overnight stay will hopefully dissuade any budding delinquent from burglarizing his neighbors' houses or selling drugs to her schoolmates."

"Troubled kids need help," Cordele said.

"That's very true," she agreed as they got out of the car and walked to the entrance. "But unfortunately, a certain percentage of them have to be locked up until some of that help 'takes,' to keep the rest of society safe. We don't lock up children for turning over outhouses around here. Some of these kids are hard-core gangbangers who've committed murder as an initiation ritual."

"They still need help."

"That's why there are people in the world like you . . . and the lady we're going to see now."

Once inside the building, Savannah and Cordele had to pass through a security checkpoint that hadn't been in place before 9-11. Even in the small, sleepy town of San Carmelita, the world had changed.

Down a hall and to the right, they found a door that bore the name ANGELA HERRIOT. Savannah knocked, and within seconds the door was opened by an elegant black woman of generous size.

Angela would have stood out in any crowd, not only because of her exceptional height and weight, but because of her brilliant personal adornment. An orange and yellow caftan swirled around her, reaching to the floor, and her jewelry was equally oversized: enormous copper earrings that dangled nearly to her shoulder, several strands of colorful beads around her neck, and rings on every finger, including her thumbs. It was safe to say that Angela Herriot was no shrinking violet. She was more like a glorious giant parrot tulip.

"Come in, Savannah, come in," she said, waving them inside the small office that was cluttered with books and stacks of papers everywhere. Having visited her office before, Savannah suspected that Angela's people skills were more acute than her organizational ones.

"This is my sister, Cordele," Savannah said. "She's visiting me from Georgia. She's studying to be a psychologist."

Angela laughed, and the deep sound of it filled the tiny room.

"I don't know whether to congratulate you or give you my condolences. It's the hardest work in the world, I believe, but I wouldn't do anything else."

Cordele blushed and nodded; she seemed a bit overwhelmed by this larger-than-life persona.

"Sit down, sit down," Angela said, pointing them toward a couple of metal folding chairs. "Sorry I don't have proper furniture, but, you know, budget cuts."

"Yes, Dirk has told me all about the belt-tightening."

"I wouldn't know about that," Angela said, pointing to her nonexistent waistline. "I gave up wearing belts in nineteen-eighty."

She pulled her own chair away from the desk and turned it to face theirs. "Sit, sit."

Savannah had noticed long ago that Angela tended to say things twice, as though to make sure no one would misunderstand what she was trying to communicate. She found the characteristic endearing, along with Angela's no-nonsense approach to almost everything.

"How can I help you, Savannah? You said you need a favor?"

"Maybe, maybe not. I'm worried about a little friend of mine, a six-year-old girl I recently met."

"Worried in what way?"

"I think she's—no, I *know* she's being neglected. I just don't know if it's a case for Child Protective Services."

Angela leaned back in her chair and toyed with one of her earrings. "What sort of neglect are we speaking of? Does she get enough to eat?"

"Probably more pizza than the FDA would recommend, but I don't think she goes hungry."

"Is she clean? Appropriately attired?"

"She could stand to have her face washed a bit more often and her hair combed. She has good clothes."

"Is she healthy?"

"Appears to be."

Angela shrugged. "Doesn't sound like a legal matter, Savannah. What are your concerns?"

"Her mother may have a substance-abuse problem, at least from time to time. I understand there's been several hospitalizations or stays at clinics."

"Does the child have proper care during those times?"

"I believe she stayed with one of her grandparents, although that may not be an option in the future."

"Then we'll have to wait until next time to deal with that."

Savannah had a sinking feeling. She had certainly experienced it before—this desire to help a child in what might be considered a borderline case. Abuse had to be fairly overt for a parent's custody to be challenged.

"She stays outside at all hours, even until midnight," Savannah offered.

"Doing what?"

"Roaming around the estate."

Angela's right eyebrow notched up a bit. "Estate? Is this a privileged family?"

"Yes, in terms of money. But her mother allows her to stay home from school anytime she likes. I suspect she's just too lazy to get her up and out the door. There's no father on the scene, and I don't think the poor kid has any quality time with her mom. The grandmother provided the closest thing the girl received to parental attention, but she recently died."

Awareness lit Angela's eyes. "Is this a case you're working on now, Savannah?"

Cordele had been sitting quietly, listening, but she chose that moment to enter the conversation. "Yes, the grandmother is Eleanor Maxwell, the woman on TV who—"

"Cordele," Savannah said softly, trying not to sound as irritated as she was, "I wasn't going to mention names just yet."

"That's okay." Angela chuckled. "I won't say anything to anyone. I loved that woman's television show! Although every time I tried her recipes they never turned out."

"I've heard that before," Savannah replied. "So, you don't think Child Services could do anything for this girl?"

Angela gave her a sympathetic smile. "You know this isn't a situation for CPS, Savannah. I'm sorry."

Savannah stood and reached to shake Angela's hand. "Thank you. I guess I wasted your time. I was just hoping."

Angela's hand closed around hers warmly. "It's never a waste of time to see you, Savannah. I'm glad you came by. And it was nice meeting you, too, Cordele. If you don't mind me asking, what sort of name is Cordele."

"Stupid," Cordele replied. "Our dad's name was Macon—you know, like the city in Georgia. So our mom decided to name all of us after Georgia towns, all nine of us—even our little brother, who's Macon, Jr."

"Oh," Angela said. "How creative of her."

"Yeah, Mom was really creative, when it came to popping out babies," Cordele said. "She wasn't much on taking care of them once they arrived. She left that up to our grandmother. We had a very troubled childhood."

Angela's sharp eyes searched Cordele's face. Then she said softly, "Isn't it wonderful that your grandmother could do that for you. Raise nine children, I mean. She must be a remarkable woman."

Cordele shrugged. "Yeah, I guess so."

"She *is,*" Savannah said. "Gran's amazing. A real blessing. Thanks again, Angela. If I can ever return the favor . . ."

"I'll give you a call. Nobody's bashful around here."

When Savannah and Cordele got back into Savannah's Mustang, Savannah turned to Cordele. "What did you think of Angela?"

"She's cool," she said with limited enthusiasm. "But I don't want to work in a lousy little office like that. I'm going to have a private practice in a nice modern building where there are doctors and lawyers and other successful professionals."

Savannah could have pointed out that the little rural town of

McGill, Georgia, didn't have any modern buildings, nice or otherwise, and that if the entire town came to Cordele for therapy once a week, she'd barely squeak out a living. She'd have to take half of her pay in the form of farm-fresh eggs and bushels of peaches and pecans. But she decided not to say anything. No point in ruffling feathers.

So she backed the car out of the spot and headed out of the parking lot. It was when they were pulling into traffic that Cordele said, "At least Mom gave you and Atlanta nice names. How'd you like to have to go through life with a dumb name like Cordele?"

Savannah sighed. "She could have named you Jesup, instead of your sister."

"Yes, but at least you can change Jesup into a nickname—Jessie. What can you do with Cordele? Cordie sounds stupid and so does Delie. Sounds like a place to buy lunchmeat. You know, I'll bet Mom did that on purpose, just to embarrass us, like in that song 'A Boy Named Sue.' Remember that?"

But Savannah didn't answer. She had stopped listening.

It was a matter of self-preservation.

Chapter 18

When Savannah answered the door, she expected to see Ryan or John standing there. But it was Dirk. She was only mildly disappointed.

"Boy, don't you look fancy-schmancy," he said as he brushed by her and walked into the house. "Going on a date?"

She could hear the jealousy under the surface—barely under—but she chose to ignore it. "Ryan and John are taking us to Chez Antoine for dinner."

"Us? I guess that means me, too." He brightened.

She tried to think of a way to break it to him that his name hadn't been on the engraved invitation. Not even close.

But before she opened her mouth, he frowned. "Wait a minute. Isn't that the French place where Ryan ordered those friggin' frog legs and tried to pass them off on me as buffalo wings?"

"Might be," she said demurely.

"Oh, well, forget about it. You couldn't get me anywhere near that place. Hell, I gag just thinkin' about it!"

He walked into the living room and plopped down on the sofa. He gave her another once-over as she sat on the other end. "You do look good, though. Is that a new dress?"

She had worn the sapphire blue silk wraparound several times

in his presence, but Dirk wasn't exactly a fashion hound. He could remember every detail of clothing on a suspect, but not a silk dress.

"I've had it awhile," she said, adjusting the pearl necklace that dipped enticingly into her cleavage.

He noticed that. Dirk might not give a dang about fashion, but he was all male.

"I just dropped by to see what you got outta Burt today." He glanced again at her neckline. "If you wore that dress, you could've probably got him to confess to anything."

She batted her eyelashes. "Why, thank you, kind sir. But I was wearing slacks and a sweater. And I didn't even talk to him."

"Oh, man . . . then the whole day's down the drain." He flung himself backward on the sofa, arms outspread, as though he'd been shot. Dirk could be a bit overly dramatic sometimes. "I hate this damned job. I'm gonna become a professional wrestler or somethin'."

"Well, before you go climbing into a pair of rhinestone-studded bloomers, let me tell you what I saw—or rather, *who* I saw with him. Right there in Starbucks, in front of God and everybody. Givin' him a little kiss. Lettin' him slide his hand down on her heinie."

He perked right up. "Really? Who?"

"Kaitlin Dover."

His enthusiasm quickly waned. Savannah understood; an avowed pessimist could celebrate only in spurts. "That doesn't mean they knocked off ol' Eleanor, or even that she's the one Eleanor was referring to in her diary. It just means they're foolin' around."

"It doesn't really even mean that. They could just be thinking about it."

"Naw, if he got a butt squeeze in a public place, they've done it."

"You know that for a fact?"

"Oh, sure. Every teenage boy knows you don't grope a girl's rear for the first time in a public place. If she's gonna slap you, it

should be in private—less embarrassing that way. I'm surprised you don't know that, Van."

"I was never a teenage boy. Thank God." She glanced up the staircase. "Listen, I don't want to cut you short, but I was helping Cordele get dressed up. She's a little nervous about going out to a fancy restaurant. There hasn't been a lot of five-star dining in her experience."

"Yeah, yeah . . . I know. Get lost." He hauled himself off the sofa. "I know when I'm not wanted."

"Oh, please." She groaned. "I get enough of that whiny crap without you chiming in."

After shoving him out the door, she hurried back up to her guest room, where she found Cordele standing in front of a full-length mirror, eyeing herself with skepticism.

"I look like a country hick," she said, frowning at her image.

She was wearing her usual uniform of a white cotton shirt, black skirt, and black penny loafers. In honor of the occasion, she had pinned a black onyx brooch under her chin. Her hair was slicked straight back.

She didn't look like a hick, but she certainly could have passed herself off as an undertaker.

"Come in my room, sweetie, and let's see what I can dig up for you."

"Are you kidding?" she said, following her down the hall. "I could never wear your clothes. They'd hang on me. I'm much smaller through the hips than—"

"Can it, Cordele, before I smack you upside the head."

Savannah walked into her bedroom and opened the closet door. She dug around in the back and came out with one of her "hooker stroll" outfits that she had used for vice undercover work.

Cordele's eyes bugged at the black leather miniskirt and the red sequined sweater with its ostrich-feather trim. "I'm not wearing that getup! What have you even got clothes like that for? Never mind, I don't even want to know, but I ain't wearing it."

"I wouldn't *let* you wear it, turkey butt. But it does have some accessories that we could use."

She peeled off a few items and laid them on the dresser. Then she turned to Cordele. "Come here, punkin', and let's spruce you up a bit."

"Oh, first I'm a turkey butt and now I'm punkin'," she grumbled as she walked over to Savannah and submitted herself.

"They're all terms of endearment. Be still."

Savannah removed the brooch, set it aside, and unfastened Cordele's top three buttons. She spread the collar apart and clasped an antique necklace of tarnished silver and pale blue stones around her neck. "I have earrings to match this over there in the jewelry box," she said. "They'll show up pretty with your short hair."

She took a belt made of black satin with plaited cording and tied it around Cordele's waist, which she had to admit was considerably smaller than hers.

"We still wear the same size shoe, don't we?" Savannah asked, turning to her closet.

"I guess so. What's the matter with my shoes?"

"Nothing's the matter with anything. But it's fun to dress up sometimes. Remember when we used to get into Gran's old trunks and play with her . . . never mind." She had learned the hard way not to stroll down memory's long and winding road with Miss Cordele.

"Slip off those loafers and try these on," she said, holding out a pair of high-heeled sandals with a sexy ankle strap.

"Oh, I couldn't." But Cordele's eyes were gleaming with anticipation.

"Sure you could. Slap some red polish on those toenails—there's a bottle in the bathroom medicine chest—and put those heels on. You'll be the original glamorpuss."

She giggled. "Do you really think I have time? Ryan and John could be here any minute."

"Eh, if they arrive, I'll keep 'em occupied downstairs. It'll be worth the wait."

* * *

Savannah could tell, just by looking at her sister across the table, that Cordele was having the time of her life. But she wasn't surprised. Ryan and John had a way of creating magic for anyone they entertained.

And they were an entertaining pair.

They had driven the ladies to Chez Antoine in their classic Bentley; Cordele had been ecstatic. They had given Savannah a perfect lavender rose, Cordele a white one. Again, she had been agog. Ryan had noticed the sexy sandals and red toenails—after Savannah had given him a discreet wink and nod toward Cordele's feet—and he had complimented her profusely. That was, undoubtedly, the point when Cordele had fallen hopelessly in love.

Upon arriving at the restaurant, Antoine himself, a slick little Frenchman in a tuxedo, had gushed over them, kissing their hands and commenting on the high-heeled sandals without any prompting from Savannah. His high level of enthusiasm about those shoes caused Savannah to conclude that he must have a foot fetish.

He ushered them to their favorite booth, which was wonderfully private, surrounded by palms and partitioned off with dividers made of sparkling beveled glass framed in brass.

Between their before-dinner cocktails and appetizers, John had regaled them with tales of his interactions with British nobility while still a "lad" in England. Ryan added his own bit of blarney, relating some of his adventures while guarding the bodies of the rich and famous in Hollywood.

But sooner or later, the conversation had to turn to "shop talk." And it was halfway through their chateaubriand that Ryan asked, "How's the case going?"

"Nowhere fast," Savannah replied. "We thought it might be that Streck guy, the accountant. But the D.A. brought in some hotshot CPA who looked over those files we had, and they say it wasn't to his advantage to murder her right now. That doesn't mean he's totally in the clear, but we're looking elsewhere."

From the corner of her eye, Savannah saw Cordele sigh and

start picking at her food. Apparently, this line of conversation wasn't as exciting as movie stars and the British royal family.

Too bad, she thought. She never missed an opportunity to bounce ideas off Ryan and John. Their combined experiences in the FBI had made them first-rate detectives in their own right. And there was no point in letting all that expertise go to waste.

"How about the former husband?" John suggested. "I do believe you mentioned that it was the lady herself who initiated the divorce proceedings. Perhaps he was bitter."

"We did just find out that he's carrying on with the woman who produced Eleanor's TV show."

"Hmmm." Ryan took a sip of his merlot. "What would they have to gain from Eleanor's death?"

"Nothing that's obvious at this point. Dirk's checking."

"How about the servants on the estate?" John asked. "You know, we always say it was the butler who did it."

"There's no butler. Just a maid and a chauffeur-sometimes-handyman. They seem like decent people. I doubt that Eleanor left them anything in her will or anything like that, so no motive there."

"I suppose that leaves the daughter," Ryan said. "Didn't you mention that she's an unpleasant person who had a rocky relationship with her mother?"

At Savannah's left, Cordele perked up. "Eleanor Maxwell's daughter didn't like her mom?" she asked.

"No," Savannah replied. "She was quite outspoken about what a crummy mother Eleanor had been and how messed up her life was because of her mom."

"Figures," Cordele said, stabbing at her meat with her knife. "A mom can really mess you up. A rotten one, that is."

There was a brief, heavy silence around the table. Ryan broke it. "Do you think it might have been the daughter? Was she that upset with her mother?"

"Maybe. She's hot-tempered and selfish. Doesn't appear to be overcome with grief at Eleanor's passing. She told her own daughter that now that Grandma's gone, they're rich."

"I would take a very close look at that young lady," John said. "She sounds like the most likely of your suspects at the moment."

"It isn't her," Cordele said softly but with quiet authority. "She didn't kill her mother."

They all three turned and stared at her, a bit surprised, but Cordele was looking down at her plate.

"Really?" John said. "Would you care to elaborate? We'd like to hear your opinion on the subject."

Cordele looked up. "You would?"

"Of course," Savannah said. Though she was doubtful.

"Okay." Cordele laid down her knife and fork and dabbed at her mouth with her napkin before answering. "If this woman goes around telling everybody how much she hates her mom . . . if she blames her for everything that's wrong in her life . . . if she feels like her mother neglected or abused her . . . then she would have still been hoping."

"Hoping for what?" Savannah said.

"That her mother would change. That she'd become a better person. That she'd realize how much she had hurt her kid and try to make it better somehow. And as long as her mom was alive . . . there was still a chance."

Savannah swallowed hard, nearly choking. She could hear the conviction in her sister's voice, the hurt, the longing. Cordele still hadn't given up on their mother.

Long ago, Savannah had resigned herself to the fact that Shirley Reid was very probably a lost cause. She was going to spend her days sleeping and her nights sitting on that bar stool under the autographed picture of Elvis, smoking and belting back the booze. She would sit there until she was carried out of the bar and taken to the local funeral home.

She was never going to walk up to one of her nine children and say, "I realize how selfishly I've spent my life and how much that has hurt you. Please forgive me." It simply wasn't going to happen.

Savannah had finally realized that she was never going to have

a "good" mom. She had Shirley. And Shirley was Shirley. End of story.

Apparently, Cordele hadn't realized that yet. She was still hoping. And as a result, she was still hurting.

Savannah glanced across the table at John, then to her right at Ryan. She saw the compassion in their eyes as they studied Cordele's face and mulled over her words. They knew, too.

"You may very well be right, my dear," John said as he reached over and covered Cordele's hand with his own.

"An excellent insight," Ryan agreed.

Savannah smiled at her sister. "Yes, thanks, Cordele . . . for your input. We'll have to think about that one."

Cordele looked up as a waiter passed by with the dessert tray, displaying a plethora of orgasmically rich treats. "Dessert?" she said, brightening. "Do you think they have some kind of cheesecake? I love cheesecake."

"I'm absolutely certain I saw a praline-caramel cheesecake on that tray," John said.

"Good. I'm going to have a piece." Cordele smiled at Savannah, looked around the posh restaurant and at her handsome hosts. "After all," she said, "this is definitely a special occasion!"

Savannah nodded. Looking at her sister, she understood a little bit better, she loved a little bit more. "Yes, it certainly is," she said.

Chapter 19

The next morning when Savannah visited Dirk at the station house, she wasn't so lucky as before. Rather than having the place to themselves, it was teeming with charcoal gray suits and monochromatic shirts and ties.

Her least favorite member of the brass, Police Chief Norman Hillquist, walked by her chair, which was next to Dirk's desk, and said, "Have you got business here, Reid? 'Cause if you don't, get moving."

"Yes sir, Chief Hillquist," she said, far too brightly. She gave him a dimpled grin, but her eyes were ice. "I'm reporting a crime to this here detective. He's taking my statement."

She turned to Dirk. "As I was saying, Detective Coulter, last night my home was invaded by some little green guys with antennae on their heads. I think they said they were from Neptune. They told me they were going to help me get revenge on anybody who'd ever screwed me over in the past. Then they beamed me up to their mother ship where their leader had his way with me. And what a way it was, I tell you! A whole new way, like I'll bet you never even thought of! I know I sure hadn't."

Hillquist glared at her another moment, then walked away, disappearing into his office with the other stuffed suits. Just before they closed the door behind them, she heard somebody

mention something about it being the fourth "budget meeting" of the month.

"Eh, may he fall down a flight o' stairs," she muttered before turning to Dirk, who was sitting there, grinning at her. "Where were we?"

"You were drinking my coffee, eating my donuts, and telling me that you're going to track down Kaitlin Dover today and have a girl-to-girl talk with her."

She reached over, nabbed his cup, and drank the last sip. "And you're running background checks on Louise, Marie, and Sydney."

"Right. And Kaitlin and the ex-hubby, too."

"What a busy boy you are. I'll call you later."

He didn't answer; he already had his nose buried in the computer screen and was cursing it again.

On her way out, Savannah passed by the chief's office and looked in the large window. The blinds were open, and she could see the ring of execs sitting around, discussing the dismal subject of San Carmelita's fiscal budget. She paused at the glass and waited for Hillquist to look up.

When she caught his eye, she stuck her forefingers up on either side of her head and wiggled them like antennae.

If looks could have killed, she'd have been gasping her last breath. Chief Hillquist was not amused.

"Ah, get over yourself," she mumbled, then walked away. "Some guys just got no sense of humor. Too much starch in the shorts, I suspect, givin' their wienies a rash."

Dirk had gone into the DMV records and retrieved Kaitlin Dover's address for Savannah. She decided to just drop by her house and take a chance that she might find her there. If not, she figured that a little look around the place wouldn't hurt. At least, not if she didn't get caught.

Kaitlin lived in the pleasant town of Arroyo Verde, which was about halfway between San Carmelita and Hollywood. Twenty minutes on the freeway, and she was there.

Although Arroyo Verde was inland and had no ocean front like San Carmelita, the area had an appeal all its own, surrounded by hills that looked as though they had been covered with a tawny suede. Somebody had gone crazy in the Parks Department and planted a zillion palm trees within the city limits. There seemed to be a playground or picnic area on every other block.

Kaitlin Dover's subdivision was a maze of streets lined by large Spanish-style homes with plenty of red-tiled roofs, gleaming white stucco, wrought iron, and bougainvillea climbing everywhere. Any one of the massive houses set alone on a hill would have been impressive. But crammed so closely together, each one looking almost identical to the rest, they seemed to lack character.

Savannah found the street named La Rosa and Kaitlin's house number. Like the others, it looked new and even though the lawn was fairly brown from the restrictions on watering, the yard was well-tended.

Apparently, producing gourmet TV shows paid some bucks—more than private detecting, for sure.

One door of the two-car garage was open, and inside Savannah could see a red Lexus SC430. She recognized it as the one that had been parked at the Maxwells' during the tapings.

Maybe she had lucked out and found the lady of the house at home.

She walked up the perfectly edged sidewalk to the front door and rang the bell. Moments later, Kaitlin Dover opened the door, and Savannah thought maybe she should buy some Lotto tickets on her way home. This seemed to be her day.

The producer was wearing jeans and a faded Hard Rock Café T-shirt. She wasn't wearing makeup, and her red hair was practically standing on end. Savannah guessed by her drowsy eyes that she had been napping.

"Hi," Savannah said, "remember me?"

Kaitlin's face fell the moment she recognized Savannah. "How could I forget?" she said. "You were part of the worst day of my life."

Savannah knew what she was referring to, but she couldn't resist needling her just a little. "And that would have been . . . ?"

Kaitlin's eyes widened. "When Eleanor died, of course."

"Oh, *that* day."

"Well . . . it . . . it was awful . . . seeing my friend die in front of me like that," she stammered. "I'm surprised you don't understand."

"Oh, I understand. It was pretty damned awful for me, having a client die in my arms."

Suddenly, Kaitlin seemed less traumatized and more suspicious. She glanced out at Savannah's car parked in front of her house and then looked Savannah up and down. "What do you want?" she said.

"To talk to you, if you don't mind. I'm investigating Eleanor's murder. You do know by now that it's been determined to be a homicide?"

"Ah, yes . . . I heard. It's just terrible. But what do you want with me?"

"Just to talk."

"About what?"

"Burton Maxwell."

Savannah had learned long ago that a sharp verbal jab to the diaphragm could have highly entertaining and informative results.

And Kaitlin Dover looked as if she had just taken a roundhouse kick to the solar plexus. "What? Why Burt? What are you insinuating?"

"Me? Insinuating? Nothing at all." Savannah gave her a smile—a grin, actually, similar to what a cat might wear just before attacking a chipmunk. "I was just wondering if maybe you could think of any reason why he might want his ex-wife dead?"

Kaitlin's mouth opened and closed several times, but nothing came out.

"Maybe if he had a girlfriend, or—"

The door slammed shut in her face.

Oh well, she thought. It certainly isn't the first time. Finding oneself suddenly staring at a closed door and having one's ears ringing from the concussion of the slam was a necessary evil in her business.

As she walked back to her car, Savannah wondered if, indeed, she should pick up those Lotto tickets. The visit, although short, had been quite effective. She enjoyed shaking suspects up a bit in a murder investigation. It made them nervous, and nervous people made mistakes.

Sometimes it worked.

She wondered if Kaitlin was dialing Burt Maxwell at that very moment. Gleefully, she imagined what the producer would tell her lover, and his reaction.

Yes, Savannah thought as she drove away. She had accomplished exactly what she'd wanted. She would buy those tickets after all.

For lunch, Savannah drove up to a Burger Haven window and ordered a chicken sandwich, fries, and an iced tea. Since she had a couple of phone calls to make, she stayed in her car in the parking lot to eat. If there was one thing she just couldn't abide, it was loudmouthed people who sat in restaurants and chattered on about nothing and everything on their cell phones. Her prejudice even extended to less peaceful, fast-food eateries, like Burger Haven. She figured that if she didn't want to be bored spitless by other people's inane conversations, the least she could do was not inflict her own on others.

"How's it going?" she asked with her first call, which was to Tammy. Predictably, she was at Savannah's house, manning the Moonlight Magnolia desk.

"Just one call from a guy who wants his wife tailed, thinks she's doing the deed with their kid's football coach."

"Did you tell him we don't do foolie-aroundie tailies?"

"Yep. He wanted to know what kind of private investigators we are, then."

"Ones with better things to do than hang around outside quickie motels and take nasty pictures. Anything else?"

"A few more calls from reporters wanting to know about Eleanor Maxwell. Rosemary Hulse from the local paper dropped by in person. I stopped Cordele from talking to her."

"Thank you. What's she doing?"

"Sitting on a chaise in the backyard, writing in her journal. She does that a lot. I think she keeps track of everything that happens—or doesn't happen—to her."

"I'm sure she does," Savannah mumbled. "It's part of keeping a running tab on who messed her up and who owes her what in life."

She rolled down the car window and tossed her leftover fries onto the asphalt, where they were quickly snatched up by a waiting flock of seagulls—or "shit hawks," as Dirk indelicately called them.

"What?" Tammy said. "I didn't hear you."

"It's just as well. Did you get anything more on Eleanor's sister, Elizabeth?"

"Still working on it. She's mostly been in the restaurant business and living in the same studio apartment for years. Not much of a personal life that I can uncover. Orders a lot of her clothes from catalogs."

"You can tell that just from the Internet?"

"Wanna know her size and color choices?"

Savannah shook her head. "Scary stuff."

"Oops, got another call. Probably a reporter. Hold on."

Savannah munched the remainder of her sandwich while Tammy talked on the other line and watched a haggard young mother herd five children of stairstep sizes across the parking lot to the door of the restaurant. Recalling the Reid horde, Savannah wondered, as she often had, how Granny Reid had survived—let alone thrived—while raising nine "younguns," as she fondly referred to them. The woman should have been nominated for sainthood. Cordele could complain all she wanted about her upbringing, but Savannah felt enormously blessed when she thought of hers.

But she didn't have long to reminisce. In only a few seconds, Tammy returned. "It was Dirko looking for you; says call him on his cell."

"Gotcha. Tell Cordele I'll see her for dinner. You can join us if you want."

A hesitation, then no answer.

Savannah laughed. "I was kidding. Go home as soon as you finish checking out Elizabeth. Just leave your notes on the desk. I'll call you if I have any questions."

"Thank you," Tammy gushed, as though she'd been spared from a lethal injection.

"No problem. I understand."

Savannah drained the rest of her tea while she called Dirk. "Where are you?" she asked unceremoniously. They had long ago abandoned the common courtesies of "hello" and "good-bye."

"On my way to the Maxwell place," was the curt reply.

"Want company?"

"Yeah."

"I'll be there in ten."

Traffic was light, and Savannah arrived at the Maxwell gates in only six minutes, beating Dirk. Once again she punched the security code on the pad and let herself inside, wondering how long she could get away with what was little better than breaking and entering. If Louise were to really make a stink about her trespassing, she could probably get her arrested, but what Louise didn't know . . . couldn't cause Savannah any problems.

The thought occurred to her that she should just wait for Dirk before doing any sort of exploring on her own. But then, waiting had never been one of her favorite pastimes. If nothing else, maybe she could find Gilly and keep her company for a few minutes. The child should be in school in the early afternoon on a weekday, but experience had taught Savannah that "shoulds" weren't always the case.

When Savannah parked her car in the front of the house and got out, she quickly forgot about the little girl. Loud, very adult voices were coming from the chauffeur's apartment over the garage. A man and a woman were having a heated argument about something. And although Savannah wasn't close enough to hear any details, she decided to remedy the situation right away.

Hurrying to the garage, she got as far as the bottom of the

stairs that led up to the apartment's door when the screen door banged open and a red-faced, furious Louise stomped out. "I'll call the cops if I have to," she was shouting over her shoulder. "You get your shit together and clear out of here by the time I get back from L.A., or I swear I'll throw it all in the Dumpster and change the locks on you!"

"This isn't right, Louise," a male voice shouted back. "You know it, too. You never think about anybody but yourself. You're just like your mother, you selfish bitch!"

Rather than loiter around, waiting for Louise to see her, Savannah ducked behind a tall wooden fence that enclosed several recycle garbage cans and a small Dumpster. No point in making her presence obvious at what was, obviously, an emotionally charged moment.

Let the two of them have their privacy; she was perfectly content to eavesdrop.

From between the fence slats, she watched as Louise marched past the cars parked along the driveway and up the road to her gatekeeper's cottage. She was so angry she didn't even seem to notice Savannah's bright red Mustang sitting among them.

As soon as Louise reached her place, Savannah heard a car engine roar to life, and a black Lexus shot out from behind the cottage and up the road, then through the front gates. Louise must be on her way to L.A., Savannah surmised.

She wasted no time leaving her hiding place among the refuse and making her way to the staircase. Above, she could hear the slamming and banging of somebody who was grandly ticked off.

She smiled, happy to be exactly where she was at the moment. There was nothing like getting somebody when they were riled. Irate people often said all sorts of interesting things that they wouldn't have divulged under more serene circumstances.

Of course, they also tended to throw things and occasionally strike out at or shoot others . . . so she assumed a cautious posture as she crept up the staircase to the door.

Through the screen she could see Sydney ripping pictures off the wall and tossing them onto the sofa. He was muttering to

himself, and although she listened closely, she couldn't distinguish any particular words. And his handsome face looked as stricken as he was angry.

"Sydney," she said, softly knocking on the door frame. "It's me, Savannah Reid. May I come in?"

He turned to the door and stared vacantly at her for several long seconds before recognition dawned in his eyes. At first, she thought he was going to burst into tears, but he seemed to gather himself and his volatile feelings together and walked over to the door. She stepped back as he pushed it open and allowed her inside.

Dressed in a grease-stained T-shirt and jeans that had seen better days, he looked the part of a handyman more than that of an elegant, tea-serving butler.

His dark hair with its silver sideburns was mussed and his eyes bloodshot. She thought she could smell booze on his breath.

He looked terribly unhappy.

"Are you all right?" she asked. "I saw Louise leaving and . . ."

"She fired me," he said. "I've worked for her family for eight years, and she comes in here and says, 'Get out. I don't want you around anymore.' She fired Marie, too."

Savannah thought of Marie and her cozy apartment that she had made into a comfortable home. She looked around Sydney Linton's place and, even though it wasn't as quaint as Marie's, it looked comfortable, as if he had been settled in for a long time.

One entire wall was covered with a giant state-of-the-art entertainment center with a big-screen television and high-tech stereo system. The other walls were adorned with posters of vintage automobiles.

In a place of prominence over the gray leather sofa hung a childish crayon drawing done on a piece of cardboard and framed with red construction paper. The picture was of three people: a man, a woman in a black and white uniform with a white cap, and a little girl. All three were holding hands, the girl in the middle. Behind them, suspended beneath a beaming sun and a slightly crooked rainbow, was a long black automobile that must have been the classic Jaguar in the garage.

Savannah thought of what Louise had said about throwing his belongings into the Dumpster, and she winced.

Everybody lost a job from time to time. But these people were losing more than a place of employment; they were being torn out of their homes, as well. It was a lot for anyone to handle on top of the previous week's stresses.

"I'm so sorry," Savannah said, "for you and for Marie, too. But, you know, you have certain rights as a tenant, and Louise can't demand that you vacate the premises in a matter of hours. As much as she likes to think she's in charge, she has to play by the rules, too."

He gave a wry chuckle. "Since when? When you've got the money—or your parents do—you've got the power. That's the way of the world."

"Not always. You and Marie should stand up for your rights. Don't take it lying down."

He shrugged and moved some of the pictures off the sofa. "I guess I'm folding, but I don't really want to be around here anymore. I've had enough. The only reason why I was staying was because of little Gilly. With Marie and me gone—and her grandmother, too—I hate to think what life's going to be like for her. That pup is cute, but it doesn't take the place of a human being who cares about you. And we all know that Louise doesn't give a damn about the kid."

Savannah opened her mouth to say something about the legal system stepping in on Gilly's behalf, but decided to keep it to herself. What could she tell him anyway? According to Angela, there wasn't much anyone could do at the moment.

"Maybe Gilly's situation will improve," she said. "Either way, you and Marie aren't responsible for her. I'm sure you've already given her all you can in the way of love and support." She nodded to the picture on the wall. "Looks like it made an impression on her. She'll keep that sense of having been loved, even after you're gone."

Sydney glanced at the picture, and Savannah was pretty sure she saw the glimmer of tears in his eyes.

"How's Marie taking it . . . being let go, that is?" she asked.

"Better than I am. At least she didn't get into a screaming match with Louise." Having moved most of the pictures from the sofa, he plopped down on it. Motioning to the other end, he added, "Have a seat if you want. I'm not in the mood to start packing yet."

"Listen, Detective Coulter is on his way here—I just spoke to him on the phone—and you can explain your situation to him. He can put the fear o' God into Louise, make her go through the proper procedures to evict you, buy you some time."

"I only need a couple of days to find another place and pack up."

"I understand."

Savannah heard a car in the driveway, and she was pretty sure she recognized the wheeze and sputter as the driver killed the engine. "Speak of the devil, and he'll appear," she said, going over to the screen door and looking out. "Yes, it's Coulter all right."

She opened the door and leaned out. "Dirk. Up here," she called.

Dirk quickly climbed the stairs and entered the apartment. He looked tired and aggravated, but Savannah didn't read much into that. Dirk was frequently both.

"What's up?" he asked, looking from her to Sydney.

"Louise is cleaning house, so to speak," she told him. "She just canned both Sydney here and Marie, the housekeeper."

"Why? She'll still need help with this place . . . assuming she inherits it," Dirk said. "I can't imagine her mowing the grass and washing the windows."

"That'll be the day, when that spoiled brat does any kind of real work," Sydney said. He was still sitting on the sofa, looking dejected, his head in his hands.

Dirk took a couple of steps toward him. "I was going to talk to Marie about this, but you might know as well as her."

"What's that?" Sydney looked up, mildly interested.

"I was wondering what pharmacy you guys used. Not Eleanor; I know she got her prescriptions from Sav-Mor on Nelson Highway. But how about everybody else around here?"

"You mean me . . . and Marie?" Sydney asked.

"And Louise."

Sydney shrugged. "I'm not sure about Marie. She's asked me to pick up aspirin for her at the grocery store a few times when she had a headache. I don't take any kind of prescription medications." He thought for a moment, then perked up. "I've seen a little white delivery car from The Rx Shop parked up at Louise's—for a long time, too. In fact, I was wondering if . . ."

His voice trailed away and he looked uncomfortable. Dirk and Savannah both leaned forward a bit.

"Yes?" Dirk asked.

"Well, I don't know for sure, so I hate to say anything."

"Say it," Savannah prodded. "Louise just canned you and threatened to dump your stuff in the trash. Now's not the time to be worrying about discretion."

"Okay," he said. "A few times last month I saw that car up there for a long time, like more than an hour each time—longer than you need to make a delivery. And then I saw this young, skinny kid come out of Louise's with a big, sappy grin on his face. I wondered at the time if maybe . . . you know . . ."

"Louise was gettin' a little extra-special attention with her deliveries?" Dirk supplied.

"Yeah. It wouldn't be the first time," Sydney admitted. "Louise gets around."

"So I gather." Savannah thought of the various affairs she had learned about in the past few days and decided that the inhabitants and visitors to the Maxwell estate weren't exactly hard up in the hanky-panky department.

"So, where is this Rx Shop?" Dirk asked.

"Oh, I don't know." Sydney gave a vague wave of his hand. "Down the road a ways, I think, in one of those strip malls north of here on the highway."

"Thanks," Dirk said. "I owe you one."

Savannah walked over and laced her arm through Dirk's. "And we know exactly how you can repay him," she said. "You see, somebody needs to have a little talk with Miss Louise about what she can and can't do with . . ."

Chapter 20

Rx Shop in the Sunset View Mall was a member of an endangered species: a privately owned pharmacy that still served ice cream cones, sundaes, and malted shakes at a marble-topped counter. The place reminded Savannah of the tiny drugstore in McGill, Georgia, where she had been treated to a one-scoop cone on Saturday afternoons while running errands for Gran. It had been a rare treat and one that she had savored deep in her soul.

Over the years Savannah had become quite the connoisseur of ice cream, having sampled all the Baskin Robbins flavors as well as the Ben & Jerry's assortment and Breyer's best. But no ice cream had ever tasted as good as that single scoop of strawberry served at a cold marble counter, in an air-conditioned store on a hot and humid Georgia afternoon.

It was a simpler, sweeter time, when five cents could buy complete happiness.

Like that store, this one had that distinctive drugstore smell, a mixture of ice cream and candies, perfumes and soaps, mothballs and an underlying, clinical scent of pharmaceuticals.

She followed Dirk to the back of the store where the wall bore one sign that said PRESCRIPTION DROP-OFF and another that said PRESCRIPTION PICK-UP. There was a grim determination in his

walk and a grouchier than usual frown on his face, so she decided to just coast along in his wake, to watch and listen.

Behind the counter stood a large, stout, elderly woman in a white smock who made Grouchy Dirk look like Mr. Smiley Face. A small plastic name tag on her lapel identified her simply as MILDRED. Her steel gray hair matched the color of her eyes, as she glared at Dirk over the wire-rimmed glasses that rested on her long, narrow nose.

"What?" she snapped.

Standing behind Dirk, Savannah wondered if she was this crabby with her paying customers, or if she could sense that Dirk wasn't there to fork over money. But Dirk wasn't the sort to be deterred by a chilly greeting. He flipped out his badge and shoved it so close to the end of her nose that she had to take a step backward just to see it. "SCPD," he barked back, just as curtly.

"I'm busy," she said, turning away from him and occupying herself with her pills and bottles on the other side of the counter.

"So am I," he said. "I'm investigating a murder. You wanna talk here or down at the station?"

Savannah grinned to herself. Dirk wasn't likely to haul any hardworking pharmacist off to the station house just to answer a few simple questions. Unless, of course, she really pissed him off.

The druggist didn't reply, but she laid down the bottle she was filling and gave him her undivided glare.

Dirk reached into his shirt pocket and pulled out a slip of paper. "I need to know if you have any"—he consulted his note—"phenylprophedrine in stock."

"No," she said. "That's been pulled off the shelves."

"And after you pulled whatever you had off the shelves," he said with exaggerated patience, "what did you do with it?"

"We usually send recalled drugs back to the manufacturer for a refund."

"And is that what you did with your phenylprophedrine?"

Savannah saw a flicker of doubt in those gray eyes before she said, "I believe so."

Dirk gave her a smile that looked more like a snarl. “Would you please check your records? I need to know for sure.”

“Why?”

“Because I’m a curious sort of guy. That’s what you—the hard-working taxpayer—pay me the big bucks for. Please check. I’ll wait.”

Meanwhile, a female customer had approached and was waiting and watching at the counter.

The druggist returned his acrid smile and said, “I’ll check for you . . . as soon as I’m finished with this lady.”

The instant she turned to wait on the woman, Mildred’s whole demeanor changed to one of complete courtesy and cheer. “Good afternoon, Mrs. Simington,” she gushed. “And how can I help you today?”

Dirk turned to Savannah. “You know, when punk gangster kids give me no respect, I take it in stride. But this gal is your average Jane Q. Public. What’s she got against me to give me a hard time like that?”

“I don’t know, darlin’,” Savannah replied, squeezing his arm at the elbow. “Cordele would probably say your pharmacist here has authority issues . . . or maybe she has a problem with tall, dark, handsome men. Maybe your mere presence stirs deeply buried desires that are simmering below the surface of her id or ego, or something, threatening to—”

“Oh, shut up,” he said, yanking his arm away. “I know when you’re messin’ with me.”

“Tall, dark, handsome—and sharp as a basketball! No wonder she’s intimidated!”

Mildred took her good, easy time while waiting on her customer, then sauntered over to a counter where a computer displayed a kaleidoscope screensaver pattern. She began to type, and a blue screen with a detailed list appeared. Eventually, she returned to the counter where Dirk and Savannah were waiting.

“We had thirty-six bottles in stock. We pulled them off the shelves,” she recited in a monotone completely void of enthusiasm.

"And did you send them back?" Dirk asked with an equally flat affect.

"Not yet."

His face lit up with a genuine smile, and Savannah could feel her own pulse quicken just a tad.

"Good. Let me see the boxes."

The steely eyes narrowed. "Do you have a search warrant?"

Dirk's eyes got just as icy. "Do I need a friggin' search warrant to count the friggin' bottles? That would mean I'd have to come back here again and have yet another one of these scintillating conversations with you. And as appealing as that may be, I—"

"All right, all right. Come on."

She directed them behind the closed counter and to a door in the back. With a key on the ring that she had in her pocket, she unlocked the door and directed them inside. "Don't touch anything," she said.

"Wouldn't dream of it," Dirk replied.

Savannah held up both hands. "Me either."

The druggist shuffled around some boxes, rearranged some, and finally thrust one of them at Dirk. "There you are," she said. "Thirty-six bottles of phenylprophedrine."

It didn't take Dirk long to count. He skimmed his fingers over the contents of the box, looked up and gave Savannah a broad grin. "Thirty-four," he said.

"Thirty-*four?*" Mildred snatched the box away from him and conducted her own tally. "You're right," she said, although her tone suggested that those words were foreign in her vocabulary. "Two of them are missing."

"Who else has access to this room?" he asked.

"Just myself and my assistant, Karen, have keys."

"Do you have a delivery boy?"

She nodded.

"A young kid, tall and skinny?"

"Well, yes. Tony's slender and tall. Why?"

"Does he ever come into this room?"

"I . . . well . . . I suppose he might from time to time . . . to get

something for me or for Karen if we ask him to." Mildred's icy crust was beginning to develop some cracks. Her voice quivered a bit as she said, "Did you say you're investigating a murder? Tony's a good kid. He'd never—"

"I didn't say he would," Dirk replied. "Where is Tony right now?"

"Out making a delivery."

"When will he be back?"

"Anytime now. Sometimes his old car breaks down and he's gone a long time, but I think it's been running better lately."

Dirk nodded. "Right. Well, before he gets back I need you to do something else for me. I need to know how many times Tony has made deliveries to a customer of yours, Louise Maxwell, and the dates of those deliveries."

"But . . . but . . ." Now Mildred's lower lip was trembling, and her hands shook as she replaced the box of phenylprophedrine on the shelf. "I don't want to get Tony in trouble. Like I said, he's a good boy, my cousin's oldest son."

"Don't worry about it, Mildred," Dirk said with only a touch of sympathy warming his words. "I've got a feeling that, with or without your help, Tony's already in trouble."

"Don't tell me you don't know Louise Maxwell, Tony, because I hate people who lie to me," Dirk told the teenager, "and you don't want me hating you right now. I'm the only friend you've got."

Tony Doyle was doing exactly what Dirk intended him to do in the "sweat box": sweat—profusely. Of course, with the temperature in the eight-by-ten-foot room being a balmy 85, Dirk, Tony, and Savannah were all three damp of brow and moist of armpit. Tony was sitting at a stainless-steel table, his hands clasped tightly in front of him.

Savannah had pulled a chair into the corner where she sat . . . and observed . . . and listened. Watching Dirk in action was always an entertaining pastime. With his flair for the dramatic, he

could have played Hamlet onstage. Only his aversion to tights and tunics had kept him from a promising acting career.

He paced, as much as the tiny room would allow, back and forth behind his interviewee, leaning over him, raising his voice until it bounced off the gray walls and rattled the kid's nerves.

"You delivered drugs to her house six times last month alone. And almost every time your 'car broke down' and you were gone for hours, right?"

Tony shrugged his shoulders, which were broad for his age. He had the build of a football player and was definitely what girls his age would have called "cute."

Savannah could imagine women her own age—and Louise's—thinking the same thing. With his curly dark hair, bright green eyes, and muscular body, she understood why Louise might have kept ordering from Rx Shop.

The question was, what else had she asked him to do?

Dirk was getting around to that.

"Did she give you an extra-special tip?" Dirk said, leaning over the boy's head and talking down at him. "Was that why you were so late getting back to the store . . . because you were busy collecting?"

"I don't know what you're talking about," Tony insisted. "I deliver a lot of stuff to a lot of people, and most of them give me a tip."

Dirk walked around the table so that he could face Tony and let the kid read his expression when he said, "You deliver a lot of phenylprophedrine? You have a lot of people who ask you to sneak that out of the back room for them . . . or is Louise the only one who offered you a little nookie in exchange for that?"

Bull's-eye. The boy's face turned a lovely shade of crimson. He stared down at his hands and clasped them even tighter.

"N-n-n-oo," he stammered.

"Oh, yeah. You did." Dirk leaned his hands on the table and stared at the boy, his face only a foot away from his. "She asked you to get her a couple of bottles of phenylprophedrine, and you

did, and you got lucky. We already know that. We know all about it. Why else do you think we dragged you in here?"

Tony's eyes darted to Dirk, to Savannah, and back. "I . . . I don't know why. I mean . . . even if I did . . . it was just two bottles of some discontinued stuff. Is the shop saying I stole from them? I can pay them back. They can take the money out of my paycheck."

"We're not worried about petty theft here," Dirk said. "Together the bottles were probably worth less than ten bucks. It's what they were used for."

Savannah watched, noting the confusion that flooded his face. Tony was a cutie, but he wasn't clever enough to be a good liar.

"What do you mean? It was cold medicine. She had a runny nose and a cough."

"Is that what she told you?" Dirk said.

"Yeah, she said that phenylprophedrine was the only thing that really dried up a cold for her, and she couldn't get it anymore because it had been pulled off the shelf."

"Do you know why it had been pulled?" Dirk asked.

Tony thought for a moment. "Yeah. It wasn't good for people with bad hearts, or something like that. But she said she was healthy, except for her stuffy nose and a cough."

"You told her it wasn't good for people with heart conditions, and she told you she was healthy?"

'Yeah . . . well . . . no. Her note said that she knew it had been pulled off the shelves because it wasn't good for some people, but she said it wouldn't hurt her, that she really needed some for her cold."

Savannah shot Dirk a quick look. "Her note?" she said. "She asked you for the phenylprophedrine in a note?"

"Yeah. She sent me notes sometimes, left them in my mail slot at work, 'cause I was always gone out on deliveries."

"What kind of notes?" Dirk asked. "Love notes, stuff like that?"

Tony blushed. "Yeah, she sent me a couple . . . you know . . . after . . ."

"After you and her got down and dirty?" Dirk added.

Nodding, he said, "Yeah. But it wasn't dirty or nothing. We were in love."

"Were?" Savannah asked. "You're not anymore?"

Tears flooded his eyes. "Well, I am, but I don't think she is. She hasn't called me, or ordered anything from the pharmacy, or left me any more notes."

"Let me guess," Dirk said dryly. "She fell out of love about the time you gave her the phenylprophedrine."

"I haven't heard anything from her since then." His confusion deepened. "Why . . . do you think that was all she was after? But it was just stupid cold medicine!"

"Are you telling me that you really don't know what she wanted that stuff for?" Dirk was leaning so close to Tony that their noses were nearly touching. "Don't lie to me, damn it. I can help you out here, boy, but if you lie to me, I'll fry your ass, I swear."

"Her note said it was for a cold. Really." Tony suddenly brightened. "Hey, I've still got it. I kept the letter. If you want to read it, you can."

Dirk smiled. Broadly. He gave Savannah a loaded look.

"Did Louise type her letters or handwrite them?" Dirk asked.

"She typed them . . . on her computer, I think. And she signed it, 'Love, Louise' with a little heart to dot the 'i.' "

"Oh, yes," Dirk said. "We definitely want to look at that letter right away."

Savannah didn't have to ask; she knew they were thinking the same thing. Wouldn't it be interesting if that note were written in a certain large Arial font?

Chapter 21

Savannah recognized the tan parchment stationery even before she got a look at the type of print on it. Tony was holding the paper out to Dirk with a trembling hand, and in his other hand he held a cigar box with several more letters on the same stationery. A treasure trove!

She could tell that Dirk was trying hard not to show his excitement as he took the page from Tony with a gloved hand and looked it over. He showed it to Savannah, and she, too, swallowed a smile.

I gotcha, you rat-bitch, Louise, she thought. Send nasty letters to your mommy, will you? Write a kid love letters and get him to help you kill her, huh?

But she said nothing . . . simply nodded.

Nothing felt better than when you got a break in a case, unless the bad guy, or gal, was also somebody you really, really disliked.

Tony seemed to sense their satisfaction, and he stopped trembling for the first time since Dirk had picked him up at the drugstore. After being questioned at the station, he had brought them to his house in downtown San Carmelita, where he lived with his mother, and invited them inside. He had practically run into his bedroom and then came out with the cigar box in hand, eager to help in any way.

Dirk never exactly bubbled over with gratitude, but he did lay a gloved hand on the kid's shoulder and say, "It's a good thing you came clean with this, Tony. This letter puts you pretty much in the clear and helps us with our case."

Tony flushed with joy that bordered on giddiness. Then a shadow of concern crossed his face. "You're not going to do anything to Louise, are you? It was just a couple of bottles of medicine, right?"

Dirk shot a guilt-laden look at Savannah, and she quickly stepped forward. "You can't worry about Louise, Tony," she said. "If she's got problems, she caused them herself."

"What do you mean?"

Savannah weighed her words, wanting to be honest with the young man, but not spill more than was necessary. She had learned long ago that in the course of an investigation, you had to dole out information strictly on a need-to-know basis.

"I mean," she said, "that Louise didn't treat you very well, Tony, and you don't owe her a thing. You just remember that, okay?"

He nodded, still looking confused. "Yeah, okay."

At that moment the front door of the house opened, and a woman who vaguely resembled Mildred the pharmacist walked inside. She didn't look at all pleased to see the gathering in her living room.

She would be even less pleased when she found out who they were and why they were talking to her son.

Dirk shoved a business card into Tony's hand and took the cigar box from under his arm. "Thanks a million, buddy," he said. "Give me a call if you have any questions. I'll be in touch."

As he and Savannah sailed past Mom, she said, "Who the hell are you?"

"Public servants, ma'am," Dirk replied. "Just servin' the public."

"Protect and serve," Savannah added as they darted out the door.

They reached the sidewalk and Dirk's Buick without further interference.

"Pretty good," he said as they climbed inside. "The kid didn't lawyer up, and he gave us our first big break."

"And his momma didn't take a bite outta your ass." She smiled and looked at the cigar box which he was slipping into a brown paper evidence bag. "All in all, not a bad afternoon's work."

When Dirk found out that he wasn't going to be able to get a search warrant for Louise's place until the next morning, Savannah decided to call it quits early and spend some quality time with her sister.

But upon arriving home, she found the reception decidedly chilly. Cordele was sitting in Savannah's favorite reading chair, writing in a rather somber-looking black journal of some sort and had little to say to her in the way of greeting. The cats sat on the ottoman in their usual places, one on either side of her feet.

At least they were happy to see her. They jumped off the footstool and ran to her, mewing, tails arched like big black question marks.

As they tangled themselves around her ankles, she bent and stroked their glossy coats, wondering as always at the quality of unconditional love offered by animals.

"Okay," she said as she led them into the kitchen, "your love is somewhat dependent upon a never-ending supply of food and a clean litter box, but . . ."

After scooping some smelly goop into each of two bowls and refreshing their water, she went to the refrigerator and looked inside. "Hey, you want a glass of lemonade?" she called to Cordele. "I just squeezed it this morning. It's the real thing."

"Does it have sugar in it?" came the first words heard from the living room.

"Ye-e-es."

Whoever heard of lemonade without sugar? she thought as she poured herself a tall glass. What a chucklehead.

"I can make you some iced tea," she offered, trying to sound more generous than she felt. "No sugar."

"With caffeine?"

She gritted her teeth. "I wasn't going to *add* any, but it's just regular ol' tea, so . . ."

"Then it has caffeine. No, thank you."

"At least she said 'Thank you,'" Savannah muttered. "Otherwise I might have had to beat her into a—"

"Are you talking to me?"

"No. Just mumbling to myself." She took her lemonade and walked into the living room, resisting the urge to run upstairs to her bedroom and nail the door shut. "Are you hungry for supper yet?"

"No. I've been working on my journal this afternoon, and, to be honest, I've sort of lost my appetite."

Savannah sank wearily onto the sofa and propped her feet on the coffee table. To heck with it. Who cared if one's tabletop got scratched? Who cared if one's younger sister sat on a fence post and spun clockwise . . . or counterclockwise, for that matter?

"Lost your appetite, huh?" she said. "Been reminiscing again about rotten cats caught in briar patches?"

Cordele shot her a hostile, hurt look over the top of the journal. "No-o-o. My entries are about painful, wounding events that are a little more recent."

"How recent?"

"Yesterday. Today."

"Damn, that's what I was afraid of," Savannah mumbled and buried her nose in her lemonade glass, taking a long, long drink.

As Cordele sat, radiating disapproval, wrapped in silence, Savannah knew that she was expected to inquire. She was supposed to ask about her transgressions du jour and then beg for forgiveness.

Funny, she just wasn't in the mood to play the game.

So, she sipped her lemonade and radiated her own brand of silence. Gee, she was happy she'd come home early! Who would have missed this?

"In case you're wondering . . ." Cordele began.

I wasn't. Really. I'm not that curious.

". . . I've recorded the amount of quality time you and I have shared since I arrived on Tuesday. It's now Friday. That's four days. And in those four days"—she opened her journal and scanned several pages before continuing—"we have spent a grand total of four hours and fifteen minutes of semi-intimate time together. I flew all the way to California for four hours and fifteen minutes with my oldest sister. Pretty pitiful, huh?"

Savannah set her lemonade on the coffee table. Screw the coaster. Who cared about circles when they were about to commit murder?

"How about the barbecue we had?" she asked. "That alone was four hours."

"We weren't alone. You had your friends over. It wasn't quality time."

"How about the beach?"

"That was included."

"And the mall?"

Cordele thumbed through a few pages of her journal. "It's in there. One hour and twelve minutes."

Savannah snapped. She turned on Cordele like a rabid squirrel. "Do you mean to tell me that you've been keeping track since you got here . . . right down to the minutes? Is that what you're telling me, Cordele Reid, that you've been counting the cotton-pickin' *minutes* that we've spent together and writing them down there in your little black book?"

Cordele hitched her chin upward. Her lower lip trembled. "Yes, I certainly have. Writing in my journal is a coping mechanism for me."

Savannah drew a deep breath. "Cordele, I want you to stop and think about this objectively for a moment. Doesn't that strike you as just a wee little bit anal-retentive and petty, not to mention downright stupid?"

Okay, she had meant to say that a tad more diplomatically, but . . . the words were already out . . . hanging like lead balloons in the air between them.

"Not at all," Cordele said, tears glistening in her eyes. "I

record things in my journal that are important to me. *Family* is important to me. *You*"—*gulp . . . sniff*—"are important to me."

"You're important to me, Cor—"

"Not that I can tell. You've been gone nearly the whole four days, and when you are here, you're distant, emotionally unavailable to me."

Savannah looked upward and silently prayed, Lord, help me understand my sister, like Gran said I should. Please, give me patience.

"Cordele, honey," she said slowly, deliberately, "would you please tell me what it is that you want from me? What is it that you need, darlin', that I'm not giving you?"

Cordele looked at her in wounded amazement. "What I *want* from you? What I *need?*"

Lord, could you give me that patience *right now?* 'Cause if you don't, I'm going to strangle her until her eyes pop out, and then I won't even need it.

"Yes . . . what do you want from me? Tell me, and I promise I'll do my best to—"

Cordele burst into tears. "Don't you realize that the very fact that you would have to ask me such a question shows how emotionally and spiritually distant we are?"

Savannah considered handing her the box of tissues that were on the end table, but that would involve getting within reach of her, and she didn't trust herself. So she just allowed her to go on sniffing, tissueless.

"It breaks my heart," Cordele continued, "to think how close we used to be. How we used to talk for hours about . . . things. . . ."

Savannah thought back, trying to pinpoint those happy days. "You mean, when you first started college, and we sat around trashing Mom and Dad all afternoon?"

"We weren't trashing anybody. We were exploring our feelings about our childhoods, evaluating our formative years and how those experiences affected us."

Savannah nodded. "Yes. I remember that after a lot of 'exploring,' we decided that Shirley and Macon were basically crappy

parents and that we were lucky that Gran took up the slack. It didn't take rocket science to figure that out."

"How can you be so flip about something so awful . . . just dismissing the horrors of our upbringing that way?"

"I'm not dismissing anything, Cordele. I know there were some bad times with Dad on the road, driving his rig, and Mom leaving us alone while she hung out at the bars. Her coming home drunk and getting sick on the living room floor. Us cleaning her up and putting her to bed. It wasn't fun. But most of that was before you were even born. Before Gran took us in."

Cordele tossed her journal onto the ottoman and crossed her arms over her chest. "So, what are you saying? That you had it worse than I did, because you're older?"

"This isn't some kind of sick contest, Cordele. For heaven's sake, who gives a rat's ass? So, you and I both had it rough. Big deal. There's always somebody out there who had it better than you and somebody who had it worse. What does that have to do with the present, and us sitting here in my living room in California, or whether we're going to eat pizza or broiled tofu for dinner?"

"That's so-o-o like you, Savannah . . . to live in denial."

Savannah felt it snap—her last string that connected her to sanity. She jumped up from the sofa and grabbed her lemonade. "That tears it, Cordele. If you want to call it denial, go right ahead. Label me or my attitudes any damned way you want. But I'm not going to rehash ancient history with you. I'm not going to sit around and feel sorry for myself. I already did that. But sooner or later, I decided that if I was going to get anything else accomplished in my life, I had to move on. And I'm not going back there for you or anybody. If you want to interpret that as a rejection of you as a human being . . . that's your choice."

She headed for the staircase, her own bedroom, some privacy and sanctity. But she hesitated on the bottom step and turned back to Cordele, who had stopped crying and was sitting there with her mouth hanging open, eyes lightly bugged.

"By the way. It's not *you* I'm rejecting. I love you to pieces. It's just the bitterness and the friggin' whining I can't stand."

Oh, yeah . . . that little addition helped a lot, she thought as she continued up the stairs. So glad I tagged that on the end there.

It was when she reached the top of the stairs that heard Cordele's final diagnosis floating up to her: "Denial. Denial is such a destructive force. No doubt it's the root of that food issue. . . ."

Savannah lay in her bed, reading Eleanor Maxwell's journal, as she had almost every night since her death. And while Savannah had spent most of the evening being peeved and out of sorts, thanks to her heart-to-heart with Cordele, she felt a little better having read the diary. It proved exactly what she had told Cordele in the heat of their argument: somebody, somewhere, always had it worse.

"Hindsight don't need spectacles," Gran had always said. And it seemed, as Savannah read the pages of the journal, that Eleanor should have seen it coming. Louise hated her mother with an intensity that could have motivated her to do anything, including commit murder.

This journal would prove to be a powerful piece of evidence in prosecuting her. Savannah could hardly wait to show Dirk the passage she was reading now. It had been written only three months ago.

Lou hit me with a wine bottle today. Cut my head open. Had to get five stitches. They didn't recognize me at the hospital. Wouldn't that be great if the news got hold of that? Kaitlin would throw a fit. The cops wanted me to file charges on her, but she's my kid. I know she thinks I'd do anything to her, but I wouldn't have her arrested. How's that for a mother's love? I can't be all bad, right?

Less than a week later was an even more disturbing entry:

I told Lou today that I should have pressed charges on her. She told me that if I ever did anything like that, she'd break the bottle

next time and cut my throat with it. She's always saying what a terrible mother I was, but what kind of daughter says something like that to her mom? Now that my daughter's all grown up, she hates me. My twin sister and I have always hated each other. I guess hate just runs in the family.

Savannah closed the diary, laid it on her nightstand, and turned out the lamp. She had enjoyed as much family politics—her own and Eleanor's—as she could stand for one day.

But as she drifted off to sleep, she thought of little Gilly, her small face lit with joy as she played with her new puppy. Savannah could also remember a moment there in the moonlit gazebo when the child had been speaking about her mother leaving her alone for long periods of time and about Grandma smelling like booze and talking bad. Savannah recalled the traces of bitterness and anger on that tiny face. The cycle was beginning all over again. Yes . . . it seemed that hate just ran in some families.

Savannah was awake another hour, thinking about it. But she wasn't wondering why.

Chapter 22

Savannah silently cursed Dirk, who sat across the table from her, an expectant grin on his face. He had a lot of nerve, showing up before she'd even downed her second cup of coffee and asking for a favor. A favor which he could have easily done himself—if it hadn't been for that stupid "male pride" thing.

Apparently, it wasn't easy for some men to ask another guy for help. And in Dirk's case, why should he? He had Savannah to do it for him.

As Dirk watched, tapping his fingers on the tabletop, and Cordele poked around in the refrigerator, looking for something "worth eating," as she had delicately phrased it, Savannah sat with her coffee cup in one hand and the phone in the other, waiting for Ryan to pick up on the other end. He did . . . on the third ring.

"It's Savannah," she said, instantly cheering at the sound of his deep, virile voice. A shot of Ryan in the morning was more stimulating than any caffeine.

"Dirk has a favor to ask you," she said, wrinkling her nose at Dirk.

"Oh, goody," Ryan replied. She could hear the semi-sarcastic tone. It was hard to miss. The fact had been established long ago that Dirk, Ryan, and John would probably have nothing to do

with each other were it not for the common denominator of their friendship to Savannah. "What can I do for Detective Coulter?" he said wryly.

"He wants you to put on your sexiest swim briefs—the briefer the better—and go hang out on the beach."

There was a long silence on the other end. Finally, Ryan said, "I'm afraid to ask why."

She grinned. "I understand. But if you'll slip those on and grab a beach towel and a book, we'd like to meet you at Topanga Park in an hour. Do you mind?"

Again, silence. Then, "For you, Savannah, anything."

"I love you."

"And obviously, I do you, too. See you in an hour."

As Savannah was pushing the TALK button to end the call, she glanced over at Cordele, who had suddenly emerged from the refrigerator. "Ryan Stone . . . in a skimpy swimsuit?" she said, tongue hanging slightly out. "Can I go along?"

Savannah shook her head. "No."

She stomped her foot. "Yes!"

"I said, 'No.' It's business, not pleasure."

"Since when is seeing Ryan Stone's bod in a swimsuit not a pleasure?" Cordele wanted to know.

Dirk had had enough. He pushed away from the table and stood. "You broads are disgusting, you know that? And you talk about us guys ogling chicks!"

"Oh, shut up, Dirk," Savannah replied, burying her face in her cup. "After all, Ryan in a swimsuit was your big idea."

Dirk grunted and left the room.

"See ya in an hour," Savannah called after him. She heard the front door slam.

"I wanna go!" Cordele whined. "I mean it, Savannah! I really, really wanna go! And you'd better let me."

Savannah took a deep breath and another drink of coffee. "No."

* * *

An hour later, Savannah, Dirk, and Ryan rendezvoused at the Topanga State Park, a beach reserve that was conveniently located only about a quarter of a mile from the Maxwell estate. Ryan was wearing a navy polo shirt and white walking shorts, but he quickly assured her that he had a pair of red Speedos underneath.

"I wasn't going to drive around town in them," he told Dirk, whose perpetual frown had deepened upon seeing his attire. "Not even for you." He turned back to Savannah. "What's this all about, anyway?"

She pulled a pair of binoculars off the Buick's dash and beckoned him. "Follow me."

They walked to a small cliff that had wooden steps leading to the beach. She pointed down the stretch of sand to a tiny cove and handed him the binoculars.

"Check out the blonde in the pink bikini lying there on the towel," she told him.

He looked through the glasses and focused. "Yeah. So?"

Dirk gave her a quick look and a smirk. Savannah's nostrils flared, so he swallowed whatever he was going to say.

"We need you to keep her busy for as long as you can," Savannah said.

"Yeah, at least half an hour," Dirk added. "I gotta search her place, and I don't want her comin' home till we're done."

"Do you have a warrant?" Ryan asked, still looking through the binoculars.

"Yeah, but I don't wanna give her a heads-up that we're lookin' at her just yet," Dirk replied. "Not till I see what I've got on her, if anything."

Ryan handed the glasses back to Savannah and started to peel off his polo shirt. A second later, the shorts came off, and Savannah could no longer speak.

Glancing at his watch, Ryan said, "Half an hour, starting now."

Dirk looked at his. "Yeah. Startin' now."

Ryan went back to his car, tossed the clothes inside, and re-

trieved a San Carmelita Yacht Club towel. Tossing it over his shoulder, he headed for the steps and the beach.

"You wanna stick your eyes back in your head?" Dirk finally said, shaking Savannah's arm.

She continued to stare at what had to be the most incredibly perfect male body on the planet. The broad shoulders, the toned muscles, the tiny waist and hips, the legs that—

"You comin' or not?" Dirk said as he left her and marched back to the car.

"Coming?" she whispered as she continued to stare, transfixed, at the retreating figure on the beach. "No . . . but I'm sure a-breathin' hard."

Louise's cottage was no neater or cleaner than Savannah remembered it. If anything, even more movie magazines, tabloid papers, empty fast-food containers, and soda cans lay about, littering every horizontal surface in sight. The place stank of garbage.

Savannah thought of little Gilly, and her heart ached that a child, presumably born to wealth, was being raised in such squalor. The only sign of joy in the small house was a smattering of plastic dog toys scattered around the floor.

But they saw no sign of the dog, Gilly, or Louise—who was at that moment, being entertained by the charming Ryan Stone.

Tammy had met Savannah and Dirk outside the mansion's gates, and they had entered the cottage together. For the first time since Eleanor's demise, Savannah had some real hope that she and her friends were within reach of a solution to her murder.

"Gloves," Dirk said as he slipped on a pair of his own and offered some to the ladies.

Savannah could recall a day—that didn't seem so long ago—when being a peace officer or a private investigator could be done with one's bare hands. But no more. If you weren't afraid of catching a deadly bug from somebody or safeguarding potential evidence, you were warding off the possibility of being accused

on the stand of having done a sloppy crime-scene inspection, thereby jeopardizing the prosecution's case.

Whatever the precautions, Savannah longed for the good ol' days when her sweaty palms hadn't been encased in latex and the only gloves she owned were the yellow ones under the bathroom sink, that she used to clean her toilet.

"There's the computer," Tammy piped up. "Want me to get started there?"

"That's what we brought you for," Dirk grumbled. "Certainly wasn't for your good looks."

"No, the only one along for his looks was Ryan," Savannah said as she followed Tammy over to a corner desk and an old, enormous and bulky desktop PC that sat on it. "Jeez, Tam . . . you should get a load of Ryan in a swimsuit. He"—she cut an eye over to Dirk and added—"never mind. I'll tell ya later."

Tammy sat down at the desk and switched on the computer. Savannah hovered over her shoulder as Dirk walked around, opening drawers, cupboards, and closets.

"Let's see what we've got here," Tammy said as she browsed the desktop screen of the computer. "Windows '98 . . . some computer games that are probably Gilly's . . . Internet access . . . a bunch of downloaded music."

"Did she write those damned letters on there or not?" Dirk snapped as he meandered over toward them, having momentarily satisfied his curiosity about the rest of the apartment.

"Just give me a minute, will you?" Tammy barked back. "Just how irritating can you be, Dirko? I—wait a minute. Here we are. I'm into her word-processing program."

Savannah leaned over her, staring at the screen. "What's the default font?" she asked, barely daring to breathe.

Tammy's face widened with a broad smile. "Arial . . . 14."

"Yes!" Savannah started pulling the desk drawers open. "Whatcha wanna bet I find that tan parchment stationery here, too?"

"What's a default font?" Dirk asked.

Savannah smiled to herself, knowing what it must have cost him to ask. Dirk didn't relish looking uninformed under any circumstances, but especially in front of Tammy, whom he regarded as a bothersome kid sister.

"The default font, Arial 14," Tammy explained without any note of haughtiness, "is just the style and size of print that she has the computer set to type."

"It's not like a typewriter?" Dirk asked. "It can type different ways?"

"Many, many ways and sizes," she told him. "It's all adjustable by the settings, and she's got hers set to the same as the threatening letters were."

"Can you tell if she typed those exact letters on this?" Dirk asked. "I know some guys at the lab can go into a computer and see what the user's been doing on it."

"That's what I'm checking right now." Tammy continued to click and move around the screen with a level of skill that easily impressed both Savannah and Dirk.

"There's hardly anything in her documents file, except some stuff that might have been school homework for Gilly. Nothing here that's like those letters," she said.

"Shoot," Savannah said as she opened the bottom drawer of the desk and looked inside. "I was hoping—well, you know what I was hoping."

"Yeah, we all were," Tammy replied, continuing to type and click away. "But I didn't really expect to find the letters among her documents. If she's smart, she would have deleted them."

"Deleted?" Dirk sounded crushed.

"Yeah, but . . ." Tammy suddenly brightened. "Now *that's* what I was hoping for!"

Savannah stopped her search and stood straight. Dirk leaned over until his head was obscuring both of their views of the monitor screen. "What?" he asked. "What? What?"

"She didn't empty her recycle bin."

"Empty the garbage?" Savannah asked. "What are you talking about?"

Tammy tapped a tiny symbol on the computer screen that looked like a miniature garbage can with white papers sticking out the top. "When you delete something in the computer, it goes into the 'trash.' But it's not really, truly gone until you also empty what they call the 'recycle bin.' "

"Can you see what she put in there?" Dirk asked.

"I sure can. Hold on. . . ."

Nobody breathed as Tammy clicked on the little garbage pail and a list of documents popped up. They had been labeled: "Mom 1, Mom 2, and Mom 3."

One by one, Tammy opened the letters on the screen, and they read the threats that they had practically memorized from the letters that Eleanor had given Savannah.

"We've got her!" Dirk said. "I'm going to cart this whole computer thing down to the lab, and have them print this stuff out. Wait'll the D.A. gets a load of this."

Savannah had resumed her search for the paper, and it was in the bottom of the lower drawer that she found it: a box of parchment stationery of assorted colors, including tan. She pulled out the box and handed it to Dirk with a smile. "And let your D.A. stick that in his pipe and smoke it, along with what they get from the computer there."

Tammy closed down the PC, then stood. "When are you going to arrest her?" she asked Dirk.

He grinned . . . and it occurred to Savannah that when he smiled, Dirk really was quite a good-looking guy. Not gorgeous, like Ryan. But he had a certain street-worn appeal.

Unfortunately, he only smiled like that when he was about to bust somebody.

"How's about right now?" he said. "You girls wanna come along for the fun?"

He didn't have to ask twice.

Chapter 23

When Savannah, Dirk, and Tammy found Louise on the beach, she was so totally enthralled with Ryan and her conversation with him that she didn't even notice the threesome approaching from behind.

Ryan glanced their way for only a second, but it was long enough for Savannah to give him a thumbs-up and for him to smile and nod imperceptibly.

As they made their way along the beach, Savannah could feel the loose sand slipping into her loafers, but she didn't mind at all. She wouldn't have minded if there had been sharks nipping at her ankles. Taking in Louise's hot-pink bikini trimmed in lime green and the provocative way she had posed herself, lying on one side, playing with her long blond hair as she chatted with Ryan, Savannah had to control herself not to cackle like the wicked witch in the story of Snow White.

The gal who considered herself the "fairest of them all" was about to get herself busted—and by Dirk, who absolutely loved to make an arrest when he felt one was warranted. Savannah could tell by the smirk on his face as he strode through the sand beside her that he was overjoyed with this turn of events.

And several steps behind them was an equally cheerful Tammy.

Dirk wasted no time. He walked up behind Louise, reached down, grabbed her arm, and in one smooth movement, hauled her to her feet.

"Hey! What the hell do you think you're doing?" she shrieked, wriggling around like a worm on a hot sidewalk. "Let go of me!"

But Dirk didn't let go. He had grabbed much bigger and meaner characters than Louise and hadn't let go. In seconds, he had her hands behind her and her wrists cuffed.

Ryan stood, brushed the sand off his legs, and picked up his towel. "I suppose my work is done here," he said.

"Your . . . your work?" Louise whirled on him—at least, as well as she could, considering the fact that Dirk was holding her in a death grip. "What do you mean, 'work'? Are you part of this . . . this . . . ?"

"Arrest," Dirk supplied. "It's called a felony arrest."

"But we were getting along really good and—" Louise shook her head, as though unable to absorb the realities unfolding around her.

"Actually," Ryan said, "we weren't really clicking as well as you thought. You see"—he looked her up and down—"you're just not my type."

She looked crushed. "You don't like blondes?"

"Oh, no. I love blondes . . . brunettes . . . redheads." He flashed her a breathtaking smile.

Dirk snorted and Tammy giggled.

"I just don't like *you.*"

"But . . . but . . ." Louise looked as if she were going to burst into tears any moment as Ryan tossed his towel over his shoulder and strolled away.

"See you guys later," he said. "We'll bring the champagne. About seven this evening?"

"You got it," Savannah told him.

"Champagne?" Louise tried to jerk her arm out of Dirk's grasp and yelped at the pain it cost her. "Somebody tell me what is going on around here."

"I'd be happy to," Dirk replied. "I am placing you under arrest for the murder of your mother, Eleanor Maxwell. You have the right to remain silent. If you give up that right, anything you say can and will be used against you in a court of law. . . ."

"Murder my mother?" Louise glanced over her shoulder and gave him a hate-filled look. "How could I kill her? I told you I haven't even had contact with her for ages."

"Yeah, and that was a lie," Savannah said. "Thanks to you, she was recently in the hospital, getting her head sewn up. I'd say that's some pretty close and personal contact."

Dirk continued to read Louise her rights as he turned her around and pushed her down the beach toward the path that led back to the house. The second he had finished, she asserted one of her basic rights.

"I want my lawyer," she said. "I'm not saying a word until I talk to Marty."

"You better pick another lawyer," Savannah told her. "Marty's got some serious problems of his own. He's in the pokey himself right now."

"For what?" she demanded.

"For stealing all of your mom's money," Dirk told her. "You know—the money you killed her for."

"He *stole* it? How? You mean, like embezzled it? *All* of it?" She was looking pale under her tan, and Savannah almost felt sorry for her. Within a space of three minutes she had been dumped by a gorgeous man she had just met, arrested for murder, and told she was flat broke.

But then . . . Savannah smiled to herself and flashed forward to an evening of sipping celebratory champagne . . . it couldn't have happened to a more deserving person than Louise Maxwell.

As soon as Dirk left with Louise in tow, Savannah paid a quick visit to Marie's cottage and asked her to take care of Gilly when she got home from school—maybe even for a few days, as Louise would be "away." Marie had happily agreed and hadn't asked the

usual, nosy questions that might have been expected under the circumstances.

Savannah decided that if she ever won the lottery and could afford a seaside mansion, she wanted a housekeeper just like Marie. Discreet and not overly curious. Two excellent qualities in domestic help.

Having the issue of Gilly resolved for the time being, Savannah left the Maxwell estate with a lighter heart than she'd had in many days.

She dropped Tammy off at her apartment complex and turned her Mustang toward the grocery store and her mind toward the night's culinary festivities. As usual when they wrapped up a case, the Moonlight Magnolia crew would get together, eat and drink too much, and slap each other on the back, verbally and literally.

It made life worth living.

Her menu was coming together in her head: a honey-baked ham, some of her own potato salad, sliced fresh tomatoes, and maybe she'd throw together some onion rolls. Pecan pie and ice cream for dessert.

And, of course, Ryan would bring a bottle of Dom Pérignon, that delightful champagne that positively exploded with a million tiny bubbles against your tongue and lifted your spirits to all new heights.

Yes, the evening would be a pleasant one, to be sure. Cordele's nose would probably be out of joint that they were entertaining Savannah's friends rather than spending "quality" time together, discussing the bad ol' days, but . . . what the heck?

This was such a perfect day—with Louise's arrest and all—that Savannah was determined that nothing would ruin it for her.

Nothing . . . except a phone call from Dirk, just as she was picking out tomatoes in the produce section.

"It ain't goin' so good over here," were his opening words.

Savannah dropped her choices into a plastic bag and tied the top, holding the cell phone between her chin and shoulder.

"Have you got Louise in the sweat box?" she asked.

"Yeah, but she ain't sweatin'."

"Turn up the heat."

"It's already up to ninety, and she's cool bordering on frosty. Says she was out of town the whole week around when the kid from the drugstore says she had him get that medicine for her."

She dropped the phone and had to fish it out of some nearby bell peppers. "Out of town? Doing what?"

"She says she was cleaning out in a drug rehab center in San Diego."

"Well, was she?"

"I don't know. I called down there and they're checking. Gonna get back to me. Can you do me a solid?"

Savannah looked at the contents of her grocery cart and could feel the evening and all its celebrations slipping away. "Sure," she said. "What is it?"

"I wanna stay here in case the clinic calls and keep leanin' on her. Can you go over to the drugstore and ask that kid again if he's got the date right? I already called, and he's there for the next forty-five minutes."

She sighed. "No problem," she said. "I'm on my way."

Savannah found Tony in the pharmacy's storage room breaking down empty cardboard boxes. He didn't seem surprised to see her. Apparently Mildred had told him about Dirk's call.

He also didn't appear particularly happy to see her, but then, that was to be expected. There was nothing quite like the grim possibility of another round in the sweat box to dampen one's spirits.

"Don't worry," she told him right away. "I just wanted to make sure of a couple of things that we talked about the other day."

"Yeah, okay."

He put away the utility knife he'd been using and sat down on a nearby box. "What's up?"

"The date that you gave us . . . the day that you actually took

those bottles out of the storage closet here and gave them to Louise, are you sure about that?"

He folded his hands and stared down at them. Savannah could see that he was, quite literally, white-knuckling it. "Yeah," he said. "I'm sure."

"May I ask how you can be so sure of the exact date?"

He nodded and looked terribly sad for one so young. "I remember because it was my birthday. And I was really looking forward to seeing her."

"Did she know it was your birthday?" Savannah asked, preparing to hate Louise all the more if she had implicated this kid in a murder plot on his birthday. But then, somebody who would poison her own mother wouldn't have qualms about something as mundane as using a teenage boy who was deeply, helplessly in lust with her.

"Yeah . . . I guess she did," he said. "I mean, I told her it was going to be when we talked the week before on the phone."

"Did she mention it when you saw her? Like wish you happy birthday, or—"

"Naw. I didn't even get to actually see her that day."

A bell went off in Savannah's brain—an unpleasant one that sounded a lot like a neighbor's car alarm going off in the middle of the night. "You didn't see Louise?" she said. "But you said you gave her the bottles of medicine."

"I left them there between the screen and the door, like the note said."

Savannah recalled, word for word, the contents of the letter that he had handed over to them. "But I read the note. It didn't say anything like that."

"Not *that* note," he said. "The note that was stuck to the door when I got there."

Savannah held up one hand. "Just a minute. Let me get this straight. She left you that letter in your cubbyhole at work—the one you gave to us—asking you to bring the stuff out to her. But then, when you took it to her cottage there on the estate, she

wasn't there, just a note on the door asking you to leave it behind the screen?"

He nodded. "Yeah. And that's why I was so bummed. Here I do this thing for her—stealing something from my work—and taking it out to her, and she wasn't even there to meet me. And her knowing it was my birthday and all."

"I can see why you were disappointed."

Tony wasn't the only one who was bummed, she thought. She wasn't exactly thrilled with this new turn of events herself. Dirk would be even less happy.

"Have you seen Louise or spoken to her since then?" she asked.

He shook his head. "Nope. I kept waiting for her to at least call and say 'Thanks for the stuff,' but when she didn't, I figured it was over."

He looked up at Savannah with eyes that registered his hurt, but also some wisdom born of painful experience.

"Yes," she said, "that was smart on your part, dropping her, that is. You're a good guy; you can do a lot better than her."

He shrugged. "I don't really want anything to do with any girls right now. No offense, but they're more trouble than they're worth."

Savannah laughed and patted him on the shoulder. "Can't argue with you there, Tony, my man. As a single person myself, I can say . . . it may not be as much fun but it's a whole heap simpler. You take it easy now, hear?"

"Yeah. Okay. Did that help you with your investigation?"

She tried to paste on a cheerful face. "Oh, yes. That was a major help. Thanks."

As she walked away, she muttered, "With help like that, I think I'll just go hang myself. And Dirk will probably wanna swing right alongside me."

Savannah sat at her kitchen table, staring dejectedly at the phone in front of her. Through the archway leading into the liv-

ing room, she could see Cordele in her usual spot, the wingback chair, reading, cats on either side of her feet. Or at least Cordele was pretending to read while Savannah made her unpleasant calls. She hadn't turned a page since Savannah had begun.

The first call had been to Ryan and John to tell them to keep the champagne on ice but tonight's cork-popping was on hold. They had been kind and sympathetic. As investigators themselves, they knew the pain of having a case unravel in your hands.

The next call would be less pleasant, she knew.

Dirk had a growl in his voice the instant he picked up at the station house. "Coulter."

"Reid," she responded, equally brusque. "Still frosty around there?"

"Got icicles hanging from my nose. She ain't budgin' from the 'I was in rehab' bit. What about the kid?"

"He never saw her. Said that when he dropped off the pills at her place, she didn't answer. There was a typed note on the door telling him to leave it inside the screen."

"Damn! Anybody could have written that."

"Yeah, on her computer even, if she wasn't home."

She heard the heavy sigh on the other end. "Just like anybody could have written those letters on her computer, too. And if they had a sample of her signature, they could have copied it at the bottom."

"Believe me, I've thought of all of that. I've also thought about the fact that nobody on that estate seemed to ever lock their doors. I guess they figured the security gate took care of everything. So anybody on the grounds could have come and gone from that cottage pretty easily when Gilly was at school and Louise was rehabbing."

"You're just full of sunshine and light," he said.

"Hey, that's the way the cornbread crumbles. Did you get any confirmation from that clinic in San Diego that she was there?"

"Yeah, she was there. Just like she said."

"Shit."

"My sentiments exactly. I'm gonna have to kick her loose, you know."

Savannah's stomach twisted at the thought of Louise Maxwell winning the round—maybe even the fight. "Yeah, I know," she said. "Suppose you could lose the paperwork for a little while?"

He chuckled. "It's already been misplaced for over an hour. Let's see . . . it's almost seven now. I figure it'll show up about eight or nine."

"You're a bad boy."

"You don't know the half of it, baby."

Savannah heard a beep on her "call waiting."

"I've got another call. Talk to you later. Chin up."

"Yeah, yeah, yeah . . ."

She pushed the FLASH button. "Hello?"

"Savannah," said a deep, rich, female voice, "this is Angela Herriot."

"Angela! How nice to hear from you. Are you at work this late?"

"Always. Listen, I had some paperwork come across my desk today, and I thought I should give you a call. . . ."

Savannah sat, listening, for the next few minutes. Part of her—the professional, the detective—was excited by what she was hearing. But the less cerebral, more human side of her grieved.

That was the problem with searching for the truth. Sometimes, often, in fact, when you uncovered a buried secret, you wished you had just left it lying in its shallow grave.

Yes, she thought, it probably would have been better for everybody.

Chapter 24

By the time Savannah reached the Maxwell estate, it was nearly eight o'clock in the evening. After finding no one at home in either the mansion, the gatekeeper's cottage, or the chauffeur's apartment, she approached the gardener's cottage where Marie lived . . . at least until Louise could legally evict her.

The door to the little house stood open a foot or so, and Savannah could hear Marie's gentle voice coming from inside. She walked quietly to the door and peeked in. Marie was sitting in her rocking chair with Gilly in her lap. Marie was reading her a Dr. Seuss book. The child was munching on one of Marie's amazing oatmeal cookies and thoroughly enjoying the story and the attention.

Savannah hated to interrupt.

She felt that she had already interrupted this child's life far too much, but . . .

Knocking on the door, she said, "Excuse me, ladies, but could I have a word with you, Marie?"

Marie glanced up, startled. But Gilly gave Savannah a bright smile.

"Hi, Savannah," she said, waving with her cookie.

"Hi yourself, dumplin'."

Gilly laughed. "Do you know that you talk funny? You call people silly names."

"Only people I like." She stepped through the door and into the cozy living room. "I was just wondering," she said to Marie, "if you happen to know where Sydney is? I knocked at his apartment door, but he didn't answer and I didn't see the Jag in the garage."

Something crossed Marie's eyes, a certain knowing sadness that Savannah herself could feel deep inside.

"Every evening after dinner he goes to the Lucky Shamrock for happy hour. It's a little Irish pub on the beach north of here."

"I know the place. He goes there every night?"

"He has one beer and hangs out with some guys there for a while. He usually comes home right about this time. If you like, I'll make you a cup of mint tea and you can wait for him here."

"Yes!" Gilly said. "Stay here with us and listen to the story. It's about the cat in the hat."

"I'd like to, Gilly." She turned for the door. "But it'll have to wait until another time. You ladies enjoy your book and your cookies. Thanks, Marie."

Marie just nodded, the sadness lingering in her eyes.

It occurred to Savannah that an observant and discreet housekeeper knew a lot, yet had no one to share that knowledge with. What a lonely occupation, she thought as she left the cottage. What a burdensome, lonely job.

The Lucky Shamrock didn't look much like a place that had been smiled upon by Lady Luck. Sitting directly on the beach, it had no protection from the salt air and ocean winds that had taken their toll on the once-white clapboard structure.

The pub's single ornamentation was a neon green shamrock that glowed in the window next to a sign advertising Guinness. The Maxwells' classic Jaguar was parked right by the front door.

Savannah parked near the back of the lot, got out of her car, and started to walk to the door. She wasn't exactly sure what she

was going to say to Sydney Linton, or how she would say it. But she figured the words would come, as they usually did, when she needed them.

Before she reached the pub's entrance, the door opened and Sydney walked out with a friend. She stopped where she was, standing in the shadows at the edge of the parking lot, and watched.

The two men chatted for a moment, then the stranger walked to a nearby pickup and drove away.

Savannah was about to continue across the lot and call out his name when she realized he wasn't returning right away to the Jag. Instead, he stopped and looked around him in a manner that she could only classify as "suspicious."

Stepping deeper into the shadows, she watched and waited to see what he would do next.

After seeing no one, he walked quickly to the opposite side of the lot and toward the back of the building, where a large Dumpster sat against a crooked wooden fence. Again, he glanced around. Savannah held her breath, hoping he wouldn't see or sense her watching him there in the darkness.

As though gathering his resolve, he sprinted over to the Dumpster and lifted the lid. He looked inside for only a split second, then closed it and strode back to the Jaguar.

Savannah swallowed the words she had been preparing for him. She wouldn't need them. In the past minute she had seen more than he would have ever told her, no matter what she had said to him.

She waited for him to pull out of the parking lot and disappear down the highway before she left her hiding place and walked over to the Dumpster. Opening the lid, she could see that it was brimming with typical "bar" garbage.

Mulling over the implications, she left the container and walked across the lot and into the bar. The smell of booze and stale smoke hit her as she walked through the door—along with a belt of loud country music from the jukebox.

Several interested male eyes followed her as she made her way to the bar, where a round, red-faced bartender was drawing draughts into mugs.

"Whatcha drinking, ma'am?" he asked.

"Nothing, thanks," she replied, leaning over the bar, practically shouting to be heard above the music. "I was just wondering—when is your garbage collected?"

"What?" He looked at her as if she were impaired. "First thing in the morning. Why?"

"What day?" she asked.

"Thursday. Tomorrow. Why?"

"So, that Dumpster out there in your parking lot hasn't been dumped since last Thursday morning?"

"Yeah. That's right. They'll pick it up about six tomorrow morning. Why?"

She shrugged and gave him a dimpled smile. "Aw, nothing. I just keep track of stuff like that."

"O-o-okay. Whatever you say."

She walked out of the bar and back to her car. Getting into the Mustang, she took her phone out of her purse and called Dirk.

"You gotta meet me at the Lucky Shamrock tomorrow morning before six," she said, suddenly feeling tired, and old, and used up. This job would put her in her grave. She should have followed her childhood dream and become a go-go dancer. "And bring some rubber gloves, boots, and overalls. You're gonna need 'em."

Dawn's early light found Savannah, Dirk, and Tammy hip deep in garbage. Standing in the back of one of San Carmelita's finest refuse-collection trucks, they were sifting through the Lucky Shamrock's disposables. The truck's three crewmen milled around in the pub's parking lot, sending poisoned glances their way, unhappy to have their daily routine interrupted by a curt detective with a badge and a couple of women in shapeless overalls and yellow slicker boots.

"Could be worse," Savannah said as she shoved aside some

lemon peels, shriveled lime slices, and soggy napkins. "Could be hospital garbage. Remember when we had to look for hypodermic needles in Community General's trash?"

"Now *that* was scary," Tammy agreed with a shudder.

"Would you two broads can it?" Dirk growled as he dug in with his yellow rubber gloves. "The last thing I need is a couple of Pollyannas telling me that rummaging through a heap of stinkin' garbage before I've even had my morning coffee is a good thing."

"In your ear sideways, Coulter," Savannah replied, tossing a wad of wet paper towels in the vicinity of his head. "At least I was smart enough to wait until the truck got here and dumped the load upside down. You were ready to go combing through the whole mess."

"Yeah, and you're just so sure it was on the bottom of the Dumpster. What if it wasn't?"

"Then I'm wrong. But I'll bet it is. I told you: The last time this trash was picked up was last Thursday, a week ago today. Eleanor died a week ago Wednesday. I'm telling you, Sydney dropped the empty bottles—and probably the empty capsules, too—in here on Thursday night, when he came by for his nightly beer."

Dirk grumbled under his breath.

"What did you say?" Savannah asked, straightening up and stretching the kinks out of her back for a moment.

"I said—we're going through all of this crap just because you saw a guy walk over to the Dumpster and look inside. Big deal."

"Not only that. There's also the phone call from Angela. She—"

"Hey! I think I've got something here!" Tammy shouted. She lifted up a white plastic bag that had a familiar logo printed on the side.

"Rx Shop!" Savannah tromped through the refuse to Tammy's side and took the sack from her. Eagerly she opened it and found two brown plastic bottles inside. They were empty.

Even Dirk's scowl melted into a grin as he glanced into the bag and read the labels on the bottles: phenylprophedrine.

"All right!" he said. "Let's get these suckers over to the lab pronto."

Savannah glanced at her watch. "There won't be anybody there yet. Not for a couple of hours."

"So we'll be there when they open," Dirk said, holding up the garbage-smeared bag with two fingers and looking at it like it contained a winning lottery ticket.

"*You'll* be there when they open," Savannah said. "I'm going home to take a bath and drink a pot of coffee. And you're going to call me as soon as you know whether they lifted any prints. The very instant—you hear me, boy?"

Dirk gave her an almost sad, sympathetic look. "I thought you didn't want it to be him."

"I don't," she said. "But at this point . . . I just want it to be over."

Savannah lay soaking in her clawfoot bathtub, her favorite mountains of jasmine-scented bubbles up to her chin, the blinds pulled against the midday sun, and candles lit.

But it wasn't working.

The smell of garbage was long gone, but her nerves were still twisted into knots. She kept glancing over at her cell phone on top of the hamper, willing it to ring—and somehow hoping it wouldn't.

Until she heard the words . . . she wouldn't know for sure.

The phone rang, and she jumped, her heart suddenly pounding so hard she could hear her pulse thudding in her ears.

She grabbed it and punched the TALK button. "Yeah," she said.

"Three clear prints," Dirk said on the other end. "Two on one of the bottles. One on the sack."

"His?"

"Yeah. One of them on the bottle is a match to his DMV thumbprint."

She swallowed hard. "Let me go out there first and talk to him."

"Alone?"

"Yeah. He's not going to hurt me, Dirk. He only had the one murder in him, believe me."

The long silence on the other end told her that Dirk wasn't convinced. But finally, he said, "Will you wear a wire?"

She didn't need anybody to tell her that a wire was a good idea and not just for her own security. There was nothing like a taped confession to assure a conviction—if you could get one.

"Yeah," she said. "I'll go in wired. But I'm going to try to talk him into coming in on his own. And you've gotta let me. Hear?"

"I hear ya, Van. He won't even know we're there if that's the way you want it."

She thought of Sydney with a white towel over his arm, serving tea to a little girl decked out in a fancy bonnet and feather boa. She thought of the crayon drawing proudly displayed on Sydney's living-room wall over his sofa. "Yes," she said. "That's absolutely the way I want it."

With a microphone taped to her chest and her Beretta in its holster beneath her blazer, Savannah got out of her Mustang and walked across the parking area to the Maxwells' garage.

"The Jag's here," she said softly to the microphone in the vicinity of her left breast. "I'm going up to the apartment."

But having climbed the steps and knocked several times on the door, she neither saw nor heard anyone.

"Gonna walk around the grounds," she told Dirk, Tammy, Ryan, and John, who were waiting just outside the gates on the highway. They were inside John's van, which was packed with the latest high-tech surveillance equipment.

Dirk could have used departmental issue microphones and receivers, but heck . . . John's toys were more advanced and therefore more fun to play with.

Not in a million years would Dirk have admitted that he felt better having the two of them along with him and Tammy, serving backup for Savannah.

"I think I hear somebody around the side of the house," she

said as she walked between the mansion and garage, passing an herb garden and a fountain birdbath.

"Okay," she whispered, "I see him. He's with Gilly. Looks like they're . . . building something."

As Savannah neared the spot under a tree where they were, she could see that Sydney was on his knees, painting a small house bright pink. Gilly stood nearby and looked as if she were giving him directions as he brushed on the paint. Mona Lisa scampered at her feet.

Savannah's heartstrings gave a painful twang.

He was building the girl a doghouse for her new pup—a house that matched the mansion, right down to the steep-pitched roof and white gingerbread trim.

Not for the first time, Savannah marveled at the complexity of the human spirit—how a person could be such a bewildering mixture of good and evil.

As she approached, they both saw her and called out greetings. The puppy came romping across the grass to attack her shoe. She reached down and scooped her up. The dog rewarded her with a wet lick on her cheek.

"Look! Look!" Gilly shouted, pointing to the doghouse. "Sydney's made Mona a cool place to sleep. It looks like my grandma's house and mine too. See?"

"I sure do," Savannah said. She turned to Sydney, who was still kneeling on the grass, paintbrush in hand. "That's the most beautiful doghouse I've ever seen in my life. You did a good job, Syd."

He gave her a pleased smile and a nod. But then he took a second look. Something in her face must have clued him that all wasn't well. He placed the brush in the paint can, stood, and wiped his hands on a rag that hung from his belt.

"What's up, Savannah?" he said, trying to sound casual, but she could hear the tension in his voice.

Gilly heard it, too. She looked from Savannah, to him, and back to Savannah. "Yeah, what's up?" she asked.

Savannah handed her the puppy. "Is your mom at home, sweet stuff?"

"Yeah, but she doesn't want me to bother her. She's been all nervous since she got back from wherever she was, and she took a bunch of her nervous pills. She told me to get lost and not be a nuisance."

"Oh, okay. How about Marie?" Savannah asked.

"She's home. I saw her a while ago."

"Then would you do something for me? Would you go knock on her door and tell her I'm here talking to Sydney. Ask her if she would please watch you for a little while. Okay?"

The girl's bottom lip trembled, and she looked down at the pink and white confection of a doghouse. "Why can't I stay here with you guys? I want to watch Sydney paint Mona's house."

"Sydney and I have to talk about some grown-up stuff," Savannah told her. "I'm sorry, but you really need to go stay with Marie for a while."

Gilly huffed and puffed a couple of times, but she finally walked away, holding the puppy close to the front of her T-shirt. "All right, Mona," she muttered as she left, "we know when we're not wanted. They've got 'grown-up stuff' to do."

After the child had gone, Savannah and Sydney were silent, a thick tension in the air between them. Finally, he said, "So . . . what is it? What do you want with me?"

Savannah locked eyes with him and took a step closer. "I know you did it, Sydney. And I'm pretty sure I know why. I think if you turn yourself in, you might be able to cut some kind of deal."

"What are you talking about?" He kept wiping his hands on the cloth and staring at them as though they belonged to someone else.

"Don't, Sydney. We don't have time to play games. I know you killed Eleanor. You're the one who put the phenylprophedrine in the cocoa, knowing that she was going use it in her cake that night. I know you put the empty bottles and capsules back into

the plastic bag from the pharmacy and threw it into the Dumpster by the Lucky Shamrock, where you have your beer every night."

He shook his head. "No. It wasn't me. It was the person who sent those threatening letters. It was Louise. You know that. That's why the cops arrested her."

"And they also released her, as you know."

"Yeah. I was wondering why they let her go."

"Because they found out that she wasn't even in town when that kid from the pharmacy dropped off the phenylprophedrine. That means somebody else sent him the love letter, asking him to get the stuff for her, and they signed the note with her name—a pretty good copy of her signature."

"But the threatening letters . . . ?"

"Same thing. You got into her cottage and typed them up. You figured if you used Louise's computer and her stationery, we'd figure it was her."

"Why would I do that?"

"To kill two birds with one stone . . . so to speak. If you murdered Eleanor and framed Louise, they would both be out of the picture and then maybe you could get custody of your daughter."

He sighed deeply, and his shoulders sagged as though he were deflating. "How do you know she's mine?"

"I have a good friend who's in Child Protective Services. She saw your paperwork, your petition for custody, based on the fact that you're Gilly's biological father and that Louise is an unfit parent."

"Louise *is* unfit."

"I know. So, why didn't you make a legal play for the girl a long time ago? Why kill Eleanor and set up Louise?"

He looked at her with haunted eyes. "Don't you think I tried that? I did! Years ago, when Gilly was still a baby. But Eleanor had the money and the power. I had nothing but this measly job, which she threatened to take away from me if I pursued the case. I even offered to marry Louise, begged her to let me be a proper father to my little girl. But other than that brief affair we had

when I first started working here, she didn't want any part of me. I was just the chauffeur."

"So, you kept working here, taking Eleanor's abuse for all these years, to be close to Gilly?"

"Sure. I certainly didn't do it for the money. But as long as I was working here, I could see her every day, take care of her sometimes, be a positive influence on her."

Savannah flashed back for a moment on the scene at the studio, when she had held Eleanor Maxwell in her arms and felt the life drain out of her.

"I feel for you, Sydney," she said, "but it wasn't a very positive influence you exerted on your daughter's life, killing her grandmother. Eleanor wasn't a very lovable person, but she didn't deserve to have her life taken away from her like that."

"Yes, I realize that. These past few days I've been thinking it over and . . . I know what I did was wrong. All I can say is, it seemed right at the time. I believe it was the only thing I could do for myself—and for Gilly."

Savannah gave him a sad smile. "You know, down where I come from, the argument 'He needed killin' can be considered a viable defense. But here in California, like most of the rest of the country, that doesn't fly. They seem to think you should leave the killing up to the justice system."

"And what do *you* think?"

"I think they've got a good point. Leaving it to the authorities is the best way to go almost every time. Sydney, a lot of us have good reasons to want to knock off somebody. But mostly, we don't actually do it. You did it. You're gonna have to pay the price."

He knelt on the grass, took the brush out of the paint can, and wiped it off. Then he replaced the lid on the can. Without looking up, he said, "I guess your cop buddy knows you're here right now."

"Yes, he knows. I asked him if I could come talk to you, give you a chance to come in on your own."

He tapped the lid of the can with the handle of the brush, seal-

ing it. "That's about the only thing I can do, under the circumstances, huh?"

"Yes, with your prints on that pharmacy bag, he has all he needs to arrest you for murder. You should turn yourself in, express your remorse, all that. As it is, you're looking at first-degree homicide, premeditated . . . the works. You could get the death penalty. You have to do everything you can to help yourself."

He stood and looked toward Marie's gardener's cottage where his daughter was. Tears filled his eyes and spilled down his face. "And who's going to help Gilly once I'm gone?"

"I will," Savannah told him. "I'm sure that Marie will. We'll do everything we can for her."

"Thank you."

"Can I give you a ride to the station?"

He nodded.

"Then, let's go."

Chapter 25

The champagne was cold, the food good, the company excellent . . . but as Savannah looked around her dinner table at her Moonlight Magnolia cohorts, she couldn't say she was in a particularly celebratory mood.

Sitting next to her at the table, John seemed to sense her sadness. He turned to her, reached for her hand, and enclosed it between his. "What's wrong, love?" he said, searching her eyes. "You're usually in a cheery state of mind when you've nabbed a scoundrel. You seem rather melancholy this evening."

"I guess that's because I don't really consider this guy a scoundrel. Just a man who did something very wrong and very foolish."

From across the table, Cordele was watching and listening. She seemed to have something to say, but was holding back.

"Go on . . . spit it out," Savannah told her. "Obviously you have an opinion on the subject."

Cordele shrugged. "I was just thinking about a conversation you and I had about how important justice is. You seemed to think then that the only way to have justice was to punish the criminal. Looks like maybe you've changed your mind."

The rest of the table fell silent, and Savannah could feel Dirk

and Tammy staring at her, maybe waiting for a Reid family fight to break out.

But she was too tired and too depressed to fight.

"I haven't changed my mind, Cordele," she said. "Sydney Linton took a life, and he'll get what he deserves. I just feel sorry for little Gilly. She'll find out about all of this sooner or later, and—as you would put it—she'll have some major issues to work out because of it."

"I thought you talked to Angela Herriot about Gilly this afternoon," Tammy said.

"I did. She said she'd send a social worker right out to evaluate the situation. And I also talked to Burt Maxwell about his daughter's drug problems and the need for a stable, healthy environment for his granddaughter—especially now that Sydney won't be on the scene."

"What did he say?" Ryan asked.

"He assured me that he'll look into getting custody of Gilly. He also said that he'll make sure Louise doesn't fire Marie. Apparently he has financial resources of his own that Martin Streck hadn't plundered. He may even move back to the mansion and keep Gilly there. I got the idea that he and Kaitlin might be considering something permanent in the way of a relationship."

"That'd be good for the kid, too," Dirk said.

"That's what I figured."

"She's going to be fine, love," John said, squeezing her hand. "You worry too much."

Cordele gave Savannah a warm smile across the table that she wasn't expecting. "My older sister has a big heart where kids are concerned," she said. "Always has had. She and my grandmother practically raised us, you know."

Savannah held her breath, waiting for the other shoe to drop . . . the part about how awful everything had been in spite of her and Gran's efforts. But it didn't. Cordele ended her statement there, on that rare note of praise.

"How fortunate for you that—" Ryan's words were interrupted by a loud pounding on the front door.

Savannah glanced at her watch. It was nine o'clock. A little late for company. Especially visitors that practically knocked your door off its hinges.

"Who the heck is that?" she said, getting to her feet.

Three more volleys resounded through the house before Savannah could reach the door and open it. Standing there on her porch was a red-faced, furious Louise Maxwell.

Savannah opened the screen and stepped outside. She certainly didn't intend to invite any sort of Louise into her house, let alone an angry one.

"What do you want, and why are you bothering me at my home?" she demanded.

Louise shook an angry finger in her face. "*You* . . . are trying to get my kid taken away from me! A social worker came out to my place this afternoon. Said he was working for Child Protective Services, investigating a complaint that Gilly isn't being properly taken care of."

"Is everything all right out there?" Dirk said from just inside the door.

From the corner of her eye, Savannah could see all her friends and Cordele standing behind him with serious, ready-to-do-battle looks on their faces.

"Everything's just fine," she said. "Louise here isn't happy that I reported her to the CPS."

"Then it *was* you!" Louise was practically spitting, she was so furious. She took a step closer to Savannah. "He wouldn't tell me who reported me, but my dad says you called him, too, this afternoon and complained about the way I take care of my kid."

"You don't take care of your kid. That's the problem. Gilly's taking care of herself. She—"

Crack.

Savannah saw it coming. And for a split second, she considered blocking the hand that reached out and slapped her across the

cheek. With her karate skills, she could have easily grabbed Louise's arm in mid-strike, twisted it, and sent her to the porch deck with one easy movement.

But sometimes . . . karate just wasn't enough.

She let Louise slap her.

Then she pulled back her arm, made a fist, and let it fly. A moment later, Louise was doing a graceful somersault off the porch and onto the sidewalk. Her landing, however, was far less elegant than her flight.

Louise ended up flat on her back, where she rolled around on the ground, shrieking in pain and holding her jaw. From the cracking sound Savannah had heard when she'd made contact, she guessed was at least dislocated, if not broken.

"I'm going to sue you," Louise yelled as she scrambled to her feet, still holding her face with both hands. "I'm going to have you arrested, you lousy bitch. I'm going to—"

"Oh, shut up and go home," Savannah told her. Then she chuckled. "You might wanna stop by the hospital on the way, though, and get that jaw x-rayed."

It wasn't until Savannah was back in her house with the door closed behind her, her friends and sister gathered around her, that she started to genuinely feel happy again.

Maybe she'd gotten a guy arrested today for murder, a guy that she really liked. But she'd also had the privilege of decking Louise Maxwell.

The day wasn't a complete write-off.

After the Magnolia team had finished celebrating and had gone home, Savannah sat in the living room with Cordele, who seemed a bit less morose than usual. It was a welcome change.

"I was thinking of going home tomorrow," she said as she reached for Diamante and pulled the cat onto the sofa beside her. "Classes start up again in about a week and a half, and I've got things to do at home."

"That's too bad," Savannah said, stretching her legs out on the

ottoman and settling back in her chair. "I was thinking that since my case is closed, I'm pretty much free and clear for a few days."

Cordele perked up. "Yes . . . and . . . ?"

"And I was thinking that since my sister is visiting me all the way from Georgia, maybe we could spend some quality time together. We could hop in the Mustang and head up the Pacific Coast Highway. Drive up to Big Sur, hike around in the woods up there, walk on the beach, hang out, you know."

"Really?"

"Sure. Why not? I'm not exactly rolling in the dough, so we'll have to stay in cheap motels and eat fast food . . . or cheap produce, if you prefer."

"Fast food's okay, once in a while."

"Sound good?"

"Sounds great!"

"There's just one thing."

Cordele's smile evaporated. "I know, I know . . . no talking about the past."

"No talking about *bad* things in the past. We can't pretend that our childhoods were rosy, but we can set them aside for a few days and get to know each other all over again in the present, can't we?"

Cordele studied Savannah's face for a long time, then said, "That's what you do, isn't it? You just 'set it aside.' That's how you cope with what happened to us."

"I have to, Cordele. It's the only way I can live."

"Then you've really forgiven them—Mom and Dad?"

"If you mean, have I forgotten what happened? No. I remember. But I deliberately make myself not dwell on it. It's over."

"Don't you feel like . . ." Cordele paused, searching for the words. "Like they still owe you somehow for what they did . . . for what they didn't do?"

"No. They don't owe me squat. To want something from them is to be tied to them, waiting for something I'm never going to get. Why bother?"

Cordele sniffed and reached for the box of tissues on the end table. "I wonder if Mom and Dad did their best. I wonder if they were lousy parents because they didn't know any better or just didn't give a damn."

"Who knows? Who cares?"

When Savannah saw the look of pain cross her sister's face, she left her chair and moved over to the sofa to sit beside her.

"*I* care," Cordele said. "That's who."

Savannah took her in her arms and rocked her, as she had when she was a child. She smoothed the short dark hair. "I know you care, sweetie," she said. "I know you want to know. But hell, *they* probably don't even know. At this rate, you're going to spend your whole life trying to figure out what was inside somebody else's head. You're going to take all those classes and read all those books, and search your memory and your soul and you're still never going to know."

Cordele pulled back enough to look into her sister's eyes. "So what do I do?" she asked. "How do I stop?"

"One day, one moment at a time. As many times as you need to, tell yourself, 'It's over. It's gone. It doesn't matter anymore.' Just like you do with those books you love so much, you turn the page. Same book, okay, but new chapter."

Cordele dried her eyes and blew her nose. A faint smile played across her face. "Can we really go on a road trip up the coast?"

"You're damned tootin'! First thing tomorrow morning, right after breakfast. Okay?"

Cordele's smile broadened, and Savannah caught a glimpse of a little girl she had known long ago in Georgia, one she still loved dearly.

"Okay," Cordele said. She drew a deep breath of resolve. "And we're going to turn the page and write a new chapter."

Savannah kissed her sister's tear-damp cheeks. "Sugar darlin', the best is yet to come!"